I WILL FIND YOU

JESSICA HUNTLEY

INKUBATOR
BOOKS

Published by Inkubator Books
www.inkubatorbooks.com

Copyright © 2025 by Jessica Huntley

Jessica Huntley has asserted her right to be identified as the author of this work.

ISBN (eBook): 978-1-83756-581-8
ISBN (Paperback): 978-1-83756-582-5
ISBN (Hardback): 978-1-83756-583-2

I WILL FIND YOU is a work of fiction. People, places, events, and situations are the product of the author's imagination. Any resemblance to actual persons, living or dead is entirely coincidental.

No part of this book may be reproduced, stored in any retrieval system, or transmitted by any means without the prior written permission of the publisher.

PART 1

1

BONNIE

NOW

Standing in the ranger hut, I shift my weight from one booted foot to the next as my eyes scan the array of warnings, posters and notices on the board by the door. No one else is reading them, but I can't tear my eyes away. I'm transfixed by their dramatic and foreboding titles.

The Dangers of Frostbite and What to Look out For.

If Your Fingertips Are Black, It's Already Too Late.

Climbing Accidents and How to Avoid Them.

Broken Bones Equals Death out Here.

I lean in closer to a particular poster that has a very graphic picture of a broken leg where the bone is protruding through the skin, like a sapling that's been snapped by vicious winds. Saliva fills my mouth as I quickly look at something else.

At first, my eyes don't notice the small, grainy newspaper article that's pinned in the bottom corner of the notice board, but one word in the title jumps out at me as my brain catches up to what I've just read.

I scan back for a second pass.

As I read, bending slightly at the waist to bring my eyes in line with the article, my sole focus is drawn to it, even when a noisy group of hikers walk past me. It tugs on my natural curious instinct of finding out the truth about the weird and wonderful. The story that's captivating my attention is from November 2009 and has the headline: *Is the White Witch Real?* It's written by an expert hiker and mountaineer called Barry Bolder, which immediately makes the corners of my lips curl into a smirk. Whether it's a made-up name for the paper, I don't know, but it's very fitting. He seemed convinced that a woman with pure white hair lived in the Swiss Alps and that she was a danger to local hikers and tourists, having murdered several people over the past forty-seven years.

Once I've finished reading, including his very graphic explanation of how she had turned into a cannibal, I glance over at my husband, who's deep in conversation with the ranger in charge of delivering the safety briefing that's due to start in ten minutes. It's typical of Steffan to chat with the ranger. He's probably talking his ear off about all the hiking expeditions he's been on over the years and how he scaled K2 in an almost record-breaking time, missing out on the world record by merely three seconds.

A smile appears on my face as I watch him, leaning casually on one hip, as he talks to the ranger, who is nodding along with a wide-eyed expression on his face. I bet he wasn't expecting someone more experienced than him to be in his safety briefing today. But that's the truth. Steffan is a very knowledgeable mountaineer. True, he doesn't have a fitting and unique name like Barry Bolder, but Steffan Phillips is, and always will be, the only person I'd want taking me on my very first mountaineering expedition.

Turning back to the article, I reach up my hand and, as casually as I can, pull it free from its pin, fold it up and slide it into the inside pocket of my bright purple jacket; the same pocket where I keep a Swiss army knife that Steffan forced me to pack (just in case). I'm not sure why I take the article; a memento, perhaps, but it feels like something makes me do it. The White Witch of the Alps sounds like one of those local legends, myths or folklores, and I've always enjoyed reading and learning about those types of things.

For our honeymoon, Steffan and I drove up to Scotland and stayed by Loch Ness because I was convinced I'd spot Nessie. I took a flask of coffee and stayed up until three in the morning on the shores with night-vision goggles. I took a pair of binoculars and made at least a dozen boat rides up and down the Loch. I did not spot anything other than birds and fish, as it turned out, and I was bitterly disappointed to return to Wales having not debunked the centuries-old myth of the Loch Ness Monster.

But that's me. I'm a naturally curious person.

Steffan steps away from the ranger after giving him a handshake and returns to my side.

'Making friends?' I ask with a slight jest to my voice.

'It always pays to get to know the locals,' replies Steffan with a wink.

'Does he live here?'

'Yeah, all his life.'

'So... he does know more than you about mountaineering.'

Steffan scoffs. 'Hardly.' He says it in a way that tells me he's joking. It's true Steffan has a competitive side, but he's never been over-the-top about it.

My hand slides into the inside pocket of my jacket, ready to retrieve the article and tell Steffan all about it, but the ranger clears his throat, and the safety briefing begins. Steffan has made it perfectly clear on several occasions that I need to pay attention, so I forget about the article and pin all my focus on the ranger instead as he welcomes us and the fifteen or so other hikers to the start of our thirty-nine-day trek, which will take us from St. Moritz (where we are now) through the southern Alps and end at Lake Geneva. We're navigating along the Alpine Passes Trail, one of Switzerland's wildest and most challenging routes, only to be undertaken by expert climbers, hikers and mountaineers (or someone who's stupid and fancies a challenge). The ranger, who introduces himself as Johan, tells us that the Alpine Passes Trail is full of rugged terrain, remote valleys, and has peaks of up to 4,000 metres.

My eyes lose focus on Johan and stare past him, out the window beyond where the Swiss Alps are waiting to be explored. They are so beautiful that it's hard to believe they're even real. From the snow-capped summits to the deep, dark forests, the rugged ridges and the treacherous mountain trails, the Swiss Alps are a hiker's dream.

But to me, they're my worst nightmare.

Johan's still talking. I find myself shifting my weight from one hip to the other, itching to get moving. My feet are primed and ready to go, safely cocooned in a pair of new hiking boots that could have done with being broken in a bit more. They are stiff and cumbersome, but Steffan assures me they'll soon be stained with my sweat and blood. I thought he was joking at first, but then I realised he wasn't.

Steffan, as professional and serious as always, is listening intently to every word Johan's saying. I expect he could run this briefing himself without even having to think about it. He's probably listened to hundreds of them in his time.

Stick to the marked routes.

Don't take unnecessary risks.

Always ensure you have enough food and water for a minimum of two days.

Stop and tend to any blisters before they become too bad.

Listen to your mountain expert leader.

Take cover during a storm.

All common sense so far.

Johan moves on to explaining, in minute detail, how to tie a rope and use the climbing rigs situated at some of the trickier paths. Some paths require rock-climbing skills and expertise with climbing gear, but I've already done all this with Steffan before we left. Plus, I'm sure he'll remind me when we get to those points in our hike. Despite his knowledge, his eyes and attention are still glued to Johan, soaking it all in. He also speaks about the dangers of climbing and how a serious injury out here can quickly turn an enjoyable hike into a death sentence. As he explains what to do in the case of a serious injury, my stomach flips and drops like I'm on a rollercoaster.

Johan is now speaking about the cosy accommodation cabins dotted along the routes, informing us that we need to check into each one so they can keep track of us along the way. Little does Johan know that Steffan and I will be avoiding using the luxury of overnight cabins for the most part, opting for rough sleeping in a tent instead. Maybe not every night, but there will come a point where we will be straying away from the marked route and going against the safety advice being provided to us.

We have our reasons.

Johan finishes by telling the group that around fifty hikers die or disappear in the Swiss Alps every year, never to be found or heard from again, and that's enough to send a cold shiver from the base of my spine up to the back of my neck. A lump forms in my throat as I stare out at the mountains again.

Everyone claps after the briefing is over and the group begin to disperse, chatting amongst themselves, all buzzing with excitement, giddy to explore the wilderness.

Steffan takes a deep breath and turns to me. 'You ready?'

'Um, yeah, just a minute.'

I stand rooted to the spot while Steffan walks out of the ranger hut and into the cool autumn air. Because, unlike everyone else in this group, I'm not buzzing with excitement at the prospect of hiking in the Swiss Alps. I'd rather not be here at all. I'd rather be anywhere else, yet here I am, about to embark on a long and dangerous journey.

The other hikers might be here for adventure and glory, but I'm not. Far from it. I'm here for a very particular reason, and I'm not leaving until I complete what I've set out to achieve.

I don't care if it kills me.

2

ANNALISE

THEN

As she walks down the narrow alley towards the market, she wonders if it's possible to be any happier than she is at this moment. Annalise hops to the side to avoid a particularly nasty-looking pothole and then continues onwards, carrying the wicker basket she made to haul the items back from the market. It was a fun project she'd worked on at home and it had taken less time to complete than she thought. Maybe she'll make another soon. Perhaps she can sell them in the future to earn a little extra money for the home.

Today, she needs to buy half a dozen eggs, fresh vegetables and some sausages. She plans on making a sausage stew for dinner, her husband's favourite. The sun is shining the same colour and strength as her mood, almost as if it's feeding her with its rays. Yellow and strong.

At barely twenty years of age, Annalise knows how lucky she is to have a loving husband, Erik, and a place to call home. Well, not a long-term home, but a roof over her head and a warm, soft bed to sleep in at night. Her days are filled with happiness, and she keeps busy by ensuring the home is clean and tidy and dinner is on the table for when her husband returns from work in the evenings. They've only been married a year, but already she knows it's been the best year of her life, and things can only get better from here. Kids are next on their list. She and Erik have made an agreement to start trying for a child after their first year of marriage. That time has finally arrived.

As she hums her favourite tune, footsteps sound behind her. The streets are busy, so it's not a surprise. Farmers, shoppers and young children are everywhere as she steps into the market square. She loves market day, the hustle and bustle of the local farmers and producers selling their wares. Annalise loves talking to anyone and everyone she meets, always with a smile on her face. There's often not a time when she doesn't talk to people. Maybe she'll see Mary and her lovely newborn baby. Only a week old and such a darling, sweet thing. She's counting the days until she becomes a mother. She'll be a great one. She just knows it. Maybe she'll have half a dozen children. Or more. A large family is exactly what she dreams of, and she thinks Erik agrees. They haven't had that conversation yet, but in their wedding vows he promised to do whatever it takes to make her happy. A big family would make her happy.

'Good to see you, Mrs Andersson!'

Annalise turns and sees one of the market sellers waving at her. She's become quite friendly with him and his wife since moving here several months ago. She beams a smile and walks up to him. He's selling vegetables and has a wide variety available from his stall, all different colours and sizes. The choice is almost overwhelming. Almost.

'Hello, Mr Lindberg. How are you? How is your wife? I hear she had a nasty fall.'

'Ah, she's resting. Bit of a bump, but nothing too bad. She'll be up and about in no time.'

'Glad to hear it. May I take a selection of the root vegetables, please, and a pound of potatoes?'

'You sure you can carry all that?' He nods at her wicker basket. 'It's going to be mighty heavy.'

'I'm stronger than I look,' replies Annalise with a laugh, handing over the basket.

'Aye, I meant no harm.' He takes it, blushing slightly.

While Mr Lindberg places the produce in her basket, Annalise glances around the market square. She recognises several people, including a tall, broad-shouldered man who works with Erik. She doesn't know his name, but one time when she visited Erik at work after he'd accidentally left his lunch at home, she saw him and Erik talking. Erik hadn't introduced her to the man, so that's why she doesn't know his name. He is standing on the other side of the square, staring straight at her. She holds her hand up and waves, but he doesn't return the gesture. Just continues to stare at her. After a few seconds, she feels the tiny hairs on the back of her neck tingle. She is a little embarrassed to have waved at him and not have the gesture returned, so she turns her back on the man and faces Mr Lindberg, who has finished tallying up her purchases.

She pays him and takes the basket. Now that it's full, she hooks it over her arm to carry it across the square towards the stall selling the eggs. As she walks, she glances over to where the tall man was standing before, but he's not there. It doesn't take her long to spy him again at a different location further down the square. She takes note of his appearance. He's young, around her own age, with a thick head of hair and a week's worth of stubble across his strong chin. He's still watching her. Annalise tries not to let it worry her, but why is he watching her like this? Does he want something? Why doesn't he come up to her and ask?

She arrives at the stall and buys half a dozen eggs. The seller attempts to engage her in polite conversation, but Annalise is too distracted and keeps looking over her shoulder at the man. She thanks the seller with a smile and turns around.

He's gone.

The man who was staring at her. He's no longer watching her. Where did he go?

3

BONNIE

NOW

Ten Days Later

'Steffan! Wait!' As I watch my husband disappear into the distance, it's all I can do not to sink to the ground and sob like a child. The last I see of him is his large backpack disappearing over the crest of the hill. He knows I have a blister on my left heel the size of a ten-pence piece thanks to breaking in these damn boots over the past ten days. Blisters: a hiker's worst nightmare, and something I remember Johan harping on about in detail during the safety briefing. Small in the grand scheme of things, but they can turn an enjoyable stroll into the hike from hell in a matter of minutes. Or a run, for that matter. Blisters and I are old enemies, back from when I was a runner.

Three years ago, I was basically a couch potato who'd have much rather watched people running on television, judging them from the safety of my sofa, than getting off my butt and running myself. That all changed when I had a health scare and my doctor gently suggested I lose some weight and look after myself better, so I started the Couch to 5K app plan.

Nine weeks later, I completed my first 5K in a semi-respectable time, and then I thought, why not make it ten, then twenty, then fifty. Within a year, I'd not only lost nearly four stone, but I'd completed three marathons and had entered myself into The Dragon's Back, a legendary 235-mile, six-day race across the mountains of mid-Wales. It was safe to say that running saved me, but I became very familiar with the dreaded blister, a soul-sucking wound that can reduce even the toughest of people to tears.

However, I haven't put on my running trainers in over a year, and that's because I've been training for my most challenging event yet – this hike across the Swiss Alps.

Steffan has been training me. We're at very different levels of fitness. He's not a runner. In fact, when I told him I was going to run 5K he gave me an eyebrow raise – Steffan's equivalent of a gasp. Perhaps he found it hilarious that his overweight wife was going to get herself fit. If he did think that, he didn't show it. He supported me and came to all my races, clapping and cheering as I crossed the finish lines, red in the face and drenched in sweat and more than a little stiff and sore. After the London Marathon, he even handed me a glass of champagne at the end, which I downed in one and promptly threw back up again within minutes. Not my finest moment. It was even in the paper. I'd rather not repeat the headline.

I may not have run for a long time, but I've kept the weight off. At one point a year ago, I could have sunk into a pit of despair (I did for a few weeks), and the dreaded pounds threatened to pile back on at an alarming rate. But I didn't let them. I picked myself up and continued, all thanks to my husband.

So, yes, Steffan and I are different levels of fit. He's a long-distance hiker and explorer who can trek up huge mountains with a heavy backpack day in and day out for weeks. He has plans to summit Everest next year, something I wholeheartedly support. It's been his lifelong dream to climb the tallest mountain in the world, but first, his goal is to get his inexperienced wife through the ordeal of crossing the Swiss Alps.

I know I'm in the best hands, but I can't help but feel a little resentment at my super-mega-fit husband, who is clearly finding this expedition perfectly ordinary and not at all out of his comfort zone. I, however, have been struggling with the weight of my backpack for the past ten days, something I'm not used to carrying for such long distances. As a runner, I'd only had to carry a water bottle and some energy gels. I shouldn't blame him for charging off into the distance. It's not like I'm expecting him to hold my hand over every hill and uneven piece of terrain.

Grinding my teeth, I continue to follow him. Blister or no blister, I have no choice but to continue. It's my decision to be here after all, having spent several months training for this. Steffan flat-out refused to accompany me unless I put in some sort of training first. He said it was necessary, and to attempt such a long and treacherous hike without preparation was foolish and practically a death sentence. It's not often he puts his foot down. In fact, the only other time I've known him to refuse to do something was when I wanted to take him salsa dancing for our fourth wedding anniversary. I have no idea what he has against dancing, but you'll never find Steffan on the dance floor, not even if he's wasted, which is hardly ever because he's very health conscious.

Since I stopped running a year ago, my overall fitness levels have dropped drastically. Steffan said I needed to improve my cardiovascular endurance and my strength, so every Sunday for the past few months, he's taken me out for long walks with a backpack on. My body will be pushed to the limit on this trip. I think I've reached the limit already. I'm no stranger to pain and discomfort, but hiking is altogether a different experience, one my body isn't prepared for. Even now.

Hiking in the Alps involves zero running. Zero. My previous experience of completing races is utterly pointless. The medals I've collected at the finish lines will do bugger-all in enabling me to climb a mountain. Steffan has told me in explicit, mind-numbing detail that most hikers would train for between nine and twelve months to prepare properly for this expedition. I didn't have that long, so here I am. In addition to snow and ice-climbing skills, I've also had to try and increase my long-term strength and high-altitude tolerance. It's not like we're climbing Everest and will need oxygen to complete the climbs, but on certain high ridges and anything above 2500 metres, the oxygen will be significantly lower and will test my cardiovascular system, increasing the likelihood of suffering from high-altitude sickness.

It's day ten and we haven't killed each other. Yet. We joked with our friends before we left that if our marriage can withstand this, then we can get through anything. We've never done something like this before, never stepped into each other's worlds.

It's mid-October, not exactly the perfect time of year to trek such treacherous terrain, but I didn't want to wait any longer. Once the winter well and truly sets in, it may be too late, and I'd be forced to wait another six months or more. I've waited long enough.

I need to stop and dress my wound. If I keep going, the blister's only going to get worse, bigger. I've previously had blisters so big that they covered my entire heel, and it's never a fun experience.

There's no sign of Steffan coming back. I'm not sure why he's left me behind, but I assume he has a good reason. Maybe to check out the path up ahead.

I stop, take off my pack and set it down on the snow. My shoulders and back silently scream in relief as the weight on them is released. Before carrying weight on my back, I had no idea how many different muscle groups it uses. Everything hurts. Everything. I stretch my arms above my head, unable to help letting out a small moan of discomfort.

The snow isn't too deep yet, but over the next few days, we'll be navigating the higher passes towards our destination, and at this time of year, it's normal to trek through snow several feet deep. We have snowshoes and climbing axes, everything we need in our packs, each of which weighs upwards of sixty pounds. My ultramarathon pack in the past generally weighed less than eight pounds. No wonder my shoulder and back muscles hate me. My legs are just about hanging in there, having been somewhat used to taking a pounding with the running, blister aside.

Crouching, I pull out my first aid kit and start the process of unlacing my left boot and removing my sweaty sock. The red, angry blister on my heel throbs as the cold wind brushes across it, but it's also a relief to have it out of the warm, sweaty enclosure it's been flourishing in over the past few hours since I felt the hot spot first appearing. Ooh, it's a beauty too. Time to break out the *Compeed*.

Once tended to, I slide my foot back into my sock just in time for Steffan to approach. His forehead glistens and his breathing is laboured, but I know for a fact he's in his element right now. He doesn't even look as if he's struggling. I secretly hate him, yet love him at the same time.

'Everything okay?' he asks, his hands on his hips as he looks down at me.

'I have a blister the size of Mount Everest on my heel.'

'Ouch.' Steffan chuckles as he takes off his pack and dumps it next to mine. 'I was just checking out the next pass. It's an easy route through. We might even be able to get a day ahead if we keep up the pace.'

I glance up at him and give him "the look."

'Are you okay?'

'I'm not sure I can keep this pace up for much longer. My neck, shoulders and back are on fire, and this blister has its own pulse.' I hate to complain because I know it shows weakness.

'Now you've dressed it properly, you'll be fine,' says Steffan. 'I can take some of the weight out of your pack if you want?'

'No, it's fine,' I mumble.

There's a beat of silence.

'You knew it was going to be tough going,' says Steffan.

A tear leaks out of my left eye, and I quickly wipe it away, leaving a smear across my cuff. 'I know, I know. Sorry... just... I hate blisters.'

Steffan kneels next to me and places a strong hand on my knee. 'You're doing great.'

Now I don't know whether to laugh or cry because we

both know I'm not doing great, but I am managing to hold it together and that's the main thing. I can't afford to fall apart on top of a mountain. It won't help anyone, least of all me. I have to remind myself that I'm doing this for a reason and Steffan is helping me. He's the expert out here. Not me. He did tell me it was going to be hard.

Steffan holds his hand out. I grab it and he pulls me to my feet. 'Thanks.'

Within seconds, he picks up his pack like it weighs nothing and slings it onto his back. 'You need some help with yours?'

'No, thanks. I can manage.'

I pick up my pack, which feels heavier after a break, and hoof it onto my back, stumbling slightly under the weight. The fact is, I need to be comfortable with carrying this amount of weight and if I let Steffan carry it then it won't help me. I've trained loads in the gym over the past few months, but there's only so much strength I can gain lifting barbells. I never fully appreciated the strength endurance it takes to carry weight over long distance.

'I've just checked in with the rangers and it looks like a snowstorm is on the way. They're advising everyone to seek shelter at the closest accommodation hut and wait it out or turn back and get to lower ground,' says Steffan, staring into the distance. I take a moment to admire his physique and stature. He looks like a wild mountain man, his beard rugged and scattered with early flecks of grey. His hair needs a trim, but he's always had it on the longer side, so it curls around his ears and forehead. Only once have I known him to shave it off. Never again. It made him look like a convict on death row.

'Oh,' I say. A part of me is relieved. Waiting out a storm

means I'll get some much-needed rest, but a snowstorm means it may cut us off from where we're trying to get to.

Steffan nods and tilts his head to the sky, which is a greyish blue. Plenty of cloud cover, but the sun is there somewhere, causing a yellow glow. The temperature is around two degrees, but right now I'm not really feeling the chill. I'm pretty sure my first layer of clothing is soaked with my own sweat, but the longer we stay still, the quicker the chill sets it.

'Is the storm really that bad?' I ask.

Steffan shrugs. 'They say it'll last around twelve to twenty-four hours and dump several feet of snow higher up the mountain. We should be safe where we are. The nearest cabin is about seven hours from here, but it'll take us off our planned course.'

'How long will this set us back?'

'Three days.'

'That's not too bad, I guess.'

Steffan has planned this trek meticulously, adjusting for roughly two days extra in case anything goes wrong, which is a given out here. Weather changes, paths erode, or injuries and accidents happen.

'I know,' says Steffan with a long sigh. 'But I don't think we should take a detour to the cabin.'

'What? Why not? You don't expect us to hike through a storm, do you?'

Steffan shakes his head. 'No, of course not. It's far too dangerous, but if we keep going and cut across the ridge and through a valley, we can get ahead of the worst of the storm, camp out and wait for it to pass overhead. It means we'll maybe lose half a day or less.'

I absorb his words and their meaning. 'Okay.'

He must sense my unease and hesitation because he

says, 'Don't worry, I know what I'm doing. Remember, you're with an experienced mountaineer.' He flashes those pearly white teeth at me.

I smirk. 'I remember. And we'll still reach the pass where it... I mean where you...' A lump forms in my throat, so I swallow my words back down.

'Yes. It'll take us a little longer, but we'll get there. I promise. Trust me.'

I nod, those annoying tears threatening to bubble up again.

'But for us to get ahead of the storm, you'll need to keep pace with me. We can't afford to slow down, or we may get trapped.'

'I can do it. You lead. I'll follow.'

Steffan gives me a smile, turns and walks away. I close my eyes and take a deep breath, centring myself. I can do this. I need to do this. My mind drifts back to the newspaper article I read back at the ranger hut ten days ago, the one safely folded in my pocket.

Barry Bolder was out here searching for something – *someone*.

I don't know whether he ever found her – the White Witch – but it plays on my mind as I put one foot in front of the other and follow Steffan through the snow, which gets deeper with every passing minute.

4

BONNIE

THEN

The constant worry is like a writhing snake in my gut, twisting and churning, round and round, ensuring I don't get a moment of peace, not even when I'm asleep. I'm not usually a worrier, more than happy to go through life stress-free. I have a decent, well-paying job that's dull as hell, but nothing I have to concern myself with. I don't have kids to worry about, and my husband and I are happy, for the most part. It's a lot more than most people can say, and I consider myself very lucky to be in this situation. Generally, worry only pops up when something happens, but until it does, I don't think about it. I don't ponder what could happen.

My first run-in with worry was two years ago when my heart decided to quit working properly, brought on by the excess weight I was carrying, but now that's sorted out, I don't worry about it anymore. I've started running and now, I'm the fittest I've ever been. In fact, I'm training for The Dragon's Back race, which starts in two months' time. I've been enjoying my training. I'm injury-free and feeling good.

When worry hits me like this, I tend to go for a run,

which enables my mind to relax and my body to take over for once. It's seven in the morning on a Sunday. I get up and out of bed straight away because there's no way my body will drift back to sleep, not after that harrowing nightmare. I can't even recall what it was about, only that there was screaming, lots of screaming, which was enough to wake me up with both chills and sweaty skin.

I grab my phone, which lies silent on the bedside table, pad downstairs to the kitchen in my pyjamas and fluffy socks and flick on the coffee machine, a monstrosity of a thing that Steffan insisted we have because instant coffee is, apparently, not considered proper coffee. He's a coffee snob. And now I'm one too, because whenever I am given instant coffee to drink by friends when I visit, I grimace inside as I swallow the vile stuff with a smile.

I need to leave for my long-distance training run soon. Running is the only thing that calms me, that distracts me, but I need coffee first, especially since last night I barely slept. My phone springs to life in my hand, which causes me to almost drop it. I fumble for the answer button as my heart rate skyrockets.

'Hannah,' I say, breathless. 'Hi.'

'Before you freak out, which I'm sure you are already, I've just got off the phone with Chris. They're both fine. Just some freak climbing accident, and the signal has been patchy. Steffan has some cuts and scrapes, and Chris has a twisted ankle, but otherwise they're both fine.'

The relief that floods my body makes me double over as I suck in a much-needed breath. 'Thank God.' Another deep inhale. 'Why hasn't Steffan called me?'

'Who knows? Maybe he didn't think it was that serious.'

'What do you know about what happened?'

'Chris didn't say much, just that one of the climbing ropes snapped or something and they fell and bashed themselves against the rocks, but honestly, they're both fine, and continuing with their climb today.'

I nod even though I know Hannah can't see me. 'Okay. Thanks so much for calling. We still on for our run?'

'No, sorry. That's the other reason I was calling. I'm sorry to have to do this to you last minute, but I can't join you this morning. My mum was supposed to come and collect the kids, but one of the twins woke up in the night with a cough and now the other one is copying her, and Mum doesn't want to deal with sick kids, so...'

'It's fine. Don't worry about it. I hope they feel better soon.'

'Thanks, but I'm still up for joining you at the pub at the end. The kids can tag along.'

'You sure they're well enough to come?'

'I reckon they're faking it. They were playing by themselves in their rooms and weren't coughing. The second I walked into the room, they started up. See you at The Ram about two?'

'See you then.'

'Happy running.'

'Bye, Hannah.'

'Bye, babe.'

I hang up and hold the phone to my chest, taking a deep breath. My eyes close as I breathe in and out slowly, attempting to control my rapid heartbeat, like I'd do on a run. After Steffan missed his check-in call with me last night, the worry had started, but now it's finally beginning to dissipate. The coffee machine bleeps to signal it's ready, so I press the button and watch as the dark liquid dribbles out and splashes into the cup below.

Hannah sometimes joins me on my runs. She doesn't run long-distance like I do, but sometimes she runs for maybe five miles and then turns around and heads back or takes a shortcut. She's determined to lose the last bit of weight from having the twins that's stubbornly stuck around for the past five years, but it looks like I'm heading out solo today. At least I have the prospect of a glass of wine and a roast dinner at the pub with Hannah and my lovely nephew and niece later.

FIFTEEN MINUTES LATER, I'm dressed and ready for my run. There's no point in skipping it today just because Hannah can't join me. It's my day off from work, and I always go for a long training run on Sundays. It's become my tradition – a long run followed by a meal at a local pub. Usually, Steffan would meet me at the pub at the end, but since he's been away, I've had to resort to asking Hannah or my local runner friends to accompany me, but it's too short notice to call anyone else now. It's not like I don't like running by myself. In fact, I love it, but there's nothing quite like keeping pace with someone and chatting as the miles pass by under our feet. Unless, of course, we're running across a particular technical piece of terrain, and then we have to run one behind the other.

Today, I'm heading up into the Surrey hills to one of my favourite spots; a circular route that passes through some beautiful locations, as well as throwing in some steep hills just to keep me on my toes and push my lungs and legs to the extreme.

I drive to the start location, don my small running pack and tuck my phone into the side pocket, ensuring it's connected to my Bluetooth headphones, so that if a call does come through, I won't miss it. I'm not expecting a call from Steffan for a few hours yet, but you never know.

I set off at a slow pace for my warmup, performing some side steps and butt kicks for the first two hundred yards, then settle into a smooth rhythm, checking my Garmin watch to ensure I'm running at the correct pace. I'm aiming for fifteen miles today, a feat most would gasp at, but for me it's a nice, medium run. At least, it is compared to the race I'm training towards. My lean limbs are now used to the distance, and as the ground passes beneath my feet and the miles disappear behind me, I slowly sink into a blissful state, almost catatonic as my running music mix pounds in my ears, energising me and giving me the motivation I need to keep going.

My Garmin alerts me to passing ten miles at the one-hour and forty-minute mark, which is just over a ten-minute mile pace. Not super-fast, but not my slowest either. I grab my water bottle and drink while running, slopping a little down my chin.

As soon as I've replaced the bottle, the music stops and is replaced by a ringtone. I stop in my tracks, tap my earbuds and answer, not even looking for my phone to see who's calling me.

'Hello?'

A crackle comes through my earbuds.

'Hello? Steffan, is that you?'

'H-Hello...' comes the crackly reply.

It's not Steffan. I'd know his deep, gravelly voice anywhere. Plus, this man has a thick Irish accent. I grab my phone from my pocket and glance at the screen. It's a random number I don't recognise.

'I'm afraid... news... bad... husband...'

'Hello? I'm sorry, but I can barely hear you.' I try not to shout and raise my voice, but I can't breathe properly. It's like a vice is around my chest, squeezing tighter and tighter with every inhale. 'Hello? Is my husband okay?'

'Your husband... danger...'

I hold my breath. What is this person saying? I glance at my phone again, noting that I have full signal, so it must be their line that's bad.

The line goes dead.

What the hell was that about? How can something have happened to them so quickly? Hannah only got off the phone to Chris merely hours ago, and he'd told her they were fine.

There's that worry again.

5

ANNALISE

THEN

She jerks her head from side to side, frantically searching for the man who's been watching her. Perhaps he's moved somewhere she can't see him, hiding himself from view. The thought sends another shiver across the base of her neck. The happy bubble she was in earlier has burst, now replaced by nerve-tingling fear.

She decides to head back home early, foregoing the sausages from the meat stall on the other side of the market square. She'll make something else for dinner. She also had plans to browse the haberdashery stalls for some new fabric and buttons, but she can do that another day. The basket is heavy anyway, and her biceps are already burning from the weight of the potatoes and root vegetables.

Annalise walks back along the narrow alley, the one she took to the market, every so often glancing over her shoulder in case the man is following her. Why he would be is beyond her, but then he had been staring at her for at least ten minutes while she'd shopped, so perhaps he's waiting until she's alone to speak to her. But there's no sign of him.

The tension in her shoulders starts to dissipate the farther along the alley she walks, creating more and more distance from the last place she saw him. The way he'd looked at her. It had been menacing, threatening. His dark, foreboding eyes hadn't moved.

A few more turns and she stops. Seconds later, she realises she's taken a wrong turn somewhere. Her mind had been too focused on the strange man rather than where she was going. Heaving the basket further up the crook of her arm, she turns to head back the way she came and walks straight into the man who'd been watching her.

Annalise shrieks and drops the basket.

The vegetables spread across the uneven path, and a loose potato rolls past the man and underneath a bicycle that's leaning against a wall. Her body freezes. She wants to run, but she can't do anything other than tremble. The man says nothing. Just stares, his eyes wide and barely blinking. They are so dark they are almost black, and she's hypnotised by them.

'W-What do you want?' she asks.

Silently, the man bends and picks up her basket, which only has a few items left inside. The eggs are smashed on the cobbles below, not one of them intact. He holds the basket out to her.

'You ought to be more careful,' he says, deadpan.

'I... You were watching me earlier and you gave me a fright,' she says, taking the basket from him. 'You work with Erik, is that right? I've seen you once before, a few weeks ago.'

'Yes.'

'Why were you staring at me earlier?'

There's a beat of silence as they lock eyes. Those black

eyes stare right through her. She can't look away. She can't do anything. She wants to run, to hide, to scream, to do something, but he's rendered her catatonic with one look. He doesn't answer her question with words. He merely turns away. Annalise lets out a long breath. She gulps in air so fast it gives her hiccups. She bends and retrieves the potatoes and vegetables, but the eggs are beyond saving. Blinking back warm tears, she retraces her steps to somewhere she recognises, then walks towards her home.

Why hadn't the man said anything else? Why had he been staring at her? He'd confirmed he worked with Erik, and that was it.

Something doesn't feel right, deep down in her gut. Was he supposed to make her feel uneasy? Because he'd certainly succeeded. She can't get home quickly enough, back to safety. Her feet shuffle as fast as they can go without her breaking into a jog. She's out of breath by the time she rounds the corner to where her home is situated at the end of the alley.

As Annalise arrives at her door, she reaches into the pocket of her dress and fishes out the key, sliding it into the lock.

Before she can react, fast footsteps sound behind her. She's shoved through the open door and she falls to her knees, her skin grazing against the stone floor.

The door slams behind her.

'I haven't finished with you yet,' says the gravelly voice from behind.

6

ANNALISE

NOW

The roaring fire crackles and spits as I prod at it with a large stick, attempting to turn over the top log to ensure the whole thing catches. A large pile of logs sits stacked next to the fireplace, at risk of toppling over if I add any more. I made sure to chop up enough to see me through the approaching storm. I've lived out here in the mountains long enough to read the sky like a much-beloved and dog-eared book.

The storm will approach from the east in roughly two hours and will last between twelve and twenty-four hours. The temperature will drop to minus ten, maybe colder, and the wind speed will most likely max out at seventy-two miles per hour. It's a bad one. It's likely my cabin will be buried under several feet of snow for at least two days or more.

I'm not overly worried. There is cause for concern, like there is with any storm when you're living out in the middle of nowhere with no access to amenities, but as long as I'm prepared, exactly like my husband taught me to be, then I needn't worry. I've been through worse. Much worse.

During a particularly bad storm, going back over a

decade, my husband and I were trapped in this cabin for nearly two weeks without food and with little water. It was certainly one for the record books. That is, if I kept any record books. Back in that wild storm, it got so cold and claustrophobic that I experienced severe hallucinations, I lost two of my toes and one finger to frostbite, and I ended up with a permanent cough that likes to make an appearance when it gets below a certain temperature.

It's a time I'm never likely to forget, even when my brain eventually erodes from old age. At sixty-six, I'm certainly no spring chicken, but living out here, away from civilization, from the dangers of human society and pollution, I believe I am slowing down the ageing process somewhat. Maybe not by a lot, but I reckon I have a better immune system than most people my age. Who knows, living like this could be the key to everlasting life. Perhaps I'll live to one hundred. Then again, I fear my joints and muscles aren't faring well in these harsh conditions, and I often walk with a small stoop and limp nowadays, but inside, I feel like I'm in my thirties.

It's freeing to live out here, surviving off everything the earth provides. What need is there for anything else? Back nearly fifty years ago, I lived with my then-new husband in a quaint mountain village where food could be bought from market stalls. Everything I could possibly need was at my fingertips, including running water. Now, I must search and hunt for everything my body requires. I have no access to electricity, or indoor plumbing. I must admit, I do miss the basic necessities from time to time. It would certainly make life a lot easier.

I've lived like this for a long time, even with my dear husband departing this life many years ago. I lose track of time, so I can't be certain of the exact date, but it's at least a decade since he passed. The years roll and blend into one. I've learned to tell the passing of time through the changing of the seasons, but it's difficult to keep track of exactly how many winters I've spent here.

When my dear Erik died, I struggled in isolation and grief. It happened so fast; I hadn't been prepared, and I hadn't realised just how lonely and quiet it would be without his constant presence, not to mention the extra pair of hands to chop wood, hunt for food and do all the daily chores to enable us to eat and sleep in relative comfort.

Losing him was difficult in many ways and, on several occasions over the following years, I hiked up to the nearest ridge and contemplated throwing myself off the edge, ending all my suffering. But then I'd look around at the beauty of the Swiss Alps and feel at peace. Erik's body may have died, but his spirit will live forever. And I couldn't insult his memory, his life, by killing myself. It was a dark time, a time I cannot always recall with accuracy. A lot of things happened that I don't like to dwell on, but I have now managed to move on and get my life back on track.

Now, having come to terms with his sudden passing, I still lead a lonely existence, one I sometimes hate to live, but he's still here with me in my heart. I talk to him every single day. He doesn't answer, but I know he can hear me. I don't believe in ghosts, but I do believe in a higher presence, an afterlife. It makes me feel less afraid of death.

What I wouldn't give for another chance at happiness, another chance of redemption. I have tried, several times, but my plans always fail. People have turned their backs on me, so I have no desire to help them. Maybe one day, I can repent for my sins, rather than adding to them, but not until I find someone worthy of my mercy.

I remember craving human interaction as a young woman. I would go outside just to talk to people. I was happiest when in the presence of others, but a lot has changed over the past four decades or so. I am not the young, vibrant woman I once was.

I no longer crave human interaction. I avoid it. It's safer without it. Other humans are a cancer on this world, and I am happier in my cabin, alone with nothing but my inner voice.

Sitting back down in my beloved rocking chair, I stare into the flames, listening to the crackles and pops as they engulf the wood.

Solitude is my friend now.

I don't need anyone else.

7

BONNIE

NOW

Two agonizing hours later, we reach the start of the valley pass that will, according to Steffan, get us ahead of the storm that's closing in with each passing minute. It feels like we're racing it. I know there are professional storm chasers out there, but usually they have off-road vehicles, high-tech equipment and a band of others just as crazy as them all on the same wild journey. We have none of those things, but Steffan is adamant that we're going to get ahead of it and it's perfectly safe. I trust him implicitly, even though my own thoughts betray the faith I have in him.

What if we can't outrun the storm? What if we're trapped in a massive snowdrift and freeze to death? What if we're blown off course and end up somewhere we're not supposed to be, like at the edge of a cliff?

There's that worry that seems to like to rear its ugly head a lot lately. Ever since...

My mind thinks back to Johan and his terrifyingly detailed safety briefing. Why is Steffan foregoing his advice? Does he know something about the storm that perhaps the rangers don't, or maybe he thinks they're being too strict with their safety rules?

Weather is notoriously unpredictable, especially this high up in the Alps, but at this time of year, a storm is inevitable at some point. Steffan even planned for one, having packed all the essential kit in case we are stranded somewhere without access to help and support. It looks like it's going to be a bad one too. The sky is heavy, completely white. The sun appears to have lost its battle with the snow clouds and has disappeared, taking with it the last of the warmth in the air. It'll catch everyone out here off guard if they aren't prepared. Thanks to Johan, I know dozens of hikers die every year in the Alps from poor planning, avalanches, falls and bad weather. I also did a lot of personal research, none of which filled me with confidence, but Steffan quickly put my mind at ease. He knows what he's doing.

Steffan assures me that, as long as we keep up this pace, we'll reach the other side of the pass in plenty of time, enabling us to miss most of the storm, but my body is failing me, and I eventually succumb to its demand to stop and rest. He needed me to keep up with him, but it's impossible.

My legs buckle as I heave the pack off my burning shoulders. Tears sting my eyes as Steffan rushes to my side. Thankfully, he knows better than to tell me to get up and continue. He crouches next to me as the wind buffets around us, making it difficult to even hear each other. Both of us have our hoods up around our thick, woollen hats.

'It's not much further,' he says over the whooshing noise of the wind.

'I just need to rest for a minute,' I shout back.

Steffan nods and stands, leaving me sitting on the

ground. My butt is soaking wet and now that I've stopped, the wind chill is causing the sweat on my exposed face to turn to ice. I'd murder a hot chocolate right about now, or a hot water bottle.

The thing is, I'm putting faith in my husband to get us through this pass and out the other side. I know he's an expert in mountaineering. It's something he constantly feels he needs to remind me. Not in a boasting or arrogant way, but in a way that assures me I'm in safe hands. He updates his skills every year, ensuring he knows everything there is to know about the skill of climbing a mountain. He even went away last year to learn how to dig a snow tunnel, should he be buried by an avalanche. When he was a child, he completed the Duke of Edinburgh Award and has an array of badges and medals for climbing that I only found out about a few years ago.

So why did the accident happen last year?

It's a question I often ponder, torturing myself over and over.

I take a moment to compose myself, watching Steffan while he checks and re-checks the map and the route card. Then he takes out his GPS. Checks the map again.

Steffan is tall and lean. He has muscle, but he's not a gym addict. His legs are ripped. I think his calves are my favourite part of him. He moves effortlessly across the rugged ground, barely even slowing down as he climbs up a nearby steep slope, using the contours of the mountain rather than walking straight up it. Where is he going? What is he doing?

He checks the GPS again.

My stomach turns over on itself. Something is wrong.

He spends days studying every contour of the map and planning every stopover and detail before attempting a climb or trek. He writes out a route card, which he keeps in his pack, only bringing it out when he needs to double-check a route marker. He's confidant and direct, which is why the fact he's checking the route card and the GPS more than usual is giving me a sinking feeling in the pit of my stomach.

'Are we lost?' I shout up to him after he's checked the card for the fifth time in the past two minutes.

Steffan jogs down the slope and joins me. We're on a steep section of a climb and the snow is getting deeper, making each movement quite treacherous. One wrong footing and we'll slide all the way down to the bottom, probably hitting every rock on the way.

I wonder if Barry made it up this far?

I'm not quite sure why I keep thinking about Barry. Did he ever find the White Witch, or did he give up after finding nothing? Did he get trapped in a snowstorm or fall off a cliff? I should have asked Johan. He might have known something about it.

If he did succumb to the elements or get lost somehow, the chances of his body being found are slim to none. Wolves and birds of prey will have picked his body clean by now. A shudder ripples through me at the morbid thought.

You can't think like that.

'No, we're not lost. I know exactly where we are,' replies Steffan confidently.

'And where is that?'

'I think I've marked the route card up wrong, that's all.' I notice he doesn't answer my question.

'What do you mean?' My voice raises an octave.

'I think I may have written down a coordinate wrong.'

'Why are you even looking at the route card when we're

on a different path than you originally planned because of the storm?'

He doesn't answer. Frustration is brewing inside, like a kettle of water, fizzing and bubbling, just on the verge of boiling, but not quite there yet. I mustn't push him. I just need to give him time to sort out the map and figure out what's gone wrong. It must be very easy to go off-course when the weather is bad and visibility is so low. The mountains and peaks around us are completely invisible now, lost somewhere in the white void around us.

But no matter how hard I try, I can't stop thinking about the accident last year. I know Steffan blames himself and has beaten himself up numerous times over it, so that's why I can't say too much right now. I don't want to make him feel that I'm judging him or putting him under any pressure, but there is pressure, building just under the surface. I can't help it. Something has gone wrong, and he doesn't want to admit it.

'It's fine,' he says after thirty seconds of silence when only the wind whistles. 'We're on the right route. It's fine. I'll go off the map. It's fine.' His body language tells me he's confident.

Do I point out that he's used the word *fine* three times in a single paragraph?

Are we lost and he's trying to cover up the fact?

The irony of the typical husband-and-wife argument isn't lost on me, but this isn't a simple case of taking a wrong turn down a road while out on a Sunday drive. We're miles from anywhere and halfway up a mountain in the Swiss Alps with a raging storm closing in with every passing minute. It's not like we can stop and ask for directions either. Every other hiker in the vicinity will be hunkered down in a cabin or further down the mountain where the worst of the storm won't reach.

Steffan bends down next to me. 'Are you sure you can do this?' he asks. 'I know I'm asking a lot of you. I know I'm pushing you, but it's not much further.'

'I... I'm just worried we may be lost.'

Steffan chuckles. 'I can promise you we are not lost. We're going the right way. We've just taken a different route than I thought.'

'The snow is getting really bad.'

'I know. I'm sorry, but it's not much further.'

'We can't keep going for much longer in this weather. It's only going to get worse.'

'I know.'

I bite my tongue, knowing that I'm coming across as complaining. 'Where is the nearest cabin?' I ask, my voice low and croaky against the wind and snow buffeting my face.

Steffan glances at the map, squinting his eyes. Thanks to the ever-approaching weather system, the light is fading fast. It's not due to get dark for another three hours but tell that to the sky above that's threatening to explode with snow any second.

'There isn't one for miles. There's no way we'd make it to any of them without getting caught in the storm. The only thing we can do now is keep going and find a place to hunker down for the night.'

The idea of spending a freezing night in a two-person tent with my husband while a snowstorm rages outside is not my idea of a fun time, even if it does sound cosy.

'Okay,' I say, because what else is there to say?

The temperature has plummeted to around zero, maybe less. Before we take off again, I add an extra layer underneath my waterproof jacket. It's going to be slow going because of the deep snow and steep climb. My hands are freezing, so I put on my gloves too, my fingers trembling as I pull my scarf up so that it covers my nose.

Neither of us speaks as we continue. It's best not to expend energy and risk unsettling our breathing by talking. I don't complain. I don't ask questions. I just keep moving, putting one foot in front of the other, placing my unwavering faith and trust in Steffan, who I know will guide us to safety.

He has to. Because if he doesn't, we're going to die out here.

And that's not an exaggeration.

8

BONNIE

NOW

An hour later, my body is on the verge of giving up and shutting down completely. How long does it take for a person to freeze to death? How cold does it need to be? I didn't come across that bit of information during my research. It feels as if there's ice in my veins, and my joints are seizing up.

I can't feel the tips of my fingers. That's not a good sign, and I'm pretty sure that was an early symptom of frostbite. I've heard frostbite is painful, but right now I can't sense anything from my knuckles down. Does that mean it's too late and my fingers have already turned black beneath my gloves and they're going to drop off? Isn't that what one of the posters back in the ranger hut said? Maybe it doesn't even happen that way, but I dare not remove my gloves in case the movement causes damage.

My tears freeze against my cheeks and, because I've got a scarf covering my nose, the condensation from my warm breath instantly causes ice crystals to appear. The wind is so strong I can't stand upright without being buffeted to the side. I'm having to crawl through the deep snow, one miniscule step at a time. I place my left foot in front of me, but it sinks straight down through the soft drift. We haven't put on our snowshoes yet, but it's getting to that point now where if we don't, I fear I may sink into a snowdrift and never come back up for air.

How long have we been walking now? Although I'd barely call it *walking*. We're crawling. I can't see a damn thing apart from Steffan's glow stick that's stuck on his pack about seven feet in front of me. It's my only frame of reference to know I'm going forwards, otherwise it would be easy to blindly crawl around in circles. Sometimes I wonder if I've lost sight of him completely and I'm following some unknown glowing spot in front of me. How can Steffan even see where he's going? Again, my unwavering faith in him is the only thing that keeps me going, keeps me on track and moving forwards, even if it feels like walking through thick glue.

My left foot sinks again.

I'm stuck.

Why won't my leg move? Has it frozen solid or am I trapped? Fear engulfs me as my brain fills in the pieces of the puzzle as to what may have happened a year ago. I wasn't there. I don't know what happened, but it feels as if I'm experiencing parts of what happened, walking in the footsteps of the past.

'Steffan!'

Within seconds, he's at my side. I have no idea how he heard me through the howling wind, but he did. And he's here.

'You're okay. Calm down. Your foot is just wedged in a crevice. Hold still.' Steffan awkwardly crouches and grabs my ankle, yanking it upwards. I whimper, but there's no pain, so I don't think I've injured myself.

'Steffan, we're going to die out here,' I say with an over-dramatic sob.

'No, we're not. Come on. Don't give up on me now.'

'How much further?'

'Once we've reached the end of this ridge, we'll start heading down into a valley. We'll find somewhere to stop there.'

He doesn't say how much longer we have left on this ridge, but his words are enough to calm my panic and put my racing mind at ease.

'You're doing great,' he says. 'This storm is worse than I imagined. I'm sorry. We should have sought a nearby cabin instead. I can't believe...' He shakes his head, the words he wants to say left unsaid. I know what he was about to say.

I can't believe I let this happen again.

I grasp his arm, squeezing it through the thick layers of his winter jacket and thermals. Now, it's my turn to reassure him. I want him to know that I trust his judgment. It does the job. He nods, straightening up and pulling me to my feet.

From somewhere deep down, I summon the strength to follow him across the ridge, attempting to put the dangers out of my mind. One wrong step and we could slip and fall off the edge or crash down into a deep crevice, breaking a leg in the process. Or worse, our necks. Damn Johan and his safety briefing. If he could see us now, he'd be disappointed that we took such a dangerous risk to try and outpace the impending storm rather than seek shelter.

More minutes pass. Maybe hours; I'm not sure how long it's been, but finally, it feels as if we're going downhill and not up.

Thank God!

The snow is still deep, the wind is getting stronger, but at least going down means we're getting off the ridge and out of the worst of the elements, which means we can start seeking shelter. Although, God knows where. Maybe a cave under a rock or an overhang, perhaps.

As I scramble over snowdrifts, attempting to step in Steffan's footprints, to make it a little easier for myself, something dark catches my eye.

I turn and blink, my eyelids feeling heavy thanks to the ice crystals that have formed on my lashes. I'm surprised they haven't frozen together already.

The object looks out of place amongst the mountains and snowy trees. It shouldn't be there. I can barely see it. Perhaps my eyes are playing tricks on me or I'm hallucinating. Didn't Johan say hallucinations were one of the first signs of hypothermia, along with numb fingertips?

Is that a... *cabin*?

'Steffan!' I shout. He's managed to stretch out the distance between us, thanks to my slow progress. He can't hear me. Summoning some strength from somewhere, I increase my pace, but my legs are half-frozen and half-jelly. 'Steffan!' I think my vocal cords are frozen too. 'Steffan!'

This time, he turns.

Rather than shouting again, I point to the right where the cabin is, gesturing wildly in case he can't see it. It's not a large cabin and, from what I can see, there are no lights on inside, but it's shelter, and that's exactly what we need.

Steffan stomps over to me. 'What is it?'

'A cabin!' My voice gets lost in the wind.

He's got his snow goggles on, so I can't see his line of vision, but he must see the cabin too. 'Shit,' he says. 'It must be an old, abandoned accommodation cabin. It's not marked on the route anywhere.'

'We begin a slow stomp towards the front door. The cabin looks a little worse for wear, sandwiched between trees and rock and snow. It's barely visible through the blizzard, but just as I reach it, a faint yellow light flickers through the boarded-up window next to the door.

My heart almost stops.

There's someone in there.

Perhaps they're lost and trapped here too. Whatever the reason for the faint light appearing, I know I'm now minutes away from salvation and shelter. My breathing rate increases.

'Bonnie! Stop. You don't know who's in there. Let me.' Steffan reaches my side and grabs my arm, pulling me away from the door.

Steffan grabs the doorknob and twists, but it doesn't move. Is it frozen shut or locked? He hammers his fist against the door. There's no answer, so I repeat the process of banging. My hands are so cold that the gesture barely registers. The light still flickers, but then it dims slightly. Did I imagine it? Am I so desperate to be saved that my mind is showing me what I want to see? It's a real cabin, though. Steffan can see it too. I'm not wrong about that.

I keep pounding against the door even after he's stopped.

'It's locked,' shouts Steffan over the howling wind. The wind and snow are now so strong his voice comes out as a whisper. It's hard to see him, even standing so close. If this door doesn't open, then it's over for us. I can't go on another step.

Forever passes by.

Steffan takes my arm and pulls me away from the door.

He's giving up, and I can feel my heart doing the same. Am I accepting my fate, my death? But just as I turn my back, the light flickers again, illuminating a small portion of my face with a warm glow.

I turn fast, just as the door opens and a small, frail face peers out at us, using the door as a shield against the wind and snow hammering against it.

We're saved.

9

ANNALISE

NOW

Standing up from my wooden rocking chair, I shuffle into the kitchen area of the three-room cabin, readjusting my warm, wool hat that's pulled low over my forehead and ears. In the colder months, I keep it on constantly to stop my body heat escaping. My mother always told me that heat escapes out of the top of your head the quickest. I'm not too sure whether it's true, but I've used a thick hat even indoors ever since when it's needed.

My cabin consists of one bedroom and one large living area, which includes a table and a bucket for washing the dishes, plus a tiny room to use as a bathroom. Over the years, Erik and I collected and built many items to add to the cabin to make it more homely; a fireplace, a camp bed, a wooden chest, various pots and pans and a large rug across the floor. It's not much, but it's home, although *prison* is more of a correct term at times.

Erik built the entire cabin with his own hands – perfect for just the two of us. We never had children, though not from lack of trying. Having children was obviously never in the cards for us, despite wanting them from the very start of our marriage. Back then, before it happened, we'd been blissfully happy, full of life and excitement for the years ahead, but happiness has a way of dissipating rather quickly when a catastrophic event halts you in your tracks like a sledgehammer to a sheet of ice.

And that's exactly what happened.

I fancy another cup of herbal tea, something I use to help me sleep or numb the aches and pains of hard labour and old age, but I don't want to waste water, not with a storm on the way, so I forgo the luxury. I've stocked up on enough water, food and firewood to last me two weeks if I'm careful. I'm an expert at managing my rations. Erik taught me a lot of things, including how to be resourceful and make quick, rational decisions. I loved that about him. I could always count on him to keep me safe from harm, from myself or anyone else. At the start, at least. Things change.

Everything I eat and drink is from nature. I've turned into a skilful hunter and gatherer over the years, catching and killing my own food – mostly rabbits and marmots – foraging for edible plants, as well as growing my own vegetables. It can be difficult to store food for a long time, especially meat, but I've devised a way of keeping it cool, even in the summer months; an ingenious solution, if I do say so myself.

The open fireplace is used to heat the room, cook my food and boil water. It's a perfect setup. I couldn't ask for anything else. Sometimes, if the snow covers the chimney, it can stop me from lighting it, but that only happens on very rare occasions, and the fire is enough to keep this cabin warm enough throughout the winter months. Plus, the chimney is a valuable air hole for when the cabin gets buried in snow.

The whole cabin trembles against the howling gale

outside. I knew it would be a bad storm. God help any hikers caught out in it. I often come across hikers during my forages and hunts, but I avoid them if I can. Back in my younger days, I loved social interactions, but now it isn't my strong suit. I prefer to be a recluse than speak to another human being. That was one of the hardest things I struggled with when Erik passed; I had no one to talk to. It's another reason why I talk to my dearly beloved husband still. If I don't, I fear I may lose the ability to speak at all. Losing my voice would mean losing who I am. I don't want to disappear completely.

The fire is blazing away, heating my root vegetable and marmot stew. I blow out the candle on the nearby table, not wanting to waste it. I make the candles myself, using natural ingredients, but I'm running low on stock, so I need to spend some time making more. Perhaps I'll do it during the storm for something to keep myself occupied. The fire does a great job of lighting the room at night without the use of candles anyway.

Hobbling back over to the large pan, something I found on a mountain path many years ago, discarded by hikers, I give the stew a stir and smell the warm, earthy aromas. My left ankle has been giving me a bit of jip recently. I broke it many years ago, I forget how many exactly, and it's never healed properly. The earth provides us with what we need to survive, including plenty of herbs and flowering plants to numb pain and dull the senses. I spent many days under the influence of such plants while my ankle healed, but nothing can ever be as perfect as before it's broken. The same goes for a relationship, or marriage, I suppose. Once broken, a heart can never truly heal.

A knock makes me pause for a moment.

It must be that damn tree branch again. I've been meaning to cut it down in case it blows over in bad winds and crushes the roof.

I keep stirring the stew. It's not boiling yet, so I sit back down in my rocking chair. Erik built it for me as a fifth wedding anniversary gift all those years ago. He was such a talented man. There wasn't anything he couldn't build or make or do. This cabin is falling apart without him, but I'm doing my best to keep it liveable. I hope the storm doesn't do too much damage. I'm not sure my body could handle climbing up to the roof and fixing it or scaling a makeshift ladder to board over a broken window.

There's that knocking again. It's louder than before, more frantic.

It's not coming from the roof either.

It's coming from the front door.

Surely, it can't be what I think it is.

There's no way anyone would be out walking in this weather. The cabin isn't even on any of the recommended hiking routes. It's why we chose to build here. I've only ever had one hiker appear at my door, and that's only because he likely followed me here. My cabin is located away from human eyes, in a spot that no one has ever encountered.

But my curiosity is too strong to ignore, so I walk across the room and unlock the door, pausing a moment as my wrinkled hand rests on the latch. If I open it, there's a strong chance the wind could rip it off its hinges. All the warmth the fire has created will be lost, but the banging continues. It's relentless.

Then it stops.

I pause, wrestling with the choice to either keep the door

closed and go back to my meal, or open it and risk letting in more than the bad weather.

    I make my decision.

10

ANNALISE

THEN

There's no noise anymore, apart from her ragged breaths. Her eyes are closed, and she's listening to the air wheezing in through her nose and mouth, feeling her chest rise and fall every few seconds. It's over. It's okay. It's over now.

She lies still for a long time, silently whispering her prayer to God. She forces her eyes open, terrified of what she'll see when she does. She's not sure exactly what's happened. Time appears to have jumped ahead because now the room is silent. The man who attacked her in her own home isn't here anymore.

As her eyes adjust to her surroundings, she looks down at her body and takes note of the blood splatters on her clothes. It stains her once-yellow dress and pale skin. Her legs buckle beneath her as she attempts to stand, and she collapses back to the cold stone floor.

The front door is closed.

Even her trembling hands are stained with red. Is this her blood?

She weeps, a broken woman in more ways than one. The

man is gone. She's alone in her house, her place of refuge. Except it no longer feels safe to her, not after what's just happened within its walls. The man isn't here to hurt her anymore, but what if he returns? Should she leave and fetch Erik, or stay and risk that man coming back? She craves the warm, strong arms of her husband. She's always felt safe in his embrace before. He'll know what to do. He'll be able to tell her why the man attacked her in their home and...

A sharp pain erupts in her stomach.

How did she not notice it before?

Annalise places a hand on her abdomen, then pulls it away, revealing more bright red blood. She's bleeding. Badly. Did he stab her, or...

She can't understand any of this.

Leaving the basket that took her hours to make discarded on the floor, along with the food, she staggers to her feet, using the kitchen table in the middle of the room to steady herself. She can't go and find Erik looking like this. She'll have to change her clothes. Otherwise, people will notice. They'll stare and ask questions she's in no position to answer.

Hobbling to the bedroom she shares with Erik, she pulls out a clean dress from the wardrobe, then slips off the blood-stained one, leaving it pooled on the floor by her feet. That's when she notices more blood on her legs, trickling down in small rivers.

Her immediate thought is that she's started her monthly cycle. She had been due this week, but maybe it's to do with the wound on her stomach. Is she bleeding internally? Shame and fear envelop her. What has he done to her? Is she irreparably damaged inside? How will she ever face her husband? Will he still see her as the woman he fell in love with, the future mother of his children, or as a scarred, damaged vessel? She can't remember what's happened. It's like her brain has blocked the whole thing out. Maybe it's for the best.

Annalise shakes the dark thoughts away, knowing for a fact her beloved husband would never think those awful things about her. In sickness and in health. That's what they'd promised each other in their wedding vows. This is a sickness, but she'll recover soon. She's sure of it.

She knows she needs help, but she can't risk being seen looking like a... a what? A victim? She doesn't want to draw attention to herself, yet the thought of stumbling through the alleys alone, looking for her husband, terrifies her. What if that man is out there waiting for her to leave? What if he hasn't finished with her?

Then, a thought occurs to her. Did no one hear the struggle while she'd been attacked? Granted, after she screamed the first time, she didn't make a single sound. The seconds and minutes had ticked by at a glacial pace, each more terrifying and excruciating than the last.

But it is over now. Isn't it?

Yet, no one had come to her rescue. No one had knocked on the door to ask if she was okay. No one is coming to help her. She has to help herself. Annalise doesn't really know her neighbours well. They've only lived in the area for a few months. Erik loves to travel, to keep on the move, which is fine with her, but it means she never gets to know the area as well as she'd like. It means she doesn't know anyone well enough to ask for help or knock on their doors.

Annalise slips her foot out of her remaining shoe. Her other one must be discarded somewhere in the main room. She then steps into the clean dress, freezing as a knock sounds at the front door.

She wills her body to move.

Footsteps, loud and clear, sound from outside. She can hear them through the thin walls.

Whoever it is, it can't be her husband. He has a key. He'd have let himself in.

Who is at her door?

What do they want?

11

ANNALISE
NOW

Have I ingested too many herbs today? Am I hallucinating? It certainly wouldn't be the first time. Once, not long after Erik passed, I saw him standing in the corner of the cabin. We had a full conversation! I made sure to cut down on the herbs for a while after that, but perhaps I've been increasing them without realising, making the tea more potent.

I wedge myself against the door as I inch it open, using it as a barrier between me and the howling wind and snow outside. I must be crazy to attempt to open the door in such bad weather. When I finally get it open, the snow is so deep it's almost halfway up the door.

Two people stand in my doorway. From their difference in size, I assume one is a man and one is a woman. I can barely see their faces because they are covered with scarves and snow, giving them the appearance of two snowmen. The man is wearing some strange-looking black goggles that scare me at first. He looks alien. Both have huge packs on their backs, weighing them down like boulders.

I don't like this. I haven't seen another human being for

almost a year. Not this close anyway. I saw a large group of hikers last summer, but I kept my distance and hid in the nearby trees until they passed. Hearing their voices over the wind had given me goosebumps. I haven't been this close to another person since Erik passed. I almost want to reach out my hand and touch them, just to reassure my foggy mind that they're real.

How did these two find me? More importantly, are they crazy? They must be if they're out in this weather. I'm surprised they haven't frozen to death or accidentally walked off the edge of a cliff. It's easily done, especially in these awful conditions. I've been caught out in my fair share of storms, only surviving thanks to my quick actions of hiding under rock overhangs or in dark caves. These people must have hiked along the treacherous ridge, which is notorious for fatal accidents. I've found a body near the bottom once before, although after he landed, he must have crawled a while before he succumbed to his injuries, because I didn't find him directly at the bottom of the cliff. Of course, I left him there after raiding his supplies, but then I felt bad, so I went back and buried him. No sense in drawing in hungry wildlife. That's how I've come to own mugs, knives and forks and other cooking utensils over the years; waste not, want not.

'Hello!' shouts the woman. 'Please. Help us. We need shelter. Thank God we found you!'

I think that's what she says. It's difficult to hear her over the wind. I haven't spoken English in a very long time. Erik and I would always converse in our native tongue, but we did grow up learning English too. I do sometimes practice speaking English out loud, but it's one of those things that's dwindled over time. I can't read it, though.

'No!' I say as I move to close the door, but quick as a flash, the man steps forwards and wedges his large boot in-between the door and the frame. The woman shakes her head at him and then turns to me.

'Please... we're desperate.'

I'm not strong enough to fight the weather pushing against the door and the man's boot combined, so I reluctantly nod, bow my head in acknowledgement and allow them to step forwards into the cabin. The man grabs the door and wrestles with it as he latches the bolt across. The noise from outside dampens slightly. They are both breathing heavily and covered head to toe in snow, so I can't even see the colour of their jackets.

The woman takes off her gloves, pulls down her hood and unwraps the scarf from her face. Her cheeks are red-raw from the snow and wind, her eyelashes covered in ice crystals.

'Thank you,' she says, sounding out of breath. 'Thank you so much. You've just saved our lives.'

I stare at them, unsure what to do or say. I'm surprised I can understand them so easily. It seems my understanding of the English language hasn't diminished completely.

The man removes his goggles and hood. His unkempt beard is covered in snow, which he quickly brushes off. It lands on my floor rug. I immediately don't like him, but that's got nothing to do with him personally. After the incident all those years ago, I've never liked or trusted another man ever again. I'm sure there are lovely men all over the world, but I've yet to meet one.

'Who are you and what are you doing out here?' I ask slowly, making sure to pronounce the words as well as I can. My accent is quite thick. I take a step towards the fire where the large stick I use to stoke it is resting. I don't know these people or what they're capable of. They could be here to kill me. After what happened last time, I can't be too careful. I must be able to defend myself. Gone are the days when I welcomed people into my home with open arms. Everyone is a threat nowadays.

'I'm so sorry to intrude,' says the woman. 'We had no idea anyone was out here. My name is Bonnie and this is my husband, Steffan. We took a wrong turn and... the weather came in quicker than we expected.' The young woman shoots a desperate look at her husband. He nods but doesn't add anything else.

'Did you not know a storm was coming?' I ask, sounding like a mother scolding her naughty children. Honestly, some people are just so idiotic. One should never think they can race ahead of a storm, unless they have a death wish.

'We did, but...' The woman, Bonnie, stops and bites her lip. 'I just happened to see your cabin. We didn't realise anyone was out here. Do you live here?' Her eyes scan my humble abode, focusing on the roaring fire, which must be like a welcome beacon to them. They look half-frozen.

'Yes,' I say. 'I do.'

Silence fills the small room.

Every part of me screams to kick them out, but an ache in my gut tells me that if I do that, I may as well be signing their death warrant. How am I supposed to overpower them? It's not like I can manhandle them out the door. I'm an old woman now. Strong for my age, I'm sure, but not strong enough to shove these two back out into the cold. I sigh loudly, making it known this is a huge inconvenience to me. I don't want either of them here.

Erik always warned me to keep my distance from people,

especially after what happened. Before we arrived here, if we absolutely had to interact with others, then it was always him who spoke. I always had to hide, never show my face, not to anyone. These two have trespassed on my property and practically forced their way into my home. I've a right to defend myself if I must.

'I suppose... you'll have to stay here,' I say, mumbling the words.

The relief in Bonnie's eyes is evident. Her shoulders relax slightly, despite her still carrying her enormous pack that looks as if it weighs almost as much as she does.

'Thank you so much,' she says as she awkwardly takes the bag off her back. As she does, snow and ice scatter all over the floor. 'I don't know what we would have done if... I mean...' She stops and her eyes flood with tears.

Steffan clears his throat. 'Yes. Thank you for letting us come in,' he says in a gruff voice as he too takes off his pack. I don't mention the fact that I didn't *let* them in. He wedged his foot in the door, giving me no other choice in the matter. 'We won't be here long,' he adds. 'The storm should pass over in an hour or two.'

I chuckle as I turn and tend to the fire. 'That may be true, but I doubt you'll be able to go anywhere until the day after tomorrow at the earliest. There's a lot of snow on the way. The sky was thick with it. You'd better make yourself comfortable and bring any wet clothes over to the fire to dry. The stew is almost ready. There may be just enough for all of us.'

Both Bonnie and Steffan look at each other. I can practically hear their gurgling stomachs.

'Thank you,' says Steffan with a nod. 'But we can't accept your food. We have our own.'

'Suit yourself,' I say. 'But I assume you're only carrying enough food for your trek, so if you use it all now, you may not have enough to get you to wherever it is you're heading when you eventually leave when the snow melts.'

Steffan silently stares at me. 'You're right. Thank you. As long as you're certain.'

I nod, stir the contents in the pot. My back is turned to them, but the large stick is within reach should either of them decide to attack me. I listen as they shuffle around behind me, removing their jackets and boots. It's not overly warm inside, hence why I'm keeping my hat on and the thick shawl I made, but it's warm enough for them to remove the top layer of clothes to dry and thaw.

'It's so lovely and warm,' says Bonnie.

'Compared to outside, maybe. After an hour or two, you'll notice the cold creeping in. My husband insulated the walls and roof with tar and wool, apart from the small room over there.' I point to where the toilet room is located behind the shut door.

'Your husband? Is he here?' Bonnie glances left and right, as if she's expecting him to pop out somewhere.

'Yes, he's here. Well, not right now,' I reply, deciding to use a white lie as a defence against my new lodgers. Maybe they will be less likely to attack or harm me if they think my husband is close by or on the way back. 'He's out hunting.'

'In this weather?'

'We have several hideaways dotted around the mountains. He'll be holed up in one until the storm has passed.' I'm not too sure if either of them has bought it, but I've said it now, so there's no going back. 'Come, take a seat by the fire. My name is Annalise.' As I say my name, I reach my hand to my face and tuck a stray strand of hair back under my hat.

Come to think of it, now that they're in here and we're talking, a warm glow settles itself in my chest. As much as I hate to admit it, I have missed human interaction. In the back of my mind, Erik is sending me warnings about this couple, that I shouldn't trust them, and he's right, but human beings need others to thrive. And I've been starved of human interaction for far too long now.

Perhaps Bonnie and Steffan will be able to thaw my cold heart after all.

12

BONNIE

THEN

The phone doesn't ring again. It remains frustratingly quiet, taunting me. Now, the worry switches to something more, which builds, rising higher and higher from the pit of my stomach until I can't think straight or take a deep breath. It's like my lungs have forgotten how to inhale oxygen or all the oxygen from the air has vanished because every time I suck in a shaky breath, it burns. Worry has now turned to... I don't think there's a word for what I'm experiencing.

Panic. Sure.

Confusion. Check.

Fear. Yes, but it's more than fear. Much more.

Terror sounds about right.

There's still five miles left of my run to complete. The path I've taken is my usual circle route, which means it's quicker to keep going than turn back. I can get back to the car in less than thirty minutes if I run faster than normal, but my legs have turned to jelly in the past five minutes, and I can barely get my feet to point in the right direction. How hard is it to put one foot in front of the other? I do it every day for miles and miles at a time, but they refuse to work properly, let alone run at a decent pace.

I start walking as fast as my legs allow, constantly pressing redial on the unknown number. With every dial tone, my panic, horror and frustration increase. Why won't the damn phone ring again? I try and call the number back several dozen times, but it disconnects straight away and there's no answer machine to leave a message. I jab at the call button repeatedly, expecting it to magically answer all my burning questions, but all it does is frustrate me.

I navigate to Steffan's number and call it instead. It rings once and disconnects.

Christopher's phone doesn't even ring. Straight to voicemail.

I tilt my head to the sky and scream.

How do anxious people make it through the day with this constant gnawing ache in their gut? It's all I can think about and focus on. I trust my husband completely, but it doesn't stop me listing all the dangers and possible scenarios in my head over and over. I just want it to stop so I can go back to being the carefree, worry-free person I used to be.

Even in my dreams, it never lets up. I wake up most nights in a cold sweat, gasping for breath, and then realise that I'm safe and sound in my bed while they are out in dangerous weather conditions, trekking across the Swiss Alps, which house some of the most brutal mountains on earth.

They arrived there over two weeks ago, and I've barely heard anything since. Steffan told me that it wouldn't be possible to contact me every day, so I expected a few days without a message, but surely, it's been too long now. I should have heard something. *Anything.*

The thing is, it may be their first time climbing and hiking together, but Steffan has climbed K2 and all the other top ten highest mountains in the world. Everest will be his final challenge in two years' time, and, for some harebrained reason that I'll never understand, my baby brother wanted to join him during this training expedition. He too has climbed smaller mountains before and has hundreds of hours of hiking and climbing experience under his belt but doesn't have as much experience as my husband. Neither of them is a novice. They know what they're doing, which is why the constant worry is a surprise to me. What's so different about this expedition? Am I experiencing some strange phenomenon where I can sense something dangerous is about to happen before it does? I've heard of that happening, like when mothers just *know* something is wrong with their child, even before the doctors confirm the diagnosis. Is that what this is?

By the time I make it back to the car, my stomach is in knots and I'm not sure whether I want to puke or cry. I slide behind the wheel and take a deep breath, attempting to compose myself. I'm due to meet up with Hannah and the twins in twenty minutes at the pub. Maybe she'll be able to bring me down off this cliff edge that I seem to be standing on, barely able to keep my balance.

I drive on autopilot to the pub car park, which is only just down the road, switch off the engine and then stare ahead, my phone clutched tight in my hand.

I press the call button again and am met with the same dial tone.

What was it the person said exactly? My husband was in danger? It's an odd word to use considering his expertise. Why would he be in danger?

My phone erupts in my hand. I jab the answer button.

'Hello. Hello!'

'Bonnie...'

'Steffan! Is that you? Oh my God, are you okay? What's going on?'

'Sorry... line bad... just wanted to call... tell you... okay.'

'What? You're okay?' There's a long pause on the line. I check the call is still connected. It is. 'Hello? Steffan?'

'Yes... Okay.'

I put one finger in my left ear while pressing the phone so tight to my right it starts to hurt. 'Some man just called me and said you were in danger. It scared the life out of me.'

'Who called you?'

'I... I don't know. He didn't say his name. He just said you were in danger. Is Chris okay?'

'Yeah. Chris... fine. Bonnie... don't... answer. Don't... speak... man... again. Call later.'

'Wait... but who is he? Is it someone who's there with you?'

'No. Doesn't matter. Don't worry. Bye.'

'Okay. Bye.'

I hang up, my brow furrowed. Now, I'm even more confused than before. The relief that Steffan and Chris are okay is overwhelming, but who the hell was that man who called me?

I stare ahead at the car park in front of me, where there's only one other car. A knock sounds on the window next to me, and I leap in fright, only to see Hannah peering at me. I open the door and get out, my muscles silently screaming at me. My butt is numb, the type of numb you get when you're driving long-distance and haven't had the chance to stretch your legs or shift your position. My legs are tense and stiff, punishing me for not stretching properly after my run. Cooling down is my normal routine at the end of a long one, but after getting back to the car, I got straight in without so much as a quad stretch.

'What are you doing sitting in your car?' asks Hannah with a laugh. 'I thought you'd have a glass of pinot grigio in your hand by now.'

The twins give my legs a hug, one on each side. 'Eww, Auntie Bonnie, you smell,' says Natalie, the oldest of the two.

I chuckle, ignoring my stiff muscles and the odd phone call. 'Sorry,' I say. 'Let's sit outside so I don't stink up the place, yeah? How are you both feeling? Mummy said you had a cough.'

'We're fine,' replies Noah. The twins share a cheeky smile.

I look up at Hannah, who rolls her eyes. 'Kids,' she says with a shake of the head.

Five minutes later, Hannah and I are seated at an outside circular table with a parasol, each holding a glass of white wine, with a menu in front of us, while the twins play in the play area just off to the left. We haven't ordered yet, but I already know what I want: a full vegetarian roast dinner with all the trimmings.

'How was your run?' asks Hannah.

'It was good, thanks, apart from a weird phone call I had. It really freaked me out.' I tell her about the call and then what Steffan said too.

'This man who called you... is he someone who's with them on their trek?'

'I have no idea. I don't think so, but it seemed odd to have a call like that so soon after you confirmed they were both okay after their accident.'

Hannah frowns. 'And Chris is okay?'

'Steffan said he was.'

Hannah takes a sip of wine, then swallows. 'Weird.' We sit in silence for a moment, then she says, 'Did this guy have an Irish accent?'

'Oh my God. How did you know that?'

'He called me too. Not today. About a week or so ago. I'd completely forgotten about it until you mentioned it.'

'What did he say?' It's at this exact moment the waitress turns up and asks if we're ready to order, so we do. The twins rush over and squabble over who wants what. It takes an agonising amount of time before Hannah and I are alone again.

Hannah leans back in her chair and pushes her sunglasses up to rest on the top of her head. She has such gorgeous thick, black hair; it shines in the sun at certain angles. 'Going back to the phone call I got a week ago. He said the same thing, really. That Chris was in danger. He also said he needed to be careful, then hung up.'

'Did you ask Chris about it?'

'Of course I did. He was standing right next to me when I got the call. He went all wide-eyed when I told him about it, but then laughed it off and said it was probably a prank call or something, but whoever it was knew Chris by name, so...' She tails off and turns to watch the twins, who are arguing who gets to go down the slide first.

I take a sip of my wine. I've only had half a glass and it's already going to my head. It's never a good idea to drink alcohol after a long run, but I relish the fuzziness. Plus, I earned it.

'I wouldn't worry about it,' says Hannah.

But I do. The worry niggles at the back of my mind for the remainder of the meal.

13

BONNIE

NOW

My blood turns to ice as my brain slots together what I'm seeing. It hadn't even occurred to me outside, when I'd first spotted the cabin, or even as I'd willingly stepped over the threshold, but here she is. Annalise. An old woman who lives alone in the Swiss Alps and who appears to have... pure white hair.

I only caught a glimpse. Less than a glimpse. It was more of a flash, but I'm certain she tucked a strand of white hair back up under her wool hat. Almost certain. Ninety-five percent certain. Maybe ninety.

I think back to a particular paragraph in the article where it mentions the first official sighting of the White Witch in 1985. Apparently, a local farmer said he saw a wild woman with a streak of white in her hair stealing a lamb from his fields and carrying it off into the woods. But, according to Barry's article, it wasn't until 1997 that the name "The White Witch" officially stuck, which was made up by Fred Harrington, who's said to have spotted a woman with pure white hair chowing down on a raw deer carcass deep in the middle of the mountains. He immediately turned and ran away.

The thought sends an uncomfortable shiver up my spine as I watch Annalise lower her eyes away from me and turn to the fire. I keep my eyes on her, unable to look at anything else as my mind overruns with questions.

Is this the white witch whom Barry was searching for?

But that's ridiculous, right? Because the White Witch is merely a local legend, a tourist attraction that's been warped and altered over the years to bring new crowds to the area, more attention. Barry said so himself in his article, highlighting other local legends too; the Frost Giants ruled by the Frost King, the Witch of Belap, who's said to have been burned at the stake, and even Heidi, a renowned and much-loved urban legend going back many years, originated in the Swiss Alps.

That's what always fascinated me about urban legends and why I grew up wanting to find the Loch Ness Monster. Parents tell their children, who tell their children, who tell their friends, who tell their children. Over the years, these stories grow wings, change direction and become even more fantastic and unbelievable, constantly holding a new generation's interest, developing their fascination for all things weird, wonderful and, sometimes, downright creepy.

Am I staring at a real-life urban legend?

What's Annalise's story? Why is she living out here all by herself? Wait, she mentioned a husband, didn't she, so what's their story?

I study her closely, all too aware that I'm open-mouthed staring.

She's a little stiff and awkward as she moves, a possible limp in her gait. I'm guessing she's nearing her seventies, but

I've never been good at guessing people's ages by their appearance alone. Deep-set wrinkles surround her dark eyes, and her body looks rail thin. I can tell that even with her wearing layers of clothing by how thin her hands and face are, the blue veins on the backs of her hands almost glowing through her pale skin. Her hair is tucked up under a thick wool hat pulled low around her forehead and ears, and I want nothing more than to rush forwards and rip it off her head, settling the mystery of the White Witch once and for all.

Steffan pulls my attention away from Annalise by asking, 'Are you okay?' He nudges me lightly.

'Yes, sorry.' I hold my hands out to him. 'My fingers hurt a bit.'

Steffan takes my hands. It's difficult to see properly in this dim light. The cabin is quite dark, lots of shadowy corners, but the fire is casting enough of a glow to be able to see each other's faces. He squeezes the tip of my little finger. 'Can you feel this?'

'Yes.'

He squeezes another. 'And this?'

'A bit... Ouch!' I wrench my hand away and shake it.

Steffan smirks. 'It's okay. You're not going to lose your fingers just yet.'

'Oh, well, that's good.' I appreciate his attempt at lightening a dark moment. He moves closer to me, then wraps his arms around my body.

'I'm so sorry, Bonnie. This is all my fault.'

I bury my face into his shoulder. 'It's not your fault. We're safe. That's all that matters now.'

The cabin may be warmer than outside, but it's nowhere near as warm as an average central-heated house. I can't see any obvious cracks in the walls, which Annalise said were insulated with wool and tar, but the windows are single-pane and have boards covering them to protect against the wind and snow that's piling up outside, getting deeper by the minute.

'Are we safe in here?' I ask. 'There's no air holes.'

Steffan nods towards the fire. 'By the looks of it, there's a decent chimney and flue. It might get a bit stuffy in here, but I expect she doesn't keep the fire going all the time to allow for air flow. We'll be fine. This will be a fun story to tell the grandkids one day, right?' He moves away, letting me out of his embrace.

I chuckle. He's not wrong there, although to have grandkids, we'd need to have kids first, and that's a whole other can of worms we haven't opened yet. I love my nephew and niece, but my God, are they exhausting. I like to be able to hand them back at the end of the day after babysitting.

Steffan and I work in silence while we sort our kit out. He's used to this sort of admin, as am I to a certain extent, but when I run long-distance, I don't have as much kit to contend with.

I bend and untie the laces on my boots, but my fingers refuse to cooperate, fumbling over the thin pieces of string, which are frozen solid. Steffan may have put my mind at ease with regard to possible frostbite, but my fingers are still numb. I eventually manage to get my boots off by sitting on the floor and wrestling with them like I'm trying to wrangle an alligator. It takes far longer than I care to admit, and once they're off, I stop for a moment to recover my breath.

My body and brain are slowly thawing, a welcome benefit of the increase in temperature, but my muscles are struggling to respond to their signals.

The warm aroma of the stew bubbling in the pot over the fire distracts me for a moment. The last time Steffan and I stopped for food was roughly eight hours ago, so my empty stomach is making it clear that it needs feeding. Now that we're out of the storm and the adrenaline and near-frostbite is wearing off, my body is showing signs of exhaustion. My head is spinning and all I want to do is curl up in my sleeping bag and snooze for a whole day.

I check my Garmin. It's almost ten in the evening. Annalise said herself that it's doubtful we'll be going anywhere for at least two days, so Steffan and I may as well settle in for the long haul. I don't like the idea of staying in this cabin for two days, but there's nothing I can do about it.

We're alive. We're safe.

And quite possibly trapped in a cabin with a cannibalistic white witch.

14

BONNIE

NOW

Annalise potters around the small kitchen area in the corner. It looks to be a three-room cabin, the main room barely bigger than fifteen-by-fifteen-foot square, give or take, and two doors leading out of this room, not including the front door. I assume one is a bedroom, and one is a toilet area. There's a lingering smell the closer I get to one of the doors, which both Steffan and I are too polite to mention, but luckily, the aroma of the stew covers most of it. A large rug made of animal skins of varying colours and thicknesses is spread out on the floor. Deer mostly, I expect.

Did she say her husband built this place from the ground up, or did he just insulate the roof and walls? This cabin isn't far off from the style of the accommodation cabins dotted around the mountains, but it's much older and there are no basic amenities. There aren't any lights, other than the glow the fire is providing. I can't see any plug sockets or electrical items. The kitchen has no oven or fridge. It's just a table covered in various pots and pans and cooking utensils.

There's a large rectangle in the far corner, covered by a thick blanket. Not sure what that is. Possibly a storage chest.

It's cramped and dark. With the snow piling up outside, it feels as if we're being buried alive. Steffan has assured me that we won't run out of air, but how does he know that for sure? Won't the fire suck up all the oxygen and put us at risk of carbon monoxide poisoning? He says it may get stuffy in here, especially with three people now breathing in and out. The air already feels thicker.

Attempting to put the niggling worry at the back of my mind, I focus on the task ahead. I don't blame Steffan for the situation we're in. He made the wrong choice, that's all. Yes, we should have sought shelter earlier rather than push on to try and get ahead of the storm, but the only reason he wanted to keep going was because he knew how much it meant for me to be out here. Maybe he thought that if we stopped, there was a chance I might not want to continue.

The truth is, I can't stop, and even being trapped inside this cabin won't stop me.

Steffan is the only person who knows where it happened. He's leading me there because there's a reason why Steffan and I are out here. I need to see the site where the accident occurred.

I take the wet clothes over to the fire where Annalise is adding another log. There's a huge pile of them next to the fire.

'Is there somewhere I can hang these?' I ask timidly. I'm trying my best not to stare at her, but I can't seem to shift the anxiety rolling around in my stomach at the thought that she could be the woman who's been the source of so many stories and sightings. Come to think of it, if she has been living out here for several decades, the time frame would fit with the start of the legend too.

I wonder how she started living out here with her husband.

I don't know whether to be afraid or curious. Maybe a little of both. I'm certainly approaching her with trepidation.

Annalise nods and points overhead where a long piece of wire is stretching from one side of the cabin to the other; the perfect drying rack. She has many items such as cups, pots and spoons, but there are other objects located in the cabin that are clearly hand-made; the rocking chair, for example. It's rustic and quite beautifully carved and designed. A thick, musty-smelling blanket is draped across the back of the chair.

I wordlessly hang each piece of wet clothing over the wire before placing my soaking boots by the fire, along with Steffan's. I remove my socks and check out the damage to my feet. They are damp and wrinkled from the cold water that's seeped into the boots and soaked my socks, but thankfully, there's no sign of frostbite either. The *Compeed* has started to peel away from my soggy skin, so I pull it off completely, revealing the gross blister beneath. I don't bother putting another plaster on, but slip my feet into some dry socks instead.

'Thank you again,' I say. Despite her creeping me out, I am grateful she allowed us entry.

'Well, I couldn't very well leave you to freeze out there, could I? The question is what were you doing out there in the first place? But let's not worry about that now. Here, take a bowl and I'll get you some stew.' Her English is slightly fragmented, with a sing-song quality to it due to her strong accent, but it's enough for me to understand. I can't imagine she has a lot of need to speak English out here, so I'm relieved we don't have a language barrier between us.

I take the dented metal bowl she gives me. There are dried bits of food stuck around the edges. She doesn't seem to have any other bowls, so she brings a mug and a small saucepan over for her and Steffan to use to hold the food.

Taking a seat on the floor next to the fire, I turn my face towards it, allowing it to defrost my frozen nose and eyelashes. Annalise places a spoonful of stew into the bowl I'm holding. It's not a lot, but I'm in no place to complain about portion sizes. She moves awkwardly, hobbling slightly.

'It smells amazing,' I say. 'What's in it?'

'Potatoes, various herbs, carrots and marmot.'

My heart sinks.

Do I mention that I'm a strict vegetarian and have been since I was ten years old?

Either I put aside my beliefs and eat to keep up my strength, or risk becoming weak with hunger. The posters back in the ranger's hut warned about the dangers of starvation. I must keep up my calorie intake to stay strong. But the idea of swallowing meat makes my eyes water.

I stare down into the thick, gloopy stew, which does smell exceptionally good despite not looking very appetising, and my mind immediately questions what type of other animals are native to the Swiss Alps and what she must have to eat to survive. During the past few days, I've spotted ibex, golden eagles, marmots, red deer and even heard the howl of a nearby wolf. I haven't eaten meat in over twenty years, but I'm in no position to turn my nose up at a warm, hearty stew. Maybe I can eat around the lumps of marmot...

Steffan sits next to me, his legs crossed at the ankles. He

digs into his food straight away, giving me a side eye when I don't immediately start eating.

'Something the matter?' asks Annalise, frowning at me.

I look up from the bowl. 'Um, no... nothing,' I say with a forced smile.

Steffan leans over and whispers in my ear, 'Just think of it as a vicious, ugly animal and not a cute, fluffy one. It's really good, to be fair.'

I glare at Steffan for his crude remark.

Annalise turns her back to sort something out, so I use the opportunity to scoop out the lumps of red meat that I can see and deposit them in Steffan's saucepan. It feels like I'm doing something naughty behind her back, but honestly, I can't stomach eating meat on top of everything else that's happened.

Once the meat is out of my bowl, I relax a little and nibble at the food that's left. The rest of the stew is made up of potatoes and various vegetables, which are delicious. Once I've cleaned the bowl, my stomach gurgles, begging for more. It's nowhere near enough calories to replace the energy I've used during the treacherous hike to get here.

I place the bowl aside. 'That was delicious, Annalise. Thank you.'

Annalise nods and smiles as she slurps the stew from her mug. She's been using her hands to scoop up the meat and vegetables. The dark juice drips down her chin and hands. I glance at Steffan, who is just finishing his food, using a spork from his own pack. Despite having a few items of cutlery, it seems she prefers to use her hands.

Steffan puts the saucepan down and sighs. 'I reckon the storm won't last much longer.'

Annalise says nothing as she gazes into the fire. I'm not

too sure if Steffan is talking to me or Annalise, but I answer anyway. 'I guess we'll see in the morning. Are we... I mean... How far are we from the place?'

Steffan blinks several times and gulps hard, his Adam's apple bobbing. 'About a day's hike away.'

'Will this storm set us back?'

He nods. 'I think we may have to accept the fact that the snowstorm may have impeded our plans.'

'What are you saying?'

'Nothing, I just... I don't want you to get your hopes up. That's all. It's my fault. I should have seen this storm coming. It came out of nowhere.' He rubs the back of his neck and stares at the floor. I can see the weight of the world on his shoulders. He's doing his best, but even his best isn't good enough when you come up against Mother Nature. The thought of turning back and returning home without the thing we came for is enough to make me dizzy.

'I'm not leaving until we...' I'm unsure if Annalise is listening to us, or if she even cares what we're talking about, but she seems to be in her own little world. She has picked up a book and is now reading. I glance briefly at the title, but it must be in another language other than English because I can't read it.

'I know,' replies Steffan, giving my arm a gentle squeeze.

I smile weakly at him before rising to my feet. 'Um... Annalise, is there a toilet I can use, please?'

Annalise looks up without a word and points to one of the doors I saw earlier, the one with the funky odour wafting from the cracks. I walk over and open it. The thick stench hits me in the face, and I cough to control my gag reflex. I don't want to appear rude, and now I'm second-guessing whether I need a wee that bad. I do. I can't hold it. There's no way I'm going to make it through the night without relieving my bladder.

Holding my breath, I walk into the tiny room and close the door. It's completely dark, so I switch on the Garmin's light source, which turns off after ten seconds, so I keep pressing the dial as I check out my surroundings.

There's no toilet. There's a black bucket. That's it. I guess her husband hasn't got around to installing indoor plumbing. Where does she wash? What happens when the bucket is full? I can't even bring myself to look into the bucket. Don't people who live like this usually have an outhouse or something? Maybe this bucket is a temporary solution while the storm is raging outside.

Oh God, this is disgusting.

I perform the world's most awkward squat, pull down my layers and do my business. There's nowhere to wash my hands. What am I supposed to do with the bucket now?

Burning with humiliation, I return to the main room where I find Steffan sitting on the floor by himself.

'Where's Annalise?' I ask, glancing around.

'She's gone into the other room,' he replies, pointing to the second closed door, next to the one I've just come out of.

Steffan stands up and faces me. He keeps his voice low as he speaks. 'I didn't want to say this in front of Annalise, but... I'm worried, Bonnie. We shouldn't be here. We should be on the other side of the valley by now, safe and sound in a tent, away from the storm. I'm so sorry I got us into this mess. I wasn't thinking.'

'Steffan, it's fine, okay? I don't blame you. Please, let's just get through this, get out of this cabin and then we can get back on track.'

Steffan nods, but I can see his eyes are red and watery.

'By the way... Annalise is a little creepy, right?' he says, changing the subject.

'Shhh!' I say. 'We don't know how good her hearing is.'

'It's just... she kind of smells a bit and she looks like an evil witch or something.'

I bite my tongue because he's not wrong about the smell, but it's hardly her fault if she doesn't have access to washing facilities and an appropriate waste disposal system.

'It's funny you say that because... look...' I head over to my jacket that's drying by the fire, reach into the inner pocket, bypassing the Swiss army knife, and remove the newspaper article, which is now a little soggy around the edges. My jacket may be waterproof, but coming up against gale-force wind and snow is bound to test its limitations.

'What's that?'

'I saw it at the ranger's hut while you and Johan were chatting.' I hand him the article and watch his face as he reads it, holding it close to the fire for light. It doesn't take him long. He looks up at me and smirks.

'Bonnie, you don't seriously believe this, do you?'

'I don't know,' I answer with a shrug.

'Look, I know you like your urban myths and whatnot, but do you really think that frail old woman tracks down lonely hikers, snatches them from the trails and takes them back to her lair to kill and eat them?'

Now that it's been said out loud, I can hear how ridiculous and far-fetched it sounds. As usual, I've let my imagination run away with me.

Steffan points at a part in the article. 'Look, it even says that there's no physical proof that this woman even exists. She's, apparently, notoriously fast, agile and exceptionally good at camouflage, despite her white hair. As far as I can see, Annalise doesn't have white hair and she's certainly not agile.'

I take the article back from him and look down at it, scanning over a particular paragraph that leaps out.

Hikers who have experienced frostbite, been close to starvation or fallen off cliffs and trapped themselves are all susceptible to hallucinations and vivid imagery. Many hikers go missing every year in the Alps. Some are found dead. Some are found alive. And some are never found again. But no one has ever come face to face with the so-called White Witch and brought back substantial evidence that she is real.

'You're right,' I say.

'I know you're scared. I am too, but we shouldn't be afraid of Annalise. Besides, if she comes at us with a knife and fork, I'll protect you.' He's trying to make me feel better with humour, but it doesn't help.

We're disturbed by the sound of a door opening, and Annalise emerges from the adjoining room. I quickly hide the article behind my back. I truly hope she didn't overhear us talking about her just then, but if she did hear us, she makes no comment.

Annalise walks towards me with a pile of blankets in her arms. She hands them to me. They smell musty and... some other smells I don't want to think about.

'I have no spare pillows,' she says. 'Feel free to make a bed in front of the fire. It should stay burning through the night, but if it starts to die, then put on another log if you need to. Don't worry if it goes out. There'll be enough residual warmth to last a few hours.' She turns and walks back out of the room, closing the door. How does she stay warm in there? Perhaps she's used to it by now.

'Thank you,' I call out just as she shuts the door.

Steffan grabs one of the blankets from me. 'I'll make up the beds. Holy shit, that stinks.' He shoves the blanket back at me.

'I guess we'll be using our own sleeping bags then,' I say.

'Um, yeah,' replies Steffan, crouching to retrieve them from our packs.

I watch as he makes two beds on the floor near the fire. He takes out our sleeping bags and uses a couple of his jackets that aren't wet as pillows. A few minutes later, we snuggle up together as close as we can get. I pull the sleeping bag up to my chin and lie on my back in the crook of his arm.

Steffan falls asleep almost instantly, but I don't.

My head slowly turns, and I look at the closed door to where Annalise is sleeping. There's a part of me that wishes I could lock the door somehow, trapping her inside. Steffan may not believe she's the White Witch, but my brain still isn't convinced.

It's going to be a long night.

15

BONNIE

NOW

As expected, my brain doesn't shut off. It whirls and spins and keeps going over the same thing: Annalise being the White Witch. I keep telling myself to stop it, quit being so ridiculous, but then it comes up with even more ludicrous questions, like, what if that wasn't marmot she fed us earlier? Granted, I didn't eat it myself, but Steffan did. Did he eat human flesh?

My stomach churns and forces me to swallow the influx of saliva in my mouth. I gingerly sit up, careful not to disturb Steffan, and fetch my water bottle, then take a small sip to quench my dry throat. The fire is dwindling. Didn't Annalise say to top it up with another log to keep it going overnight?

Steffan's soft snores tell me he's out for the count. Hardly anything wakes Steffan when he's in a deep sleep. I once got back from a night out with Hannah, proceeded to trip over every stair on the way up to the bedroom, then pulled the duvet off the bed, leaving him with nothing to cover himself. He didn't even notice until he found me curled up in a foetal position on the floor with the duvet wrapped around me the next morning.

Slowly, I push back my sleeping bag and shuffle towards the fire. The heat feels good against my face, so I stay there for a moment with my eyes closed, listening to the quiet crackle of the low flames. The wind outside is so strong that it's whistling down the chimney, threatening to extinguish them. I place a new log on it, hoping it's enough to save it. I don't relish being in the pitch black and freezing cold. We need to save the batteries in our torches and electronics.

Thankfully, the log catches fire after a few minutes and starts to flicker back to life. I rub my hands together, noticing that the tips of a few of my fingers are still tingly. Then, I glance over my shoulder at the closed door to Annalise's bedroom.

A thought pops into my head before I can stop it. Maybe if I can prove she isn't the White Witch, it will put my mind at ease. There must be something in this cabin that will tell me a bit more about her. If she does kill hikers, then perhaps she takes their items. Maybe that's why she has cups and cutlery.

Leaving Steffan in peace, I quietly get to my feet and grab my torch from my pack. The light from the fire only reaches a little way across the room. The first thing I'm looking into is the large rectangle over in the corner covered by a blanket.

Every step I take makes the floorboards creak. I trip over the damn rug on the floor, thanks to my muscles still not responding properly. It's like my whole body is numb. I hold my breath, waiting to see if Annalise comes out of her bedroom to see what the noise was, but all is still and quiet, except for the thumping of my own heart and the soft snores from Steffan.

I tiptoe across to the corner and remove all the items stacked on top of the rectangle. There's a lantern, a load of home-made candles, a few books and blankets. Once they're on the floor, I grasp the edge of the blanket covering it and pull it off, revealing a wooden chest.

All breath leaves my lungs as I consciously tell my brain to breathe and calm down.

What's she hiding in here?

There doesn't seem to be any sort of lock. Why would there be? She and her husband live alone. For all I know, this is the chest where they keep extra blankets or clothes. Holding the torch in one shaky hand, I use the other to lift the lid of the chest, which is surprisingly heavy.

I let out a long breath when I see no dead body staring back at me. Me and my overactive imagination getting the better of me again.

Using my free hand, I search through the items inside. There are various books in English, maps, clothing items and even some random coins. I assume she finds things on paths, items that have been accidentally dropped by hikers.

There are also quite a few modern objects, like a couple of phones, watches and a pair of earbuds, none of which I'm sure Annalise has any use for, but why are they in here? If a hiker accidentally dropped one of these items, then I'd have thought they would have tried to go back to find it. How did she get hold of these? Did she purposefully steal them?

I try and switch one of the phones on, but it's dead. Finding these things does nothing to quell the idea of her being the White Witch. In fact, they only add to my burning questions. Why would she take these?

Then, I see something that catches the light of the torch and makes my blood turn to ice once again.

A watch.

Not just any watch. It looks scarily familiar. It can't be...

I read the inscription on the back of the dial to be sure.

I'm right. It is familiar.

It's the watch that I gave to my brother, Christopher, on his twenty-first birthday.

PART 2

16

BONNIE

NOW

My tongue sticks to the roof of my mouth as all moisture evaporates. What does this mean? Why does she have my brother's watch? Did he drop it while hiking out here a year ago with Steffan, or...

An ache forms in my gut. No, that's not what happened, and I know that for a fact. The only logical explanation I can come up with is that she took it from him after finding his body.

Christopher is dead.

There's no doubt about that.

It's been almost a year since Steffan came home from his hike to the Swiss Alps without him. Two of them went, but only one came back. I think about it every damn day.

A tragic accident that Steffan blames himself for day in and day out.

The day they left for the trek, Steffan swore to me he'd keep Chris safe. He even made a joke that he couldn't promise Chris would return with all his fingers and toes due to frostbite, but at least he'd be alive. We'd laughed, but under the humour, I'd put my faith in Steffan to come through for me.

I don't blame him, though.

How can I?

Accidents happen on the mountains all the time. Even Johan told us that at the start. Steffan had been forced to make the impossible choice of risking his life to reach his body or return down the mountain alone without it. They had been climbing up an almost sheer sheet of rock and ice, pushing their skills and strength to the limit, but to them it had been an epic adventure, one they had been excited to embark on together. Steffan had been thrilled to take Chris under his wing and show him the ropes.

But the rope had slipped, come loose, and Chris slipped through Steffan's fingers and plummeted to the bottom of the cliff, dying instantly. It had happened so fast.

When Steffan finally reached safety and called for help, it was deemed too dangerous to attempt to retrieve Chris's body because a huge snowstorm was closing in and had already blocked off the access to the bottom of the cliff. It wasn't until a week later that the storm cleared, but by then the winter had well and truly set in, burying Chris' body under snow and ice.

That's why we're here now.

It's our mission to retrieve Chris's body and bring him home.

Steffan is the only person who knows where he is. But I couldn't let Steffan come back alone.

I don't care how long it takes, how long I have to stay here, I'm not going home until I find him.

But why is his watch in Annalise's wooden chest? We're still over a day's hike from the area where Chris fell. Does

Annalise travel that far afield? How could she when she hobbles around the cabin like a frail old woman? Maybe her husband found him...

Yet another impossible theory pops into my head. Did Chris somehow survive the fall, managed to make his way here and then stumbled across this cabin?

I grab the watch from the chest and hold it up to the light.

I'd recognise it anywhere. I read the inscription on the back.

Christopher – Happy 21st Birthday. You'll always be my baby brother. Love you. Bonnie xx

I hold it close to my heart for a moment, closing my eyes as I recall the memory of Chris opening his gift. It's not a flashy watch, nor was it particularly expensive, but he never took it off from the moment I gave it to him. In this moment, I feel so close to Chris, holding his watch against my heart. I know it's silly, but finding his watch is like finding a sign; a sign that I'm almost there. Like Chris is talking to me from beyond the grave, urging me to keep going.

I slip it into the pocket of my hiking trousers.

I place the blanket back over the chest and return the items to roughly the same place I found them, then shuffle back to my sleeping bag. I don't wake Steffan. I'm not even sure I want to tell him about the watch. It might send him over the edge. The slim possibility of Chris being alive after the fall would destroy him, the fact that he'd left him there.

I can't do that to Steffan, not until I have the answers I need.

I decide to keep it to myself.

THE NEXT MORNING, the fire is just about still going. I didn't get a wink of sleep, but I didn't add a second log to it either because I didn't want to leave the warm confines of my sleeping bag again. The embers of the wood glow, giving off a faint light. It's dark still.

My Garmin says it's 08:06 a.m. but not even a crack of light is coming through the window boards. Annalise has boarded them up on the inside, but I assume she's done it on the outside too, to stop the storm smashing them. It should be getting light now, so why does it still look like the middle of the night outside?

Reluctantly, I climb out of my sleeping bag, my body instantly shivering at the sudden drop in temperature. I grab a now-warm, dry jacket from the hanging wire and put it on, as well as another pair of socks, before heading to the nearest window and peering through the boards.

There's nothing but darkness.

Something's not right here.

Pressing my face against the boarded window, I try and work out what I'm seeing. Then, it hits me hard. I can't see anything out there because there's nothing to see. The snow is so deep that it's buried the whole cabin above the windows.

I know Annalise said we wouldn't be able to leave for a couple of days, but now I'm wondering if we're going to be here longer.

We're well and truly trapped in here.

And the longer we stay here, the more chance of never finding Chris's body because of the impending weather. It may already be too late. He may be buried all over again.

17

ANNALISE

NOW

I sleep well. I always do. My body has had years to acclimatize to the low temperatures and rural living. I wonder how my guests have fared overnight. It's now sometime between eight and nine in the morning. My body is my clock, and I can read it like a map. I do have a collection of watches and other forms of technology I have no idea how to use stored away, but I've never attempted to figure out how they work. There is no need. I enjoy collecting things, especially since their owners have no use for them anymore. I guess you could call them my trophies, but that makes me sound like some sort of serial killer. It's nothing like that at all. I just like collecting fascinating items with a story to tell.

As I enter the main room, Bonnie is standing by the window, attempting to look out.

It's strange having people in my home, invading it like a plague. I can count on one hand the number of people besides Erik and me who have stepped inside these walls. I've been alone for years, perfectly content with how I spend my time, even though the lack of human interaction makes me, at times, rather lonely. I have my routine, which I stick to like clockwork, a certain way to do things, and already these two are stepping in and altering it just by being here. I'm nothing if not adaptable.

No light is coming in from outside, so the overnight snowfall must be higher than the windows. That's not a good sign. It means these two won't be going anywhere for a while, which will be disappointing for them. I know from previous experience that digging out of here after a heavy snowfall not only takes a lot of time, but also skill and a lot of strength, neither of which I have left in my old age. I've learned to wait out the thaw, which can take between two days and two weeks.

I knew the storm was going to be bad, which is why I ensured I had enough provisions to last me two weeks, but with extra mouths to feed, we now only have enough food for maybe five days at most. I'm not sure how much extra food they have in their packs, but hopefully it will be enough to keep us going until the snow thaws. I'm used to going hungry, but I'm betting they're not.

Bonnie sees me. Her husband is still wrapped up in his cocoon by the fire, lightly snoring.

'You won't be able to see anything,' I say calmly.

I head to the kitchen area and fill up the kettle with water from the jerrycan, both of which I took several years ago from one of the accommodation cabins on the other side of the mountain range, back when I could walk that far. I filled up the jerrycan from the nearby spring before the storm hit.

Bonnie approaches me. 'Is the storm over?' she asks in a timid voice, as if she's concerned about waking her husband.

'Yes, it's over for now. I reckon there's still more to come.'

The colour drains from Bonnie's face. 'We're trapped. The snow is so deep.'

'Yes.'

'How long will it take to dig ourselves out?'

I pause and stare at her. 'I'm afraid digging out isn't an option.'

'Why not?'

'It is dangerous and a waste of time, considering another snowstorm is on the way. Plus, you won't get far. The cabin is situated in a valley, which means it's shaped like a bowl, and bowls fill up.'

I take the kettle over to the fire and place it on the metal shelf. Then, I add another log and stoke the embers to help it catch. The water in the kettle usually takes around five minutes to boil. I always start my day with a cup of herbal tea, but since I have guests, I added more water into the kettle and retrieved two extra metal cups from the kitchen area. All of them are chipped and dented, having been trodden on or accidentally dropped off a cliff, but they do the job.

Bonnie returns to the window, still attempting to see outside, but she won't be able to catch a glimpse of anything but darkness. Being buried in snow makes the cabin surprisingly dark, and it eventually acts as an insulator, so at least the cabin will be warm. The fire will help melt the snow from the inside, but it will still take a while to thaw. It doesn't happen quickly.

I light a candle and then use it to ignite the lantern on the covered chest.

That's strange. The items on the chest aren't where I left them last night. One or more of them have been moved ever so slightly.

I turn to Bonnie. 'I wouldn't worry, dear,' I say, noticing Bonnie nibbling on her bottom lip.

Bonnie turns and faces me. She glances at her sleeping husband and her jaw twitches. She's not happy about being trapped in here. I don't blame her. It's never a nice experience, but we're perfectly safe, unless the chimney gets covered by snow.

My eyes scan the floor where the animal skin rug is lying.

'Is everything okay?' asks Bonnie. She must have been watching me.

'Yes. I was just thinking about what to do for dinner later.'

'Aren't you worried about being trapped in here?'

'Well, yes, but it's not like it's never happened before. However, it is the first time I've been trapped inside with other people. The food and rations may not last us for very long.'

'Are you saying that if we don't get out of here in a certain time, then we'll starve to death?'

'Oh no, dear. It takes weeks to starve to death. Trust me. At least we don't have to worry about our water supply, since we can melt the snow around the cabin.'

'You don't think we'll be trapped here more than a few days, do you?'

'It's hard to tell, dear, but it's certainly a possibility.'

'What's the longest you've been trapped inside?'

'Two weeks.'

Bonnie gulps hard. 'I can't stay here, Annalise. Not that long. I... I need to get back out there. We must try and dig ourselves out. Steffan and I can do it.'

'Why are you in such a hurry to leave?' My question

must come out a little more forceful than I intended because Bonnie gulps and appears lost for words.

'I... I just...' Her eyes flick to the door then back to me. She steps backwards. Is she afraid of me?

The truth is, there's no way I can now allow Bonnie and Steffan to leave. I did my best to stop them from entering in the first place so I wouldn't have to trap them here, but they forced their way in and took the decision out of my hands. I tried to warn them, but they didn't listen.

No one can know of my existence. If Bonnie and Steffan leave and return to their lives, they will tell people about me, about the strange old woman living in the Swiss mountains. And that is something I cannot allow. I will have to keep them here somehow, but if they wish to dig, then I'll allow them to dig. It will keep them busy while I come up with a plan to keep them trapped.

'Very well,' I say with a nod. 'You may dig a tunnel, but I have no shovels to make it easier. You'll have to use your hands and perhaps some kitchen utensils. I won't be of any use to you.' I hold out my frail hands, showing her my missing finger.

Bonnie nods. 'I understand. Thank you. You'll just have to tell us which direction to dig for the shortest route back to the main path.'

'You won't get very far,' I say quietly as Bonnie approaches her husband and wakes him. I busy myself with making the tea while Steffan grumbles and sits up. I really need him to move because he's right in the way of the fire.

Once Steffan is awake and has visited the toilet, he re-enters the room like a man on a mission, hands on his hips. 'Right, let's get going,' he says.

Bonnie shakes her head. 'Steffan, we're not going anywhere anytime soon.'

Steffan's eyes flick over to the nearest window. 'Why not?'

'The snow is so deep, it's buried the cabin,' says Bonnie with a sigh.

Steffan rushes to the front door and, before I can stop him, yanks it open, only to be met with a solid wall of snow. 'Holy shit,' he says. He looks like a trapped animal, eyes wide and muscles tense, ready for fight or flight, yet unable to do either.

He shuts the front door and starts pacing, running his hands through his shaggy hair and taking deep breaths. Bonnie approaches him.

'It will be okay,' she says, but by the tone of her voice, she has no confidence in her words.

'Bonnie, I don't think you understand...' Steffan's eyes shift to mine. He clearly doesn't want me listening in on their conversation.

I hold his gaze a moment, then slowly turn my back on the couple.

My hearing is exceptional for my age.

18

BONNIE

NOW

I can understand Steffan's frustration and stress. He's never been good with enclosed spaces either, which is why he spends so much time up in the mountains. I always know when Steffan is stressed or worried because he gets this wide-eyed look and he can't keep still, like he has a proverbial itch that needs to be scratched. His hands move constantly, stroking his beard or clicking his fingers.

After a few minutes, Steffan appears to calm down and starts sorting his kit, as if he's preparing to leave. I crouch next to him.

'Steffan, we can dig out of here. There's not enough food to last much longer than a few days, a week at most, but we can melt the snow to use for drinking water. Annalise doesn't have any shovels or anything like that, though, so it might take longer to dig than normal, but I believe in you. Just tell me how I can help.' He doesn't make any move or noise to say that he's heard me, so I remain where I am. 'Steffan...'

'Yes, sorry. It's just...' Steffan pauses and takes a breath. 'Look, the truth is... I've... I've never dug a snow tunnel before, let alone done it without the proper equipment. Bonnie... I don't even know if it's *possible* to dig out of here.'

I hear his words loud and clear despite him whispering them, but they don't make any sense.

'What? I thought you went on that ice expedition course two years ago?' I remember Steffan explicitly telling me that the course covered all sorts of snow and ice drills, including avalanche survival training. He was super excited about it too. In fact, he wouldn't shut up about it for weeks when he found out he'd got a place.

Steffan refuses to meet my gaze and instead fiddles with a zip on his pack. 'I didn't go in the end.'

My skin bristles with goosebumps. 'B-But... if you didn't go on that course, then where did you go for two weeks and why did you lie about attending?' I do my best to recall those couple of weeks while he was away. He couldn't check in very often, but when he did, he said he was enjoying it and... now that I think about it, he didn't tell me much detail about the course at all when he was there. Considering how excited he was about attending, he barely told me anything about it – only that he passed at the end. He even showed me his certificate, but instead of putting it on the wall in his office like the others he gained, he put it in his desk drawer. When he returned from the course, he'd looked exhausted and slept for almost a full twenty-four hours.

So... if he wasn't on the snow and ice course... then where the hell was he?

Steffan sighs. 'It's a long story. I'm sorry I didn't tell you, but... they kicked me off the course.'

'What for?'

'I... I don't know. I didn't have the right equipment or something.'

'But I thought you said they would supply everything you needed?'

Steffan clears his throat, something I know he does when he's nervous. Why is he lying to me? What's he hiding? All I want is for him to explain why he didn't tell me at the time.

'I was... embarrassed,' he says.

'Embarrassed? Why?'

'Because... I'd made such a big deal about going, and then when I got kicked off, I was worried you'd be ashamed of me or something...' He trails off, still fiddling with the zip.

I shake my head. 'Okay, apart from that being ridiculously not true, I'd never be ashamed of you for something that wasn't your fault, but the question remains... If you weren't on the course, then where were you for two weeks? You had to go to Austria for it, right?'

Steffan nods. 'Yeah.'

'Then where were you, Steffan? Why did you lie to me?'

'I didn't lie. I just... omitted the truth.'

'Because?'

'Because...' He stops again, lowering his head. The silence seems to stretch on forever until he finally whispers, 'I went to Vegas, okay?'

All the air whooshes out of my lungs as if a vacuum has sucked it out.

No. He promised. How could he?

Steffan used to have a gambling problem before we met. He told me about it on our fourth date and admitted he was in a lot of debt, but he was getting help.

Because of his debt, we haven't been able to get a mortgage, so we're renting our house, but slowly but surely, he's been building up his credit, earning enough to cover it. It all started when his parents died when he was eighteen and he inherited a lot of money, which is the main reason why he can afford to do all these mountaineering courses and travel the world. But he didn't invest it properly at the start, and eventually the money began to run out. That's when he took up gambling. He managed to make a fair bit, but it got out of control when he began to lose large amounts of money. Around the age of twenty-five, he got his life back together, and that's when we met. He's always told me he hasn't gambled since we've been together, but now I know that's a lie.

And it's killing me.

Steffan's eyes flood with tears. 'I'm sorry, Bonnie. I wanted to tell you, but I couldn't. It was stupid to keep it from you.'

I consciously take my hand off his arm, where it's been resting since we've been talking. I don't know what I'm supposed to say. Getting into a full-blown argument won't help our current situation, but brushing over this huge lie won't do us any favours either.

'I wish you'd told me,' I whisper.

'I'm sorry.'

'We're married, Steffan. That means that whatever happens, we're in it together. Like right now. I can't do this without you, you know that, right? We're here to find Chris's body and we're trapped in a cabin under several feet of snow. I trust you to get us out of here, but that means you have to trust me too, no matter what.'

Steffan nods. 'I do trust you, Bonnie.'

'Please don't ever lie to me again.'

'I won't. I promise.'

'You're the only person in this cabin who has the experience, ability and knowledge to tunnel us out of here. Even if you haven't been on the course, you must have some idea of what to do, right?'

Steffan takes a deep breath. 'I do, but... there's a real risk of the tunnel collapsing, and, without shovels, it's going to be next to impossible to make any sort of indent in the snow. It compacts like rock, especially when it's this deep, and if it's higher than the cabin, then...' He stops. He doesn't need to finish the sentence.

'Can we at least try?'

Steffan clenches his teeth together. 'It's risky.'

'But if we stay here until the snow thaws enough for us to get out, there's a risk another storm will come, and his body will be covered in snow for another year. The sooner we get out of here, the better chance we have at finding him.'

'I know, Bonnie, but... I think it's best that we wait it out after all.'

Panic surges up through my body. I grab Steffan's arm and squeeze. 'Please,' I say. 'Please, can you at least try?' I want to add that Annalise is also freaking me out, but I decide to keep my mouth shut on that for now.

My eyes flick to Annalise, who has been busying herself in the kitchen area this whole time. I don't like the idea that she can overhear us, but I'm hoping her hearing isn't too good in her old age. Then again, even if she can hear us, it doesn't concern her. I almost blurt out about Chris's watch, but I can't risk Annalise hearing us. I'll have to wait until she's at least out of the room first.

'Fine,' replies Steffan quietly. 'I'll give it my best shot.'

I smile weakly. 'Thank you.' I know I've just guilt-tripped him into digging a tunnel, but he owes me to at least try. Once we're out of this place, I will be bringing up the whole gambling thing again, but now isn't the time.

I watch quietly while Steffan organises his supplies. He's taking stock of how much food and water we have.

'Between us, we have enough food and water to last for the next forty-eight hours. We can stretch to seventy-two if we ration it a bit more or eat and drink whatever supplies Annalise has. The thing is, we're going to need our own supplies for when we get out of this cabin and trek back to the main path to carry on towards where Chris fell, so we need to keep some back.'

'How off course are we?' I ask.

'Without knowing exactly where we are, I have no idea, but I'd say we're at least a two-day trek to the nearest cabin with food and water, or a day's trek from where Chris is, which means...'

'Which means we can't risk using any of our supplies because otherwise we'll never make it, even if we do tunnel our way out of here.'

Steffan nods. I'm sure he wants to say more but is reluctant to do so for fear of her listening in. She has been very hospitable to us since we've been here, so there's no reason to think she wouldn't share her food and water with us.

I glance over at Annalise. Steffan nudges me to get my attention, then leans in close to my left ear and whispers, 'I don't think she has a husband.'

I nod, agreeing with him. Everything in this cabin is set up for one person and one person only. I don't see any evidence of a second person living in here with her. There's one chair, one pot, one bowl, not to mention only one small bed in the bedroom. I saw it briefly last night when Annalise went to bed after giving me the blankets.

I really want to talk to Steffan more about my thoughts of her being the White Witch. Something about her doesn't sit right with me at all. She may come across as hospitable, but there's an underlying current of something sinister that I can't quite put my finger on. The fact that she had my brother's watch is a huge red flag, one I can't ignore, but perhaps there's a perfectly reasonable explanation for it. I don't know what it is, of course, not yet.

But why did she tell us she had a husband if she doesn't? Perhaps she did once, but maybe he died. Maybe Annalise told us she had a husband to make us think there was someone on their way, someone to protect her. She doesn't know us. We're strangers and she has no reason to trust us. I notice her eyes keep glancing to the large stick next to the fireplace when she's around us. She's preparing to defend herself if necessary.

I hear footsteps and look up as Annalise approaches me from behind. She hands me a cup of greenish-brown hot liquid.

'Thank you,' I say as I take it.

She smiles in response. That's when I notice her crooked, rotten teeth. In the dim light of the flames, it makes her look like an evil witch. I suppose there's no access to dentistry out here. I do my best not to stare, so I take a sip of the liquid instead. I swallow and fight against my cough reflex. It's strong, whatever it is. Some sort of herbal tea, but I can't distinguish the flavour. It's not unpleasant, but I'd prefer elderflower and mint any day.

'What do you have that we can use to dig?' asks Steffan.

'Not a lot, I'm afraid, other than cups.'

'I'll take a look around and see what I can find.'

'I'd rather you didn't,' she says quickly, stepping in front of Steffan just as he moves to walk past.

I lower the cup away from my mouth, my breath

catching in my throat. The whole time we've been in here, she hasn't made a threatening move against us, but this feels like she's defending her territory.

'No worries,' says Steffan, taking a step back. 'I'll grab the ice axes from our packs.' He moves aside to our packs, which are lying next to the fire. Annalise and I stand in silence, watching him. The hairs on the back of my neck prickle as Steffan comes up empty-handed.

'They're gone,' he says.

'What?'

'Our ice axes are both gone.'

I don't bother looking because I know Steffan wouldn't lie about something like that, but how is it possible that they are gone? Did they fall out during our trek yesterday in the storm? Or has Annalise taken them overnight? But when would she have had the chance? I was awake all night. And I didn't see them in the wooden chest where I found Chris's watch.

Annalise sighs. 'Oh well,' she says. 'I suppose you'll have to make do with the cups.' And she goes back to the kitchen, humming a tune.

Steffan and I hold each other's stares.

Is Annalise keeping us trapped in her cabin on purpose? Considering she didn't want us here at the very start when we knocked at the door, does she now not want us to leave? Is that how she's come to own so many different items? Does she trap hikers in her cabin? What does she do with them?

She's still wearing that thick hat, but the idea that she's the White Witch once again appears fresh in my mind.

I feel like we're in danger here and time is running out. If Chris's body gets buried under more snow, there's no chance of us ever finding him.

19

BONNIE

NOW

'From the front door, dig left for approximately fifteen feet, then straight on until you hit the rocks, then dig around and left and that should ensure you reach the edge of the nearest path. Use the snow you dig out for drinking water and use the pot to take it to the fire and melt as much as you can.' Annalise opens the front door to a wall of snow. It's hard to see in the dark, so I grab a torch, hoping the battery lasts for the next few hours at least.

'Is that safe?' I ask.

Annalise gives me a weird look. 'It's been good enough for me, and I'm not dead yet.'

Somehow, her words don't fill me with confidence, but at least we're not likely to run out of drinking water. Just food. Maybe air. The thought floods my mind out of nowhere.

Is it possible to run out of air being trapped in here? Fire sucks in oxygen to keep going, doesn't it? There are no windows we can open for ventilation. What if we're suffocated by carbon dioxide? Am I overthinking this? Have I thought that before? My mind is a little foggy. I have a serious case of déjà vu.

'Bonnie?'

Steffan's voice jolts me back to the room. 'Sorry, I was just... thinking.'

'Grab the pot, will you?'

Steffan heads to the front door and stands in front of the wall of snow. 'I think the best and easiest option is to dig up and out. If the snow is above the roof, then we won't be able to climb that far if the tunnel is straight up, so I suggest we dig steps into the snow and ice, enabling us to climb higher with each level.'

I nod along with his suggestion. It sounds like he knows what he's talking about, but after him revealing he never attended the ice and snow course, I'm not filled with the confidence I once had in Steffan. There's a niggle of doubt there, but he's our only hope of getting out of here as quickly as possible.

Steffan bends down and starts using a cup to dig at the snow.

This is going to take a very long time.

I hand him the pot, which he quickly fills up. I take it to the fire. Now what? There's going to be so much snow that we're going to run out of space for containers to hold the water. What are we supposed to do with it all? Drink it, yes, but there's going to be too much to use.

I watch Steffan as he continues to dig, one mind-numbing inch at a time. The sight of the snow rising above the door is unsettling, and a gnawing ache forms deep in my gut again. What if Steffan is unable to dig a tunnel or steps out? What if the snow comes crashing down on top of him, burying him alive under tons of ice? My brother's frozen corpse flashes before my eyes. This is dangerous and risky, but if we don't at least try, then we're going to run out of time before we know it.

Annalise busies herself by preparing breakfast. I feel bad that we're eating her food, but Steffan and I need the food rations in our packs for when we leave the cabin. I'd also rather not have a repeat of last night, having to hide the fact that I'm a vegetarian. I don't know why, but the idea of Annalise knowing makes me uneasy.

I help Steffan for a bit, then decide to make us both a hot drink. I use my Jetboil and a hot chocolate to share. I know I'm supposed to be saving some rations, but I really can't face whatever it is Annalise is heating up in metal cups over the fire. Maybe I'll skip breakfast. I think she's reheating more of the same food from last night. I guess the distinction between breakfast and dinner doesn't mean anything out here. Food is food.

Steffan stops briefly to chow down the food she offers when it's ready, barely taking a breath. Watching him chew on those little lumps of marmot makes me shudder.

'Are you sure you don't want any?' asks Annalise.

'No, thank you. I'm not very hungry,' I reply. It's partly true. I'm not sure whether my stomach is trying to eat itself out of hunger or swirling because of nausea.

Annalise settles in her rocking chair.

There are lots of questions I want to ask Annalise. They are rolling around in my head, making me dizzy, but I feel her hospitality and patience will only stretch so far. Does she have a radio she can use to call for help? What happens if she ever gets sick or badly injured? Is she definitely lying about having a husband? Has she ever had a husband, or did she make him up? Is she really the White Witch who kills and eats hikers? How did she come to have Chris's watch? I think of his watch, safely stored inside my jacket pocket against my rapidly beating heart. Just the thought of it there calms me. Chris is telling me it's okay. Focus on one thing at a time.

First job: get out of this cabin.

To do that, I'm going to need to keep my strength up and stay hydrated, but without scoffing all the food from our packs, that's going to be difficult to do. It means depending on Annalise to feed us.

My thoughts cast to the meat in the stew last night and what Steffan has eaten again this morning, and my hot chocolate threatens to rise back up my throat.

No. Stop it. Stop thinking that right now.

To distract myself, I help Steffan again. It's hard work, I can tell, but even after an hour, he's barely made a dent in the snow because not only does the roof of the tunnel keep collapsing because the snow is fairly soft, but the cup he's using to scrape away the snow isn't enough to be of any real value. He doesn't know how to brace it either, to stop it from collapsing. Digging a trench with no roof will take twice as long and will mean we will have to melt considerably more snow.

Another hour later, Steffan slumps to the floor, his back resting against a wall. In the torchlight, I can see the shadows under his eyes.

I go to him and place a hand on his arm, my feeble attempt to calm him. He takes a deep breath and closes his eyes.

'The snow is higher than the roof. I don't know what I'm doing. I'm sorry.'

'You're doing a great job.' I glance at the hole he's made in the snow. It's roughly big enough to fit his body.

'Thanks. Just give me a minute. I'll keep going.'

I smile, admiring his determination, and then watch as he gets back to his digging attempt. He crawls in, so I can only see his feet, and starts chipping away at the ice, but then the worst happens.

There's a shout, followed by a thud.

I scream as I realise what's happened.

The snow tunnel has collapsed on top of Steffan.

20

BONNIE

NOW

I don't even think. I scrabble at the snow on my hands and knees like a dog after a buried bone. Steffan's boots stick out of the tunnel, but the rest of him is covered with lumps of snow and ice.

'Steffan!' Grabbing his boots, I pull on them, but he doesn't budge. 'Annalise, help me!'

Without waiting for her, I grab another cup from the kitchen area and use it to dig around him. How long can he survive under the snow before he suffocates? Is he dead already? Will the weight of the snow crush the life out of him before I can get him out? Is it even possible to get him out?

His left foot twitches.

He's still alive!

'Steffan!'

I can't breathe. All I can think about is losing someone else to the ice and snow. It can't happen. I won't let it. Annalise appears at my side and, together, we manage to clear enough snow to reach his waist. I see his hand, so I grab it and inch by inch we pull him backwards out of the ice tunnel until he's lying on the floor, free but unconscious.

I clear the snow around his mouth, brushing it out of his beard that's been getting thicker and thicker lately. Leaning down, my cheek close to his mouth, I watch for the out-breath.

It's there. His chest is moving.

The relief that hits me is like a punch to the chest, and I almost fall to pieces right there and then. Annalise places a hand on my shoulder, then walks away without a word. I can't seem to find the right words to thank her for helping me rescue him, so I keep busy by checking Steffan for injuries. There's no blood. Nothing looks broken. But he's soaking wet, so I need to get him out of his wet clothes and raise his body temperature as quickly as possible.

When I look over to the fire, Annalise has already straightened out his sleeping bag and has brought over one of her foul-smelling blankets. We work in silence while I remove his boots, trousers and jacket, which has done a decent job of keeping his underclothes dry, but I strip him down to his t-shirt and shorts anyway. As I'm attempting to put on one of his dry jumpers, he groans and comes to.

'B-Bonnie?'

'Hey,' I say with tears brimming in my eyes.

'Hey,' he replies. 'I guess the tunnel idea didn't work then.'

'You could say that.'

I help him into the dry clothes, and then he sits in his sleeping bag with the funky blanket over his lap. I'm silently glad he doesn't make a comment on it.

Annalise hands him a steaming mug of herbal tea. 'Thanks,' he says, wrapping his trembling fingers around it.

'I thought I'd lost you,' I say, scooting closer to him.

'It was lucky I hadn't made it any further into the tunnel when it collapsed, otherwise you wouldn't have been able to get me out in time... Thank you... for saving me.'

We lock eyes.

There's an unspoken acknowledgement between us. He could have died, all because I convinced him to dig us out of this cabin, because I'm so desperate to reach my brother's body before more snow comes and buries him again. There may not be anything left of Chris after almost a year in the wilderness, surrounded by scavenging wolves and birds of prey. Oh God, what if his body has been picked clean and...

I close my eyes against the vivid and graphic images that flash into my mind. No. No, I can't think like that. We'll find him. We have to. I can't leave my baby brother out here all alone.

Seeing Steffan buried under the snow like that, a cold, white weight pressing down, squeezing the life out of him, made me realise just how much I love my husband. I can't lose him too. I can't.

'Of course,' I say. 'I'll always save you.'

Steffan smiles weakly. He's still shivering, but I think the hot tea, fire and blanket are helping because he doesn't look so pale anymore.

I glance back at the collapsed tunnel. 'We can't try again.'

Steffan shakes his head. 'You're right. It's too risky. We'll have to wait for the snow to melt naturally, until it's not so deep.'

'Okay,' I say. 'How long do you think it will take to melt?'

'A day or two, but if Annalise is right and there's another storm on the way...' He doesn't finish the sentence. He doesn't need to. We both know we're screwed. More than screwed. We could be here much longer than two days.

Steffan looks at me. There is remorse and guilt in his eyes. 'I'm sorry,' he says. 'If I'd gone on that course, I would know how to dig a fucking snow tunnel properly.'

I squeeze his arm a little harder as he squeezes my hand back.

'It isn't your fault,' I say. 'You didn't have the right equipment.'

Steffan blinks. 'No. I lied. I got accepted but then changed my mind and used the refund money to go to Vegas instead. I didn't even show up to the course.'

'I see...' I remove my hand from his arm.

He's lied to me. Again.

After he promised he wouldn't. He said he got removed from the course because of having the wrong equipment. If that had been the case, then it wouldn't have been so bad, but now I know he willingly and knowingly removed himself from the course, took the refund money and went off to Vegas to gamble it all away – it changes everything.

A few beats of silence pass before I reply, 'What else have you been lying about?'

'What? Nothing.'

'Why don't I believe you?'

Steffan shuffles closer to me, copying my gesture of placing his hand on my arm. I stop myself from flinching away. 'Bonnie, I promise you. I'm not lying about anything else. I'm sorry. I just panicked, okay? I didn't want you thinking any less of me.'

I don't respond. I don't know how. What am I supposed to say to that? Because I *do* think less of him, but not because of taking the money and gambling it away. Because he lied to me about it barely a few hours ago. I'm torn between feeling sorry for Steffan and resenting him for lying to me.

I leave Steffan to continue to warm up and go to Annalise, who is in the kitchen area again. She always seems to keep herself busy somehow. 'Thank you for helping me pull him out of the tunnel.'

'I did try and warn you that it was a bad idea in the first place.'

'I know. We're very grateful for your hospitality. It looks like we're going to be in here until the snow melts enough for us to be able to climb on top of it and use our snowshoes.'

She shakes her head. 'Even then, it will be a difficult journey.'

'We don't have any other choice.'

I walk over and kneel next to my pack, removing my phone from the top pocket. It's a long shot, but I switch it on and wait for it to power up. There's no signal. I wasn't expecting one, but there was a glimmer of hope for a moment. I turn it off again. I can't risk the battery running out because when we do get out of here, we're going to need it.

I sit on the floor near Steffan, fiddling with the rough skin on my fingers. The fire is dwindling now, but Annalise has made no move to place more logs on it. Perhaps she's letting it die down a bit so air can come down the chimney like Steffan said. It is getting stuffy in here, slightly harder to take a deep breath. The walls feel as if they're closing in, squeezing.

I'm at a loss for what to do next. It's so dark in here without the flames roaring, but Annalise has a couple of candles lit, which flicker ominously.

Steffan and I can't risk losing each other. We need one

another. There's still a resentment there about the lies, lingering in the background, but I know Steffan only lied to shield me from his horrible decision. He knows how much I hate gambling. I do.

My dad was a gambling addict too, and it tore my family apart. My mum left him when we lost our childhood home, and took me and Chris with her. We lost everything, and then my dad ended up homeless and living with his brother. Mum, Chris and I moved to a cheaper area, and we eventually got back on track, but it was hard work. I lost contact with my dad after that, but my mum always hated and resented him for breaking up our family, even though she was the one who left him. She said she did it to protect us from his illness because that's what it was, a sickness that kept hold of him no matter how hard he tried to fight it.

I don't want that to happen to me and Steffan. I thought he was better, that I could trust him, but now I don't know what to think. I don't like the lies. It's how it started with my dad. A small lie, followed by another until they snowballed out of control.

I trust Steffan with my life, but now, we have a whole new mountain to climb.

21

ANNALISE

NOW

Earlier, while Steffan and Bonnie had been tunnelling, I managed to retrieve some food from the cold storage area. They'd been too busy to notice what I was doing, and I was in and out within thirty seconds. There's not a great deal of room and, thanks to the freezing temperatures outside, the meat I've chosen for tonight's dinner is perfectly chilled.

It took Steffan less time than I thought to give up on digging. I expected the tunnel to collapse much sooner than it did, so he must have been doing something right, until he didn't. He may look and act like a so-called mountaineering expert, but he knows next to nothing about how to survive out here. I mean *really* survive. I know exactly how to dig and brace a snow tunnel. I've done it several times. There are also shovels hidden in my bedroom, but Steffan and Bonnie won't be having access to them. I don't know the whole story between Bonnie and Steffan, and I'm no body language expert, but I was married for over half my life. I can tell when things aren't quite right. Steffan has been lying to her, and that's never a good sign.

Erik and I didn't have the perfect marriage, but we were as close as anyone could be to their spouse, especially at the beginning, and it's those memories I cling on to, even on the darkest days. By the end, we could read the other's minds and barely needed to speak to be content in each other's company. In fact, I preferred it when Erik didn't say a word, but when I look at the couple in front of me all I see is tension and doubt, lingering like a bad smell. There's no trust there, not really. Perhaps there was once, but not now. Something has happened to drive a wedge between them. Something big.

I can't focus all my worry on them though. The state of their marriage is the least of my concerns. My main concern is how I'm going to stop them from leaving. I'm an old woman, which means brute force is not my forte. However, I do have several things up my sleeve as long as I can keep them on side.

The first thing I need to get them to do is trust me. I have a feeling it's going to take a lot of work. Bonnie may be difficult to coerce, but Steffan may be easier. Bonnie has that look in her eye that tells me she doesn't trust me, and hasn't since the start.

Considering the snow is higher than the roof and another storm is on the way, it doesn't look like they'll be attempting another escape soon.

I have some time.

I keep myself busy and prepare dinner for tonight. I enjoy cooking and sometimes I can make the process last all day. It's past lunchtime now, but I haven't made any attempt to feed them. I often skip lunch, an unnecessary meal in my view. I don't need a lot of food to sustain me and can even go several days without eating if I need to. Living out here on the food from the land, I've grown accustomed to small amounts of food and water. Steffan, however, looks as if he's struggling from the lack of food. He's also very pale after his near-death experience. He was lucky. I almost didn't help Bonnie pull him to freedom because if he had died, it would have made things that much easier for me. One less person to worry about escaping.

I've pulled out a few kidneys wrapped in leaves from the cold storage. Nothing from any animal I hunt and catch goes to waste. Even the bones get boiled in a hearty broth.

Leaving the kidneys by the embers to defrost, I turn my attention to the root vegetables. I'm planning on letting the fire die so that the chimney can ventilate the cabin for a few hours. With three people breathing oxygen, the air is getting very stale. I'll light it again tonight.

Several minutes later, I settle in my chair. I usually knit during the day, but I've run out of wool, which I hand-spin myself, so I pick up my book.

Bonnie eventually comes and sits near me. I get the feeling she's a little apprehensive about getting too close, almost as if she's afraid of being burned. We've been trapped inside for less than twenty-four hours, and already I can see the start of boredom in the couple. Steffan is attempting to get some sleep. He has his eyes closed.

'I hope you don't mind me asking, but what made you decide to live out here?' asks Bonnie. Her cheeks flush red. 'I like camping out in the wilderness from time to time, but to be totally self-sustainable and live in such harsh conditions is... Well, it's amazing. I'd love to know your story.'

I nod, appreciating her respect. This could be a good time to test her. Others have failed in the past. Of course, I won't reveal everything straight away. Not yet.

Steffan appears to be asleep already. My husband also had the uncanny ability to drift off at the drop of a hat.

'Very well,' I say. 'I shall tell you. It's a long story, but since we've got nothing but time on our hands, I shall tell you as much of it as I can.' At this point, Steffan grunts in his sleep and rolls over.

As I recount my story, I rock gently back and forth on my chair, staring into the embers.

'I was born and raised in Soglio, a small, remote village hidden within the mountains near the Swiss-Italian border. Most of the residents spoke Italian there, but I was brought up speaking Italian and English because my mother was English. She met my father while travelling and they fell in love, and she never left. It's quite romantic, really. My father was a farmer, and my mother trained to be a seamstress. Erik and I attended the same school, so we'd known each other all our lives. We grew up together. He was my first and only love, like it was written in the stars.'

Bonnie smiles at this comment, her eyes flicking towards her husband, who's still snoring softly. The colour is returning to his face.

'At age nineteen, we were married, but Erik wasn't content to live in the same village all his life. He had a taste for freedom and adventure, and I always said I would follow him to the ends of the earth if that's where he wanted to go. Thankfully, he didn't wish to travel that far, but he did wish to see what else was out there. We had very little money, but we were both from farming families and knew how to hunt and catch our own food. Erik was also an expert fisherman.' I stop for a moment, gathering my thoughts. My heart is racing as I'm speaking. I have never told this story, not out loud. I often recite it in my head to lull me to sleep at night, as my brain recalls a happier time of my life. I must be wary, though, because revealing too much information would be catastrophic. Bonnie could get the wrong impression.

'We travelled around Switzerland, Italy and Austria for a year, never settling long in one place, enjoying each other's company and the bliss of being a newly married couple, but we both longed to put down roots and start a family. Neither of us wanted to return to our hometown, so we decided to find a perfect spot to create our very own little haven. Erik, being an expert builder, built us our forever home here; the same four walls you see around us now.' I look around lovingly at the walls my husband erected and sigh. 'Unfortunately, we were not blessed with children, even though we wanted them very much. Together, we lived out our days here in peace.' A large lump forms in my throat. This is it; the first test of trust. 'I must tell you... I lied to you before. About my husband. He is not out searching for food and firewood. He died many years ago from a sudden illness that took him in a matter of days.'

Bonnie covers her mouth to stifle a gasp. 'Oh!' She's not a good actress, so I can only assume she must have deduced that my husband isn't around earlier.

'I have been alone here ever since, but even though he's died, I do not wish to return to civilization. Not now. It's been too long. I prefer to stay out here and live out the remainder of my days within the same four walls my dear husband built.'

Bonnie is silent for a moment. 'I can understand that. Your story is truly fascinating, Annalise.'

'Well, I don't know about fascinating, but it's nice to have spoken it out loud for once.'

Having not conversed with another person in so long, my

words tumbled out and, even though I have withheld some details, Bonnie and Steffan are now the only people on earth who know who I am and where I live. A part of me feels like my younger self again, back when I loved talking with people and swapping stories.

But there's no going back now. Letting her leave will pose a serious problem for me. My husband, God rest his soul, is in no danger of being arrested for what happened all those years ago, but what if this couple tell someone about the woman up in the mountains and they come looking for me? All I want now is to live out the remainder of my days in peace. Not have strangers knocking at my door, asking questions about what happened forty-odd years ago. What's done is done. There's no point in digging up the past now, is there?

'Can I ask you a question?' Bonnie asks.

'You may.'

'Have you ever heard of the legend of the White Witch?'

My eyebrows rise. 'Yes, I've heard that a few times over the years from passing hikers. You think I am her, no? The White Witch.'

Bonnie's mouth opens then quickly closes. 'No, I... I mean...'

I sigh, then with one quick swoop, pull off my hat, revealing my waist-length, dark brown hair that's speckled with grey. 'I might be a little grey in my old age, but my hair is by no means pure white.'

Bonnie's whole body appears to relax, and she lets out a small laugh. 'I'm sorry. I guess I've always been fascinated with legends and things like that.' Her eyes cast over to the covered wooden chest in the corner. Ah, now it makes sense. She's been snooping around and has likely found my stash of items inside. 'I'm sorry that Erik died. You must miss him very much,' continues Bonnie.

'I do, but he'll always be with me. The people we love never truly leave us. They're always here with us.' I place a hand over my heart.

Bonnie's eyes flood with tears as she smiles back at me.

That's when I realise that she and I have something in common.

She's lost someone too.

22

ANNALISE

THEN

The knocking at the door continues. The sound is so loud, it's as if it's being amplified, emanating from all around her. She doesn't like it. She wishes it would go away.

'Are you alright, Fröken?' a woman's voice sounds.

Annalise opens her eyes, having no idea how long they've been closed. Why is someone asking if she's all right? How would they have known that she wasn't? Did someone hear something? Had she been screaming after all?

Annalise shuffles to the door, double-checking her dress and hands for blood splatters she may have missed. Her hands are stained pink. She shields her eyes from the burning sun as she opens the door and peers out at the face of a stranger.

'Can I help you?' she asks, quickly hiding her hands behind her back. The voice belongs to a middle-aged woman who looks as if she's on her way to the market with an empty basket.

The woman smiles gently. 'I was actually knocking on

the door to ask if I could help *you*.' Her eyes scan her whole body, and Annalise instinctively steps further behind the door, shielding herself from view. 'I thought I heard shouting. I just wanted to check to see if everything was okay.'

'Oh.' Annalise smiles. Her instinct is to laugh and chat with the woman, to tell her there's been a mistake, but there hasn't been a mistake, has there? But Annalise doesn't want this woman to know what's happened. Not before Erik knows.

The woman reaches forwards to touch her – what for, she doesn't know, but Annalise flinches away. The idea of a stranger's hands, even a woman's, on her is enough to fill her with terror.

'No, please, don't touch me. Nothing has happened. I'm fine,' she says, almost tripping over her own words in her haste to get them out. *Please just leave.*

'Are you sure?' The woman's eyes keep searching, scanning behind her to see if she can see something amiss.

'No, really, I...'

The woman's eyes lower to her legs. 'T-There's blood...'

No, no, no.

The woman gasps. 'Oh, goodness. What do you need me to do? I'm a nurse. I can help.'

Annalise is thrown for a moment, but then understands what the woman must think is happening. By the look of sheer horror on the woman's face, she must assume she's started her monthly cycle.

'Please,' says Annalise. 'Can you fetch my husband? He works at the sawmill. His name is Erik Andersson.'

'Of course, but are you well otherwise? Should I fetch a doctor?'

'No, thank you. I'm fine. Please, just tell him to come

home as soon as possible.' Tears fill her eyes as the woman smiles and turns away, rushing down the nearest alley without a backwards glance. She has no idea how long it will be until Erik gets the message, and she can't risk being seen by anyone else. People ask too many questions, and she's in no position to answer them.

Annalise gently closes the door and cleans herself up again. Her hands won't stop shaking. She stares, attempting to control them with her mind, but they refuse to obey.

More time passes. How much, she doesn't know. All she knows is the next thing she hears is the soothing voice of her husband.

'Annalise.'

It jolts her back to reality as if she's been struck by lightning. She's standing in the middle of the kitchen area. How long has she been standing here?

It doesn't matter now. He's here. Erik is finally here and, more importantly, he's alone. The woman who found her earlier is nowhere to be seen. Perhaps he sent her away, telling her he could take care of her himself.

Erik scoops her into his arms as if she weighs nothing and carries her to the nearest chair, where her body finally slumps forwards. She hangs her head down between her knees, crying hard, unable to stop the tears from flowing now that she knows she's safe with her husband. He can fix this, she hopes. He can make all the pain and humiliation go away.

But he's not saying a word. Not a single word, and it's scaring her. As he takes a cool compress and begins to wipe the dried blood she's missed from her skin, his face contorts into a frown and his jaw clenches.

'I'm sorry,' she repeats, raising her head up to finally meet his eyes.

Still, he remains silent.

'Please, say something, I beg you.'

Erik gently cleans the pink stains on her hands, waiting several seconds before speaking. 'Who did this to you? What happened?' His voice is low, calm, but full of rage, ready to explode at any moment.

'I... I don't know his name, but he works with you. He followed me back from the market and ambushed me as I arrived home, pushed his way in and...'

'What does he look like?'

Annalise squeezes her eyes shut, not wanting to remember the face of her attacker, but needing to tell her husband the truth. Nausea swells as she pictures him in her mind. She'd be happy to never think about him ever again.

'Tall with broad shoulders, stubble...' She gulps back the lump in her throat and stares down at her legs, which are now free from blood, but it's left a pink stain against her pale skin. She wonders if it'll ever come out. All she wants is a warm bath, but they don't have access to one. Her limbs are heavy, and they ache as if she's just walked a hundred miles without a break.

'I know who he is. Did he...' Erik closes his eyes and breathes in deep through his nose. He turns his head away from her. Is he ashamed of her now? He can't look at her.

'I can't remember. Yes, I think so.' The tears continue to fall as she tells him what she can recall, but the images are blurry. She sobs several times as she recounts what little she can.

'I have to take care of this,' he says once she's finished the harrowing story.

'What are you going to do?'

Erik stands, placing the pink flannel beside her. 'Stay here. I'll be back soon.'

23

BONNIE

NOW

I wasn't sure whether to ask Annalise about her being the White Witch or not, but before I could change my mind, the question blurted from my lips. I kept quiet about the fact I'd found my brother's watch, though. I didn't expect her to laugh, nor did I expect her to reach up and pull off her hat, revealing her dark brown hair, speckled with grey.

It certainly isn't white.

But it doesn't mean she *isn't* the woman mentioned in the legend. Does it? Stories and tales change and adapt all the time. Humans have a notorious habit of embellishing the details, making things seem more dramatic than they are. Not always, but when it comes to urban legends, it's a high possibility. A woman with pure white hair sounds a lot creepier and more mysterious than a woman with dull brown hair.

I listen to her story so intently that I don't think I take a proper breath until it's over. It renders me almost speechless. It's beautiful, yet haunting, somehow. For her and Erik to leave their hometown and spend all those years together in the middle of nowhere, away from any form of civilisation, is a drastic choice. I wonder if there's another reason behind their decision of solitude, or whether they just loved each other so much that they didn't want anyone else to pollute their relationship.

Annalise has lost the love of her life. I know how it feels to lose someone close. Annalise has become a lonely recluse, hiding herself away in the mountains, whereas I have made it my life mission to find my brother's body and bring him home. I don't know what else to say to her. While the caring part of me wants to comfort her, another part wants to keep my distance; the part where my brain keeps flashing warning signals that she's dangerous. She had my brother's watch, which means she must know exactly where his body is. She won't know who he was to me, of course. Do I dare ask her about the watch, about why she collects items? Is it a fascinating hobby, or does she have a more morbid reason for having them?

Annalise's story rolls around in my head, repeating over and over for the rest of the day. Steffan sleeps for hours. I don't disturb him, just let him sleep, let his body recharge and recover after his harrowing brush with death.

My fingers are numb again, tingling, so I try and keep them moving by stretching and flexing them. I don't think they've warmed up properly. The tips look a little blue. Are they getting worse? Surely, they should be improving by now.

The windows are still blacked out by snow, but my watch says it's almost seven in the evening. We've been here nearly a full twenty-four hours. It feels longer. Much longer.

Annalise has been making dinner for the past two hours, chopping vegetables, stirring the large pot over the fire and adding various herbs and spices. I can't say I'm looking forward to tonight's meal, considering she's added some small red lumps to the pot. It doesn't look like marmot this time. I'm already trying to think of ways to smuggle the meat into Steffan's bowl. Why didn't I just tell her I was a vegetarian the first time? Now, I'm having to continue the charade by lying to her and faking my liking of the stew, which would be quite delicious were it not for the meat.

Where does she keep the meat anyway? How does she keep it fresh? Clearly, there's no large freezer here. Maybe it's cold enough in the cabin to keep things relatively fresh for a few days, but after a few days, I'd certainly be questioning the freshness.

I entertain myself by studying the maps and the route cards Steffan so painstakingly created before we left for the trek. I try and find where we went wrong, but I'll be honest, I hadn't been paying much attention to the ground around me, considering by the end there was a thick blanket of snow over everything and I couldn't see more than a few feet in front of me. I should have worked on my mountaineering and navigational skills before I came here. I shouldn't have left it up to Steffan to guide me the whole way, but he'd been so adamant about doing it. I know how to read a map, an essential skill even when training to run an ultra-marathon, but I've never been hugely confident in route planning and navigation.

My eyes glaze over after studying the maps for so long, and my mind keeps going back to Annalise's story. I can't imagine the pain and grief she must have suffered through alone when Erik died. She told me he died from a short illness, but I wonder what it was and how long ago he passed.

Pneumonia, perhaps? Living out here, neither of them would have access to any medical treatment.

'Dinner is ready,' says Annalise in a chirpy voice. Is it my imagination, or does she seem happy to be hosting us now?

A deep, meaty aroma fills the cabin as I take a seat close to the fire, which Annalise lit again earlier to cook the meal. She still has a candle burning, though. All our kit and clothing that was hanging wet is now warm and dry, folded and packed, ready for when we can leave, but who knows when that will be.

'Smells lovely,' I say, taking the bowl from Annalise as a queasy feeling swirls within.

Steffan sits up and starts eating straight away.

'What sort of meat is it today? You said you catch and hunt your own food.'

Annalise takes a seat in her rocking chair, which squeaks every time she rocks backwards. It's beginning to grate on my already frayed nerves. 'A bit of this and a bit of that.'

I peer into the bowl and see a lump of red meat floating at the top. 'It's very... red,' I add.

'Hmm.'

I can't do this. I can't lie to her again. Didn't I tell Steffan off earlier about lying? It only causes more problems down the road.

'Annalise, I'm sorry I didn't tell you before, but... I don't eat meat.'

The cabin falls silent. Steffan pauses with his spork halfway to his mouth and Annalise cocks her head to the side, as if she doesn't quite understand what I'm saying.

'You... don't... eat meat,' she repeats.

'Yes. I'm a vegetarian.' It dawns on me that perhaps Annalise doesn't know what that word means. If she's been up here for forty-odd years, would she have heard the word before? I know it's been around for a while, but I can't imagine it being as widely used as it is today.

'I see,' she says, looking into her own mug that she's been using to hold the stew. The chair continues rocking back and forth.

Back and forth.

Squeak. Squeak. Squeak.

Annalise makes no further comment and eats slowly, spooning the thick stew into her mouth, allowing it to dribble down her chin. She's staring at me now. Is she waiting for me to eat? Should I continue eating out of respect, or eat around the meat in the bowl? Have I offended her?

Luckily, Steffan makes the first move and digs his spork into my bowl and fishes out a couple of the lumps of meat. 'Well, whatever it is, it's delicious,' he says, shoving the meat into his mouth and chewing.

Annalise smiles, showing her rotten teeth. 'Well, at least someone is appreciative of my cooking.'

Oh God. I have. I've offended her.

'Annalise, I...'

'Don't worry, Bonnie. We're all entitled to our own opinions and way of life, but you'll find when it's a matter of life and death... you'll eat and drink just about *anything* to stay alive.' The way she emphasises the word *anything* makes my blood run cold.

What does she mean by that?

I eat the vegetables left in the stew in silence, but I've lost my appetite, so every mouthful is torture.

A few minutes later, Annalise hands us both a cup of herbal tea. The smell is even stronger than before, and it does nothing to settle my stomach, but it's warm, and that's all that matters. I'm not sure if it's because I'm getting used to the cabin's lower temperature or because the fire isn't as big as usual, but the chill is beginning to seep into my bones.

I'm not sure how, but I manage to finish the bowl of stew and the cup of tea. Annalise finishes hers and then begins to clear up the empty containers. With nothing better to do, I head to the window and look out at the snow wall, as if I'm expecting to watch it melt before my eyes.

It's late evening now, so even if I could see out, I wouldn't be able to see anything. Being trapped in this snow cabin is starting to make me itch. I scratch the side of my neck and then my arms. I've never been good with confined spaces, which is one of the reasons why I love running outside and not on a treadmill.

By the sounds of it, the storm has started up again, as Annalise predicted. The wind is whistling down the chimney, threatening to extinguish the fire, which is now dwindling to nothing more than a flicker. Another storm is the last thing we need, but we knew it was going to happen. I can't tell if it's snowing, though. Maybe it's just strong winds and won't come with more snow. I can only hope. Maybe by tomorrow morning, the snow will have vanished, and we'll be able to leave... or maybe there will be five extra feet of snow on top of us.

'I'm going to turn in early,' says Annalise. 'Sleep well.' And she's gone.

Steffan looks up at me. 'You okay?' I can barely see his facial features through the darkness. Annalise has taken the only candle, so now Steffan and I must use our torches. He turns his on and props it up so it casts its beam across the cabin.

'I'm slightly embarrassed about telling her I'm a vegetarian,' I say, keeping my voice low. 'Did you hear what she said after? I offended her.'

'Bonnie, I wouldn't worry about it. Honestly. It's better you told her than choking down lumps of meat. You stood by your morals. I'm proud of you.'

I ignore his sweet words uttered to make me feel better and say, 'What about that comment she made about eating and drinking *anything* when it's a matter of life and death?'

'Well, it's sort of true, isn't it? You hear these horror stories all the time of people resorting to hunting and killing all sorts of animals to survive. Not to mention...'

'What?'

'Nothing.'

'Go on. What were you about to say?'

Steffan's Adam's apple bobs. 'I've read stories of cannibalism too.'

'Oh my God, you're not saying...'

'What? No, of course not,' says Steffan with a laugh. 'I'm just saying... if you had the choice of eating meat or starving to death, what would you choose?'

I bite my lip. 'Well, obviously, I'd eat it then if there was no other choice, but we're not there yet, are we?'

'No, not yet.' Steffan doesn't seem to be at all concerned by her comment, so maybe I shouldn't be either, but it keeps nagging at me. It wasn't what she said so much as the way she said it.

Now that Annalise has finally left the room, I decide it's time to show Steffan the watch. I reach into my pocket and pull it out, then walk over to him and crouch down to his level.

'Look, I found this in that wooden chest over there last night.'

Steffan takes it from me. He clearly doesn't recognise it, and it's too dark to see the inscription on the back. 'It's a watch,' he says.

'It's Christopher's watch.'

Steffan frowns. 'Are you sure?'

I nod, my mouth turning dry. As I watch him turn it over, studying it, I want to reach out and grab it back from him. It's like, when I'm not touching it, Chris feels further away from me than ever. 'It's got the inscription on the back. It's too dark to see now, but I promise you it's there. I'm telling you, it's the watch I got him for his twenty-first birthday. He was wearing it when he went on the hiking trip with you, which means he was wearing it when he fell.'

Steffan hands it back to me, his hand shaking. 'Weird.'

I hold it close to my heart again, then slide it back inside my pocket. 'Don't you see what this means?' I ask. Why is he not more shocked at this revelation?

'Sure. It means Annalise somehow found his body and stole the watch off his wrist. For what reason, I don't know, but it's not like she killed him for it to sell for money, is it?'

'But why take it?'

'I don't know. She's a lonely old woman. She probably likes shiny objects and collects stuff.'

I'm silent for a moment, thinking. I'm wary to bring this up, considering how it could make Steffan feel, but I need to say it out loud or it's going to eat me alive. 'What if she didn't find his body? What if he survived the fall and...'

Steffan turns to me abruptly, as if he's just been slapped. 'Stop. Just stop. Why are you doing this to yourself, Bonnie? Chris did not survive that fall, okay? Why would you even... How could you even suggest such a thing?'

I gulp. 'I'm sorry... I didn't mean to suggest that...'

Steffan's eyes are watering. He turns his face away from me. 'Just drop it.'

I nod, returning the watch to my jacket pocket. I scratch my throat and gulp, suddenly feeling hot and dizzy. 'I'm not feeling too well.' Maybe my tiredness is catching up with me.

Steffan turns to me and places his hand against my forehead. 'Maybe you're coming down with something. Get some rest.'

He helps me sort out my sleeping bag, but by the time I crawl into it, my vision is swimming and my fine motor skills are clumsy, even worse than when I was half-frozen. What the hell is going on with me? Steffan seems fine and slowly sips his herbal tea, pulling a disgusted face every time he swallows. He eventually gives up after drinking only half of it and sets it aside.

I turn on my side. Something's wrong with me. I think Steffan is right, that I'm coming down with something, or maybe it's anxiety and stress. A similar thing happened after Chris's accident. I couldn't get out of bed for weeks, practically fermenting in my unwashed bedding until Steffan dragged me out and put me in a hot bubble bath. I couldn't eat or think straight. It wasn't until Steffan suggested going for a run that I began to come out of my brain fog.

Losing someone close is something I wouldn't wish upon my worst enemy. People who've never experienced it can never fully understand what deep-rooted grief can do to a person. It destroys them from the inside out, knowing that every day when they wake up, they'll never go back to the way things were when they were alive.

Knowing there's nothing they can do to change anything is one of the most heartbreaking and soul-sucking emotions. Grief changed me into someone I never thought I'd be.

Losing my brother didn't just break me, it destroyed who I was, and now I'm a completely different person, and I know I can never change back. They say time heals all wounds. It doesn't heal them. It merely dulls the pain on the surface, but underneath the scar is a wound so deep that it's impossible to reach the bottom.

I drift into a deep sleep. The last thing I see is Steffan coughing and slumping forwards at an awkward angle on the floor.

24

BONNIE

NOW

For the first time in over forty-eight hours, I sleep, but my dreams are not pleasant ones. They are filled with darkness, swirling winds and shouts of agony. I can't make sense of the noises and images, which roll and combine into one giant blob of… nothingness.

I need to wake up, to find a way out, but it's like I'm trapped in the storm outside the cabin, screaming into the wind, which steals my voice the instant it leaves my mouth. The next moment, I'm underneath a tonne of snow. It's pressing down on me, and I can't breathe. Every time I open my mouth, snow rushes in, blocking my airway.

I grapple with my subconscious, finally dragging myself out of my nightmare, but it hurts to do so. It feels as if I'm dragging my own mangled body across a bed of sharp icicles.

My eyes flutter open. I'm still lying on my side, the exact position I was in when I fell asleep. Steffan's body is slumped on the floor next to the fire, which is now completely extinguished. The torch he left on is the only form of light. Steffan's not in his sleeping bag. It's like he's fallen asleep sitting up and toppled over.

My vision blurs as I awkwardly roll over to face the middle of the cabin. My body refuses to allow me any more movement than that. Annalise is standing at the kitchen table. She has a small candle next to her, which is highlighting just one side of her body. The rest of her is cast in shadow. Her back is towards me. Her voice is low, quiet as she speaks.

'I'm not sure these two will make it, you know. I know a thing or two about these things. We both do, don't we?'

Who the hell is she talking to?

'Ours was a good marriage to start with, don't you think?'

Oh my God. She's talking to her dead husband as if he's in the room with her. She even turns and looks to the left as if he's standing right next to her, talking back. I can't see what she's doing, but it appears like she's chopping up food or preparing it somehow. Annalise continues to converse with her husband, even laughing, as if he's said something funny.

'These two are a problem,' she says. 'You always warned me that we couldn't trust anyone.'

She pauses for several seconds. I hold my breath, fearful that she might hear my rapid breathing.

'Ah, that's a good idea, Erik. What's that? Oh yes, don't worry, I will. They are sleeping like babies right now. I think the snow may be melting slightly in this storm. The snow doesn't appear to be as high as before. Remember when we were snowed in for two weeks? That was a hoot, wasn't it?' She laughs again, loudly. The sound fills the room. She turns and looks over her shoulder at me. I slam my eyes shut and pray she doesn't notice. I count to ten, doing my best to control my racing heart.

The fact that she's talking to Erik as if he's there is... *disturbing,* but not overly unusual for someone who's spent a decade by herself. It's the way she's speaking to him, though, like he's physically standing next to her.

My heartbeat speeds up as the cabin falls into silence. Did she see me watching her? Do I dare open my eyes? With my eyes shut, I think back to just before I fell asleep. I felt strange, woozy. After I'd spoken to Steffan about the watch, my eyes had gone all funny.

The tea.

Did she drug us with the herbal tea? She drank it herself too, but maybe she gave herself a weaker dose, or perhaps she's built up a tolerance over the years. Am I overthinking this? Has being trapped in this cabin for almost twenty-four hours made me paranoid, or am I bang on the money? Maybe Steffan is right. Maybe I'm jumping to conclusions, letting my own imagination run away with me.

I keep counting, reaching thirty, and then decide to risk opening my eyes.

Please don't be standing over me with your face only inches away from mine.

Annalise isn't standing where she was before.

My heart thuds so hard in my chest, I fear it may be audible. Where did she go? My eyes scan the cabin, but other than her bedroom, there's nowhere else she could be unless she's in the toilet room.

I shift my body again so I can look behind me, towards the fire.

There she is.

She's standing over me, staring at me with a morbid

smile, her crooked, black teeth bared like a vicious animal. A small river of saliva drips from her mouth.

A scream escapes my mouth before I can stop it.

'I'm so sorry to startle you,' she says. She bends next to me and strokes my hair. Oh my God, what is she doing? Why is she stroking my hair like I'm a sick child?

'Um... that's okay, A-Annalise.' I can't breathe.

Do not hyperventilate, Bonnie.

'Did you have a nightmare?' she asks.

'No, I... I thought I heard a noise, and it woke me.'

'Not to worry. It was probably just the wind.'

I rub my eyes, realising my vision is swimming again. Her face is blurry around the edges. 'What time is it?'

'Not quite three in the morning, dear.'

'Why are you awake at this time?' I bite my lip, wondering if I'm asking too many prying questions, but Annalise just smiles.

Annalise keeps her voice low as she answers. 'I couldn't sleep. I thought I'd make a start on preparing breakfast.'

'Right. Um... can I help at all?'

'No, thank you. I have everything under control.' Annalise reaches out her hand and strokes my hair again. I flinch slightly and then feel guilty for doing so. It's just... *creepy*.

'You have such lovely hair,' she says.

'T-Thank you. So do you,' I reply honestly. She really does. I still can't get over how white and straight it is. Mine is dark and dragged back in a messy ponytail most of the time, except now, where it's loose around my shoulders and splayed across the pillow.

Wait...

My brain catches up with my eyes.

Why the hell is her hair now white? What am I looking at? It's cascading down past her shoulders, not a fleck of brown or grey anywhere. It is pure, brilliant white, like the snow.

'Y-Your hair is...'

Annalise grins.

Oh God...

Annalise removes her hand from my hair.

My eyes glance past her towards the lumps of meat on the table. Some of them are huge! She must have caught and killed a massive animal, like a deer or...

Wait...

No, stop it.

Why has my mind gone straight there again?

My lips quiver as I ask, 'Annalise... can I ask you a personal question about your husband?'

'Of course, dear,' she replies, going back to stroking my head.

I pause for a moment, unable to drag my eyes away from the frozen meat on the table. 'What did you do with his body when he died?'

Annalise's hand stills. It's now resting on my head, and I have a horrible feeling she's about to grasp a fistful of my hair and drag me somewhere to punish me for asking such a personal and loaded question, but she doesn't.

'What an interesting question,' she says. Finally, after what feels like a lifetime, she removes her hand. 'I had to dispose of his remains privately. I couldn't have anyone knowing where he was. You understand.'

'I...' Wait, why couldn't she have anyone knowing where he was?

Annalise frowns, shaking her head, as if she's confused. 'What I mean is... I had no way of reporting his death, so...'

I gulp, but a large lump gets caught in my throat. I can't breathe.

Is she... Did she just...

'Shhh,' says Annalise. 'Sleep now. You won't remember this in the morning.'

I won't? Why won't I? What the hell was in that herbal tea?

My head spins as if I'm on a merry-go-round, and I'm forced to close my eyes against the dizziness. I sink my head into my makeshift pillow, then open my eyes again, watching as she moves away from me and back to the kitchen area.

A sinking dread is sitting at the bottom of my stomach, curdling my insides. The lump in my throat is still there. I glance over at my husband, who is sleeping peacefully. I should have trusted my gut at the start. I was right. Steffan was wrong.

Annalise no longer seems like our saviour. There is something sinister about her. I'm not imagining it. She's drugged us.

I swallow the bile bubbling at the back of my throat as tears sting my eyes. I wish I had some sort of weapon close by, but as I fight against nausea and dizziness, my eyes gradually close.

Did she kill her husband?

Has she been eating him to stay alive?

Did she... feed her husband to *us*?

25

BONNIE

THEN

The meal is delicious, and the twins are relatively well-behaved, but I can't seem to get the strange phone call out of my head. I don't know an Irish man and I'm almost certain Steffan doesn't either. Then again, I don't know everyone in Steffan's life very well to be one hundred percent sure. He knows all my friends, mainly because my only real friend is Hannah, but he comes to my work summer garden parties and the Christmas parties. He's met everyone in my life. Now that I think about it, I don't know who Steffan spends his days with when he's not at work, apart from Chris. I don't get invited to his work functions because he tells me they are so boring, and he wouldn't want to put me through it. I don't know any of his hiking and climbing friends either.

I say goodbye to Hannah and the kids at the car, then drive home on autopilot, looking forward to a hot shower to wash off the sweat that's now dried on my skin. As I pull into the driveway of our rented house, I notice a man peering through the lower window into the lounge.

I get out and slam the car door, making my presence known. 'Hi. Can I help you?' I ask, keeping hold of my car keys in my right hand.

The man doesn't jump in fright at being discovered but turns slowly, then walks towards me, both his hands in his pockets. He has thick grey hair, a little stubble around his chin, and is wearing a faded denim jacket.

'I'm looking for your husband,' he says in a thick Irish accent.

My brain clicks into gear. 'Did you call me earlier?'

'Aye, I did.'

'Well, he's not here. He's in the Swiss Alps with my brother.' I think back to what Steffan said about this guy, about not speaking to him again. 'What do you want with him?'

'When do you expect him back?' he asks, blatantly ignoring my question.

'In about two weeks.'

'That's convenient,' mutters the man. He is now standing right next to me, much closer than I'm comfortable with.

'Why do you need to speak to Steffan so badly? Is it something I can help you with?'

The man grins. 'Aye, now, nothing to worry your pretty little head about. You just let the menfolk sort this out, yeah? But I suggest you let your husband know that if he continues along this path, then things will get very difficult for him and everyone involved, including his new investment friend.'

I shake my head. 'I don't... What are you talking about?' *Investment friend?*

The man nods his head at me. 'I'll see you soon, yeah?' Then he walks away, leaving me trembling on my driveway.

I call Steffan the second I get in the door, clutching the phone between my ear and shoulder while I take my trainers off. There's no answer, so I leave a voicemail asking him to call me as soon as possible.

I almost call Hannah, but then think better of it. She'll be busy sorting the kids out and bathing them. I don't need to burden her with more stuff right now. I head upstairs, dump all my running kit, including water bottles, on the landing, and plug in my phone to charge outside the bathroom door because it only has ten percent battery left.

I strip off my running clothes, then keep the bathroom door open so I can hear it if Steffan calls me back. Sweat has cooled on my skin and my head is dizzy, my stomach slightly unsettled. Most likely from the shock of speaking to that man, who unnerved me from the start, but also from hydrating with wine rather than water after my run. At least my stomach is full of the roast dinner, and I don't have to worry about cooking for the rest of the day.

During my super-quick shower, I pop my head around the shower curtain, listening for the phone through the running water. I've just finished washing my hair and am about to rinse the bubbles out.

It's ringing!

Without switching the water off, I hop out and shuffle across the bathroom, still naked and dripping wet, shampoo trickling down the back of my neck. I grab a towel to dry my hands, then wrap it round myself, checking the screen. It's Chris.

'Hi, Chris,' I say, somewhat breathlessly.

'Hey, sis. How's it going?'

'Um, fine... How are you? Hannah said you hurt your ankle or something?'

'Oh, yeah. It's nothing. I'm fine. Listen, can I please ask you for a favour?'

'A favour? What sort of favour? This isn't like the favour you asked me for when we were kids, is it?'

Chris chuckles but then doesn't reply directly. 'The thing is... this favour. You can't tell Hannah, okay?'

'I tell Hannah everything.'

'I know, but... look, you just can't tell her *this*. Please?'

'Why not?'

'It's complicated and she wouldn't understand. Plus, there's just no need to involve her. Not right now. She has enough going on with the kids and everything and with me being away.'

I sigh, wiping water out of my left eye. 'Okay. Fine. You've convinced me. Tell me. I promise I won't tell her.'

'Thanks, sis. Okay, so I need you to go to my house, go upstairs into our bedroom, find the loose floorboard in the corner and retrieve the locked box inside, then take it to an address which I'll send you in a bit and hand it to the guy waiting there.'

I stifle a laugh because what he's saying sounds utterly ridiculous. 'Are you kidding me? That's a pretty odd favour. What's in the box?'

'If I told you it was drugs, would you believe me?'

'Ha! Not at all, especially coming from the guy who dobbed his mates in when they smoked a joint at school.'

'Will you do it?'

'I... Maybe. Can you not explain a bit more what this is about?'

'I really can't. Not right now. Steffan says it's not the right time.'

'Wait... *Steffan* knows about the box and the favour?'

'Shit... No, I just... Okay, yes, he does, but I really don't have time to explain everything now. Please, will you do it for me?'

I scratch the back of my neck. 'When do you need me to do it?'

'Now.'

'Now! I'm halfway through showering and I've just left Hannah to come home and relax for the rest of the day.'

'I wouldn't be asking if it wasn't super important.'

I squeeze the bridge of my nose and sigh again. 'Bloody hell, Chris. This is crazy. You owe me. Big.' Then I have a thought. 'Wait... does this have anything to do with an Irish guy?'

'Sorry, you broke up there. What did you say?'

'Uh, nothing. Never mind. I'll do it.'

'Thank you so much, sis. You're a life saver. I'll text you the address. Can you message me when you're done?'

'Sure.'

'Thanks. Bye, Bonnie.'

The phone goes dead.

I don't like this. Something weird is going on, and it seems both Steffan and Chris are involved somehow. What's Chris got locked in a box under the floorboards? Why is he keeping it from Hannah? Why is this happening now while they're both away?

I get back under the running water, rinse my hair, then get dressed on autopilot into my grey slacks and a black t-shirt, pulling it over my head without bothering to put on a bra. I unplug my phone, which has only charged to twenty-seven percent, then slip my feet into some other trainers.

I call Hannah as I'm walking back out to the car. 'Hey, can I come over?'

'You miss me already?'
'I'm lonely.'
'On one condition.'
'Name it.'
'Bring more wine.'
'Deal.'

26

ANNALISE

NOW

My mind often drifts back to that day all those long years ago. The memory not only plagues my dreams but constantly attacks my thoughts while I'm awake. I have tried to forget it, but when something that dreadful happens, it changes who you are as a person – not just physically, but mentally as well. I have never been able to find who I once was. I believe the Annalise before the attack is still alive inside me somewhere; the carefree, happy woman who enjoyed conversing with others and who wanted children. But the Annalise after the attack is too overpowering, too damaged for the old version to break through.

The damage done to my body that day eventually affected my ability to carry children. If that day had never happened, my life, my husband's life, would have turned out very different. We would have been parents. We wouldn't have spent the remainder of our lives hiding in the mountains. I'm almost certain of it.

It's awful and stomach-churning to think about. I purposefully didn't include the attack in my story to Bonnie because not every story needs telling. I'm sure she'll wake up confused, but it's for the best. The good thing about the herbs I use in the tea is that it can often blur your thoughts, make you forget things, depending on your current mindset. Unfortunately, no amount of the tea makes me forget that awful day, but it can dull it, at least. I even add a few extra natural ingredients to increase the potency of the tea. I've become somewhat of an expert mixologist while living here. I didn't have any other choice.

The heavy sedative effects of the valerian root I slipped into their teas also ensured I could move some things around within the cabin, but it seems Bonnie has already discovered the wooden chest full of items. The watch is missing. When she told me her name was Bonnie, I didn't realise she was the Bonnie from the engraving on the back of the watch. I'm not an expert at reading the English language, but I can recognise her name. What are the chances! It means that whoever Christopher is or was, is very important to her. Perhaps she's out here searching for him, although goodness knows why she's all the way over on this side of the mountain range. Didn't Steffan say something about them being only a day away from where they were heading? Unless they can hike fifty-odd miles in a single day, then he's a liar.

I found the watch attached to a half-eaten body about a year ago. Wolves and other scavengers had destroyed most of the flesh, so I buried what was left after taking the watch and a selection of other items. It will be nothing but bones and dust by now.

It's a shame she'll never get the chance to find him.

Bonnie and Steffan won't be leaving this cabin. I'm going to make certain of it.

Erik always taught me to stay alert, trust no one, and

ensure I was prepared in case of another attack. I learned my lesson from that day. Perhaps, if I'd been able to defend myself back then, I could have fended off that awful man, but as it happens, I didn't even manage to scream for help. Not until it was over was I able to do something about it. Erik taught me a lot of things, including how to defend myself, but he taught me too late.

A lot more happened that day than I care to remember. That's why we didn't allow that journalist to leave here either. What was his name? It began with a B. I have his phone in the wooden box somewhere. He found us years ago, several years before Erik became sick and died. I blame myself for being careless, for staying too long out in the open. I'd been collecting some vegetation that I knew grew best near some rural farms, so it was risky to get too close.

I didn't see the man until he was almost right on top of me. He kept asking me questions. He wouldn't shut up, so I ran away, but the bastard followed me, and I had no idea until he knocked on our cabin door several hours later. I had no idea why he was so fascinated with me, but then he said it. The White Witch. Erik and I had no idea what he was on about. Bonnie asked me the same thing. What white witch? Other than having pale skin, I don't know what he meant. I certainly wasn't a witch, unless that was what people called women like me who lived off what the earth provided and used various herbs and spices in their meals.

That's when I knew he couldn't be allowed to leave. We were in danger after all. Erik had been right all along.

So, he never did.

I can't trust them.

After Bonnie woke up last night and saw what I was doing, I'm thinking maybe she'll never trust me either. I'm hoping the tea will make her head too fuzzy for her to be able to remember anything, but I can't take that risk. It's a shame because I quite like Bonnie. I like her spirit. And Steffan looks so much like my husband. It's quite scary how similar they look. I don't know how I'm going to make them stay or how I'm going to stop them from leaving, but I know that I'll do anything to keep my secret.

Last night, Bonne asked me what I did with Erik's body. I almost laughed. What did she think I did with him? Did she think I'd eaten him? Luckily, the potent concoction of herbs in her tea should muddy her mind enough to make her believe she was dreaming. I can't be too careful, though.

Bonnie is stirring again. She groans as she rolls over. I'm sure her head is feeling very sore this morning, and she's probably wondering why.

'Annalise?'

I stand right over her. 'Good morning, dear.'

'I... What happened last night?'

'Last night?'

'Did we... did we talk last night?'

'Not that I know of. I went to bed early, remember? You and Steffan were both still asleep when I woke up an hour ago. I thought it was best for you to rest, but I have good news. The storm is finally over, which means it shouldn't be more than a few days before the snow starts to thaw. Perhaps Steffan can revisit his digging attempt?' With any luck, he'll make the tunnel collapse again and this time, I might not be so willing to help save him.

Bonnie sits up and places a hand on her head. 'I-I feel... awful.'

'Oh no, you poor thing. Shall I make you some tea?'

'No, no more tea... Thank you.'

Bonnie shakes as she staggers to her feet and heads for the toilet. Obviously, I haven't spent the past however many years doing my business in a bucket. There's an outhouse located next to the cabin, but thanks to the snow, it's unreachable for now, so I've had to make other arrangements. I'm too old to be prude about it, but I can tell it's an uncomfortable experience for them. I'm sure they weren't expecting to share a urine and faeces bucket during this trip.

Steffan is still out for the count. He didn't even make it to his sleeping bag before passing out. I kneel next to him, stroking his hair. His forehead is sweaty and his breathing shallow. Seems he may have picked up a chill overnight, not being wrapped in his sleeping bag. His brush with death wouldn't have helped either. Or perhaps I used too much valerian in the tea. I remember overdoing it on Erik once. By accident, of course. He hadn't been well at all, but I didn't know what else to do. He contracted pneumonia and had trouble sleeping and relaxing, so I used valerian to soothe him. Unfortunately, I used too much, and it knocked him out for two days, but when he woke up, he felt much better.

Bonnie returns to the room looking a little pale, still shaking.

'Come and sit,' I say, gesturing to the space by the fire, which is dwindling now. Bonnie's eyes scan the room, constantly flicking from one side to the other. What is she thinking? Perhaps I'm not as good at hiding my secret as I first thought. Does she remember what happened last night? The question is: if she does remember, is she going to confront me about it or try and escape without saying a word?

'Steffan,' she says, shaking him gently. 'Steffan.' When he doesn't rouse straight away, she shakes him again, more vigorously this time. 'Oh my God... What did you do to him?' The accusation in her question is perfectly clear, and I don't like her abrupt tone. 'He won't wake up. Why won't he wake up?'

Steffan groans right on cue, his eyes rolling to the back of his head.

'Steffan, can you hear me? Wake up.' Bonnie gently taps the side of his face with her hand.

He groans again. 'My head.' He can't keep his eyes open.

'He's very hot,' says Bonnie, placing her hand against his forehead. 'I think he's got a fever.'

'Probably because he didn't get inside his sleeping bag last night,' I reply.

Bonnie glares at me, her usual soft eyes much more menacing. 'Did you put something in the tea?'

'It's valerian root, a natural herbal remedy that aids a restful night's sleep. I didn't see the harm. You both needed your rest.'

Bonnie doesn't respond as she turns back to her husband. 'Steffan, are you okay?'

'My head hurts,' he says. 'I feel like I've been on a drinking binge.'

'You'll be fine in a few hours,' I say. The truth is the man doesn't look well, so it's highly likely he did pick up a chill overnight. Perhaps one of my problems will fix itself over time. 'Now, I have some things to attend to. There's fresh water over there and some leftover stew for breakfast if you'd like it.' At the mention of the stew, Bonnie pales and avoids my gaze.

27

BONNIE

NOW

Annalise shuffles into her room and shuts the door, leaving behind an eerie silence that makes my skin prickle. She said she had some things to do. What things? My head is pounding so hard I can barely think straight. Every time a thought solidifies, it dissolves before I can do anything about it. She drugged us last night without our permission. Why? She said she did it to help us sleep and relax, but is that true? And if that's true, why wouldn't she just offer it to us as a kind gesture and not do it behind our backs?

I force my brain to work, but last night is a blur and trying to put the pieces together is making me dizzy. What happened during the night? Did I wake up and speak to Annalise, or was that a dream? There are flashes of images in my mind that I could have sworn...

Why can't I remember anything clearly? Is that the work of the drugs in my system? What did she call it? Valerian root. I have heard of it before, and seen it for sale in small capsules to aid a restful sleep, bottled in a calming lavender-coloured bottle. I doubt Annalise uses the recommended daily amount for safe use. She probably used the root in its natural, raw form. Does that make it more or less potent?

While I'm attempting to think of some other facts about valerian root, Steffan shuffles into a seated position. He looks worse than I feel. His eyes don't seem to focus on anything, like he's spaced out of his head.

'You're really burning up,' I say, reaching forwards to touch his forehead. It's soaked, clammy and warm.

'I'll be fine,' he grumbles. 'We're getting out of here today.'

'I'm not sure you're in any condition to move right now. Also, the snow is still far too deep. I don't want a repeat of last time.'

'Do you want to stay here longer?'

'No, but—'

'Where's my GPS and phone? I'll check the weather app if it works out here. If the snow is starting to melt, maybe the signal will be stronger and I'll be able to contact the nearest ranger hut.'

I let out a long exhale, realising it's pointless to argue with him at this point. Now the second storm has passed overhead, it means there's no more snow on the way for the time being. It's now a matter of waiting until the snow has thawed enough for us to be able to get out the door and use our snowshoes to crawl out and find the nearest path. We need to leave. There's no doubt about it. I'm just not sure revisiting the tunnel digging is a good idea.

I leave Steffan shivering while I grab his pack. I search the top pocket and all the other ones, double-checking each one, but his GPS and phone aren't there.

'Where did you put them?' I ask.

'Top pocket.'

'They're not there.' I look again, checking all the other pockets too. 'Do you think she took them?' I ask, keeping my voice low. I check my own bag for my phone, but it's not there either. I may not remember a lot about what happened last night, but I know for a fact the last time I saw my phone, it was in my bag.

'Maybe,' replies Steffan. 'Didn't you say she had a whole chest full of phones and gadgets?'

'Yeah. Over there. It's where I found Chris's watch.'

'Sounds like she's a hoarder or something.'

'Would she even know how to use them? The phones I found were all dead. There's no electricity here to charge them.'

Steffan sighs, then runs both hands through his hair and drags his fingers down his face, leaving red vertical marks on his skin. His forehead is glistening. 'She's got us trapped here.'

'Why doesn't she want us to leave?'

'Probably worried we're going to tell someone about her living up here off grid.'

'Surely no one will care.' Steffan doesn't reply. My eyes drift to the front door. 'I think I spoke to her last night, but I can't remember. My head is so foggy. I think she was talking to herself...' I close my eyes, hoping for the memories to form and become solid enough for me to understand them. 'She was talking to her husband, I think.'

'Her dead husband?'

I bite back the sarcastic retort I want to say and instead say, 'Yes. It was weird.'

Steffan readjusts the torchlight so it's between us. 'Right, so she's nuts.' A statement, not a question.

I don't answer directly. 'She's been alone for a long time.'

'Hmm...'

'She said her husband died after a short illness.'

Steffan's eyes lower to the floor and he keeps his voice low. 'I've been thinking about Chris's watch and why it would be in Annalise's cabin.'

I shuffle closer to him, intrigued that he's brought this up on his own. When I first told him about it, he shut me down so fast I thought I'd severely upset him.

'Maybe she killed him...' he says as his gaze drifts to the floor.

Okay, that is certainly *not* what I was expecting him to say.

'Wait... What? I never said she actually killed him. I said maybe she found his body and knows where he is and...'

'But let's think about it for a minute... What if... what if Chris *did* survive the fall and she found him? We're not far from the fall site.' It's difficult for him to talk about this, I know. His voice quakes as he says Chris's name. After the accident, he barely said a word for weeks, not about what happened anyway. All his focus was on me and how I was handling my brother's death. He put aside his own grief and guilt to help me through mine.

I remember the last time I spoke to Chris on the phone. He asked me to do a random favour for him, and I'd not even told him I loved him when I said goodbye because I'd been so thrown by what he was asking me to do.

I swallow back my nerves, knowing I'm stepping into uncharted territory. 'Y-you said that he fell a long way. You said he was dead.'

Steffan holds my gaze and nods. 'He d-did, but... he hit a lot of rocks and trees on the way down and... maybe they broke his fall.'

A weird alarm bell sounds in the back of my head. 'I thought you said you didn't see him fall.'

Steffan readjusts his position next to me. 'I-I didn't. You're right. Sorry, what I meant was that maybe there were rocks and trees and stuff that broke his fall, and he ended up surviving it. Maybe he found his way here, looking for help.'

'Maybe,' I whisper, but I don't think Steffan hears me because he's already turned away, making himself comfortable. He turns his back on me and lies down.

My mind burns with a million questions. Steffan willingly started talking about Chris's accident, but now has completely shut down again. I've waited so long for him to tell me what happened, in excruciating detail, but he's never been able to tell me anything other than the basics. He told me he was dead. That was it. There was nothing he could do. I've never pushed him for more detail because I've been afraid of him piling more guilt onto himself, getting consumed by it from the inside out.

But something doesn't add up with what he's just said, and it's not sitting well with me. In fact, it's making my stomach gurgle and swirl. He's lied to me before, hasn't he? Recently. About the ice course and the reason he bailed on it. What else has he been lying about?

'Steffan,' I say quietly to his turned back. He doesn't respond, so I continue. 'Was Chris really dead when you were forced to turn around and leave him?'

The silence that lingers is enough to tell me the truth.

'Oh my God...'

Steffan turns and sits up so fast that he makes me jump. I flinch away from him as he reaches out to touch me. 'Bonnie, I swear I did everything I could to reach him, but I had to think about my safety too. I had to make the choice whether to leave him and save myself or try and save him and risk getting trapped along with him.'

No. No. No. No.

The blood rushes around my head, pounding against my skull like a drill. What is he saying? Is he seriously telling me that Chris was alive when he left him behind? He chose to save himself rather than attempt to save my brother?

My mouth opens and closes, but no sound comes out because I have no words other than very vile ones. Everything my husband has ever told me is a lie. Is he even capable of telling me the truth?

Again, he reaches out his hand towards me.

'You understand, right? Why I had to lie to you? Please believe me when I say it's been killing me ever since. Seriously. I've hated myself every single day for leaving him, but he was as good as dead, Bonnie.'

Tears well in my eyes, blurring Steffan's outline in the darkness. 'Y-You left him...'

'The weather was closing in fast. He fell and... it would have been dangerous for me to attempt to rescue him in the dark and the storm. I could have slipped, and I'd have joined him at the bottom of the cliff. I had to make a very difficult decision, and I had to make it fast.'

I see red. All the tension, the questions, the anger, the doubt come rushing out all at once. I scramble to my feet, tripping over my sleeping bag in the process.

'You made the wrong one, Steffan!' My voice comes out loud. I don't even care if Annalise hears us. Steffan joins me on his feet. Now, we're facing each other, the torch light flickering ominously between us.

'What are you saying?' he whispers angrily, his eyes glancing over to the bedroom door. He doesn't want

Annalise to hear us. 'You wish it had been me that fell and not him? Is *that* what you're telling me?'

'Yes, because then both of you would have come home, and not just you. Chris would never have left you there to die, Steffan. Never.' I urgently wipe the snot and tears from my face, but they keep coming anyway. 'You lied to me. Again. And this lie is a big one. I'm not sure I can ever forgive you for this.'

Steffan's crying too. He looks away from me. 'I'm sorry, Bonnie. I'm so, so sorry. I don't even know what to say, but you have to forgive me. You have to. I can't bear the fact you hate me. Please.'

'Why? Why should I? You lied about your gambling. You lied about what happened with Chris. What else are you lying about, Steffan? Huh?'

'Nothing.'

'That's what you said last time.' I pause for a moment, then decide to take a big risk. 'What about the Irish guy?'

Steffan stares at me like I've spoken a different language. 'What the hell are you talking about? Are you feeling okay?'

'Don't you dare try and gaslight me. Just before the accident, an Irish guy called me and came snooping around the house. I told you over the phone and you said to avoid him. What was all that about?' This time, he won't even look at me. His gaze is on the floor. 'Steffan...'

'Bonnie, it was nothing, okay? It was just some guy I owed money to. I'm sorry he came round and scared you, but trust me, it's all in the past now.'

'Chris asked me for a favour that day too.'

'I know. I was the one who told him to ask you.'

'Why?'

'Because if I had asked, you probably wouldn't have done it.'

'Okay, but... why did I have to do it in the first place?'

'The guy needed repaying sooner than we originally arranged. Both Chris and I were obviously away, so... between you and Hannah, we thought you were the best bet.'

I sigh and touch the area over my heart where the watch is stored.

Steffan slowly walks away from me and begins pacing up and down the cabin like a caged bear. I don't think I've ever seen him cry properly before. He's falling apart over this, but so am I. This is killing me. He never even cried on our wedding day or when we were told that our baby had no heartbeat after our first year of marriage. I'd broken down into pieces on that day three years ago, but Steffan just stared ahead without blinking. He took my hand and squeezed it, never saying a word to me while I splintered into a thousand pieces. We haven't tried for another baby since.

Now, I'm splintering all over again.

Is he truly sorry, or is he putting on a show? The Steffan Show. If he is, then I'm not enjoying it. One-star rating, but five stars for effort.

Steffan continues to pace, then trips over the fur rug on the floor. 'Why is this all coming out now? We have bigger problems to worry about. We need to get out of here, Bonnie,' he says. 'I can't stay here any longer. We need to—'

'What?' I ask, wondering why he's stopped talking.

Steffan reaches down and pulls the rug across the floor. 'What the fuck?'

I look down at the floor, at the square-shaped trapdoor.

28

BONNIE

NOW

Why is there a trapdoor in the floor of the cabin? It has been covered with the rug the whole time we've been here, which is why I hadn't noticed it before, but it's certainly noticeable now as Steffan drags the rug all the way off it. It's about three feet square and there's a large metal ring for a handle that, now I think about it, is large enough to cause a small lump under the rug, but I hadn't considered there was something underneath it. But both of us have tripped over it since being here.

Our argument is put on hold while we stare down at the trapdoor.

'What the hell is under there?' I ask, keeping my voice to a whisper. I shift my eyes to the bedroom door, expecting Annalise to burst through at any second and scold us for uncovering it. All sorts of answers leap into my mind, none of them good, nor reassuring.

'Maybe it's a cold hole,' replies Steffan.

'A what?'

'It's probably a very crudely made one, but it would

make sense. She has no access to electricity, no way of storing food to keep it fresh, so a cold hole would make sense, especially if she wants to store meat and stuff for longer periods of time.'

I stare at the trapdoor, my mind reeling. 'She keeps food down there?'

'Probably.'

I shudder at the thought of being inside a cold hole. I wonder how big it is. Is it big enough to fit a grown person?

As I stare at the door, debating whether to curb my morbid curiosity and open it or cover it up and pretend it doesn't exist, images of last night flicker to life in my head.

Annalise was chopping something up in the kitchen area. Did she drug us so she could freely move around without us waking up and seeing her? That's probably when she took our phones and GPS. Then there's the whole issue with the wooden chest and her hoarding of items she's either found or taken from people.

Chris's watch.

I'm still no closer to understanding why it's here, although now Steffan has admitted to Chris possibly still being alive after he fell, there's a slim chance that Chris made it this far and came across Annalise, but what did she do with him? Did he die of his injuries, or did she kill him and...

I shake my head. *Stop it.*

What about Erik, her husband? Was she telling me the truth about his death? I immediately think of the film *Psycho* and how Norman Bates kept his mother's body in the house even while it decomposed because he couldn't bear to say goodbye.

Oh God...

Before I know what I'm doing, I bend down and reach out my hand, grasping the cold metal ring. I give it a tug.

'What are you doing?' Annalise's stern voice makes me jump so violently that I almost lose my balance. I straighten up and step away from the trapdoor. I didn't even hear her open her bedroom door and enter the room. I'd been too preoccupied.

'Nothing. We just…' My heart is beating so fast, I can barely catch my breath. 'Steffan tripped over the rug and…'

'What were you two arguing about just now?' she asks.

Her change of topic throws me for a moment. Is she purposefully drawing our attention away from the trapdoor? Is it because there's something she doesn't want us to see down there?

Steffan steps forwards before I can answer, but he says what I'm thinking. 'Look, Annalise, I'm sorry, but that's none of your business.'

'I think it is when you're arguing in my home.'

A beat of silence follows where Steffan looks as if he's been winded. He takes a deep breath, composing himself. He's still not looking great. He's pale and clammy.

'Like I said, it's none of your business. I think today we'll be attempting to dig ourselves out again. We need to leave.'

Annalise glances from Steffan to me then back to Steffan. Is that fear in her eyes or anger? It's hard to tell in the gloomy darkness and flickering torchlight.

Steffan grabs his jacket, shoots me a quick look and marches towards the front door. He pulls it open, revealing the collapsed snow tunnel, but it looks different. The snow has shifted.

There, near the top of the door, is a glimmer of daylight.

It means the snow has thawed slightly.

It means there might be a chance we can dig up and climb on top of the snow.

I rush to Steffan's side, looking up at the small crack of light. The possibility of leaving has overtaken the anger and resentment I feel for Steffan right now. We can fix our mess of a marriage once we're free, even though I know, deep down, that I can never forgive him for leaving Chris the way he did.

'Is it possible to get out?' I ask eagerly.

'Maybe. If we use our snowshoes. Getting out of the cabin is our first job. Once we're out, we can head down until we find the main path, then we have a chance. The storm is over. There's no more snow on the way. It's now or never.'

'You won't make it,' says Annalise firmly.

'It's a chance we're willing to take,' snaps Steffan. It's clear that Steffan has reached the end of his polite-o-metre. He wants to get out of here as much as I do. Being trapped in this cabin for two days has revealed a lot of issues between us, uncovered a lot of truths he's been trying to keep under wraps. He's vulnerable and exposed, and he needs to get out.

Steffan starts scrabbling at the snow at the top of the door with his bare hands.

Annalise grabs my arm and pulls me over to a corner, lowering her voice as she speaks. 'Your husband is not a good man, Bonnie.'

'What? Why would you say that? Were you listening to us?'

Annalise nods slowly. As annoyed as I am about her eavesdropping, it's not like a wooden door is soundproofed. Plus, I really don't want to aggravate her even more than she already is. There's no guarantee that we will be leaving today, and I'd rather not feel the force of her wrath if we have to stay a little longer.

'They all say they're sorry the first time,' she says before turning away and tending to the fire.

She leaves me standing by myself in the corner with her words echoing around my head, unable to ignore the underlying message. Was her husband abusive towards her? Maybe her husband kept her trapped inside this cabin himself. Was she a prisoner too? It certainly puts a different perspective on things, but it's none of my business. Just like my and Steffan's issues are none of hers.

I join Steffan by the door. The temperature in the cabin is dropping by the minute. He's made a decent-sized hole in the snow, but he doesn't look well. He's covered in snow and shivering. He shouldn't be up and about, especially if he's coming down with something, but there's not a lot of options for him.

'Are you sure you're feeling okay?' I ask.

'I'm fine. I just want to get out of here and I'm sure you do too.' We share a knowing look.

There's no point in bringing up Chris again, or the whole favour thing. Not now. Once we're out of this place, then we can focus our efforts on finding him and figuring out exactly what happened that day on the mountain. And why Steffan had got my brother involved in his own debt issues.

Why did the accident happen in the first place?

Why did Steffan lie about it?

And why did Steffan leave Chris to die?

29

ANNALISE

THEN

Erik leaves, despite her desperate protests to get him to stay. She doesn't want to be alone right now. What if someone sees her through the window as they pass the house or comes knocking again and she's forced to answer the door looking like she's been in a grizzly accident? Even though her husband has cleaned her up the best he can, and she's changed her dress, the smell of blood lingers on her skin, in the air, on her clothes, metallic and sweet. Did she get some in her mouth? Is that what she can taste? Saliva floods her tongue, and she barely makes it to the kitchen sink before expelling what little she has in her stomach.

She shouldn't have let him go. What if he goes after that man and does something bad? What if he's caught? What if someone sees him? What if he gets hurt and he never makes it back home? She'll be forced to deal with this herself and she has no idea what she's supposed to do. Tomorrow doesn't exist in her mind. All that exists is this moment, this day, and anything else is merely a shadow, an optical illusion. As she lifts her head from leaning over the sink and looks out the window, she spots someone peering over the top of the hedge just outside.

Annalise shrieks as she ducks behind the worksurface, eyes wide. Who's watching her? Is it a man or a woman? Why are they trying to see into her home? All she managed to see before she ducked down was a brief glimpse of a face cast in shadow from underneath a large, brimmed hat. She wonders if it's the woman who found her earlier and ran to fetch Erik, but if it is, then why is she standing outside, hiding behind a hedge?

Keeping as low as possible, she scurries across the floor to the kitchen table, ducking under it to retrieve the knife. She's not sure why it's under the table because, originally, she left it on top so she would remember to chop the vegetables for tonight's dinner as soon as she got home from the market. Now, it's her only defence against whoever it is who's outside and looking in. She doesn't know what they think they've seen or why they're here, but she clutches the handle of the knife as if her life depends on it, with her back pressed up against the kitchen side.

Annalise stays in the same position, counting as the minutes pass. Where is Erik? What's taking him so long? She fears the worst – that he's tracked down that man, attacked him and then got hurt himself – but then, just as her legs are about to cramp from crouching for so long, the front door bursts open and Erik rushes into the house, slamming the door hard behind him before deadbolting it.

Erik rushes across the floor to her side. 'Are you all right?' he asks. He's out of breath, and there are damp patches on his light blue shirt.

'Someone is watching the house.'

'Who?'

'I don't know. I didn't see. I couldn't see.' Tears stream down her face.

'We need to leave. Now.'

'What happened?'

'I... I tried to get help, but... Annalise, you didn't tell me you attacked him.'

'What? Who?'

'The man who attacked you.'

Annalise drops the knife to the floor and grabs his arms, forcing his body to face hers. 'Erik... what are you talking about? I didn't attack anyone. He attacked me.'

'You did. You stabbed him with the knife.' He points to the knife on the floor. 'That knife!'

'What?'

'I'm sorry, Annalise. They're coming to arrest you.'

'But... I didn't do anything wrong!'

Erik strokes the side of her face. 'We need to leave right this second. We can't come back here; do you understand? We need to get out of this town fast. Right now. Pack what you need and grab what you can carry.'

Annalise nods, her body trembling. She can't remember anything, but it all makes sense now. *I killed that man in self-defence.*

'Where will we go?' she asks.

'Far away from here. Do you trust me?'

'Of course.'

'I told you I'd take care of this. I promise you I'll always take care of you, Annalise.'

'I trust you.'

30

BONNIE

NOW

I assist Steffan with making the snow hole bigger. Slowly but surely, more daylight streams into the cabin, as well as cool, fresh air that burns my lungs, but in a good way. Because the front door is open, the temperature inside the cabin has dropped, so the fire seems redundant right now with regard to heating the cabin. I add my jacket over the top of my layers to keep warm. Already, I'm feeling less claustrophobic, less like the walls are caving in, but my fingers are so raw and numb still that I'm almost useless in my efforts to help him.

Steffan is like a man possessed. Sweat pours down his forehead and into his eyes, but still, he keeps clearing snow away, not caring about it dropping to the floor of the cabin and melting. Before long, he's standing in an ever-expanding puddle.

'Bonnie, make sure all our stuff is packed and ready to go,' he says.

I nod, understanding.

Annalise has stoked the fire again and is heating up a pot of water. That's when I realise something that I didn't before. Why didn't I notice she wasn't wearing her hat? Her long hair is cascading over her shoulders. Her long, brown hair with specks of grey. Not white.

Wow, that herbal tea must have really played with my mind last night. I remember it so vividly, how it had glowed white, almost like she was some creepy angel minus the halo.

'Something the matter, dear?' asks Annalise, clearly seeing me open-mouthed staring at her again.

I blink several times. 'Yes. No. Sorry.'

Her demeanour has changed recently. I'm not sure she wants us to leave, but is that because she'll be lonely when we do or because she makes a habit of trapping hikers in her cabin and collecting their stuff? Maybe she doesn't collect items... but people.

'We'll be leaving soon,' I say.

Annalise curls her top lip up into a smile that makes her look even more deranged. 'I wish you good luck.'

Wait... Is she not going to even try and stop us? Her words do little to settle my racing mind. As I pack up our things, I remember our phones and GPS going missing yesterday, or was it this morning? Time has lost all sense or meaning lately. The only thing I know is that we need to leave as soon as possible.

'Annalise, do you happen to know where our phones and GPS are?'

'Why do you need them? They don't work here.'

'No, but we're going to need them when we leave to find our way back to the nearest walkable path.' Annalise sighs, and her refusal to answer riles me up. 'Look, I know you like... collecting things, but...'

'Collecting things?' she asks, her voice rising a couple of octaves.

'Yes.' Well, I may as well confront her about it now, get the truth out of her, since we're going to be leaving soon. 'I found the wooden chest of items.'

'I see.'

'And one of the items I found belonged to my brother, Chris.' If she's shocked by my revelation, she doesn't show it. 'I just need to know how you got it. Did you find his body or...' My words peter out because I can't bear to say them out loud.

Before Annalise can answer, Steffan lets out a whoop, then turns around to face me, puffing and panting like a freight train. 'Get your stuff. We're leaving now.'

My eyes flick up to the hole. Oh, my goodness. It's big enough to fit a person through now. We really are getting out of here! I turn to Annalise, awaiting her answer.

'Good luck to you both,' she says, turning her back on me. I'm torn between wanting to leave and yelling at her, to demand she answer my question regarding Chris. It's like she's purposefully keeping the truth from me so that I'll want to stay with her. Something isn't right with Annalise. She's hiding something from me. I still have so many questions that need to be answered. What's underneath the trapdoor? Why does she have Chris's watch? What really happened between her and her husband?

I can't stay, though. I have to leave, even if I'm leaving behind the mystery of how his watch came to be in her possession.

'Bonnie.' Steffan's voice makes me turn away from Annalise.

I feel like each of them is against me finding out the truth about Chris, each pulling me in opposite directions.

The most pressing question is – why do I even care about

this woman? Yes, she saved us from freezing to death two days ago, but she doesn't care about us, not really. The thing is, I only care about her because I need her to give me the answers I'm craving, but it looks like that's not going to happen.

I have to let it go.

I crouch next to Steffan. 'If she did take our phones and GPS, then she's refusing to give them back.'

'It's going to be next to impossible to navigate without them,' says Steffan. 'We may have to give up on finding Chris and try again another—'

'No! We can't!' My hand flies to cover my heart. It seems to be my automatic response whenever Chris's name comes up. It feels like the watch is trying to burn a hole through my heart. Chris is telling me not to give up.

'Bonnie, I don't think you understand. It would be like trying to navigate with our eyes shut. Everything out there is covered in snow, so the landmarks and paths will be invisible. How do you expect me to find where he landed without a GPS?'

'You're the expert navigator, aren't you?'

Steffan clamps his lips together, clearly biting back a retort. 'The thing is... he may not be anywhere near where he originally fell. Who knows how far he got before he... The point is, we don't know what happened to him after I left him.'

Now it's my turn to hold back a snappy retort. 'What are you saying? That we just give up on finding his body and return home?'

'That's exactly what I'm saying. I told you right at the start that there was a chance we might not find him.'

'Yes, because you knew all along that he was alive when you left him.'

Steffan shakes his head. 'Bonnie, I've said I'm sorry. I don't know what else to say.'

I grab the snowshoes from our pile of kit. 'Forget it, okay? Let's just get out of here, but I'm not leaving my brother's body up on this mountain. I'm going to find him with or without your help.'

Steffan also grabs his snowshoes and his pack, but he doesn't say a word.

Within a few minutes, we're packed up and ready to leave, but it feels wrong to leave Annalise without saying goodbye.

'Thank you,' I say to her.

She glares back at me. 'You'll be back soon,' she says. 'After all, I have something you need.'

31

ANNALISE

NOW

The thing about living out here in the wilderness for so long is that you develop a sixth sense about what's going to happen before it does. I'm not saying I can predict the future, but anyone with a brain should be able to work out that trying to navigate without a GPS through deep snow in treacherous terrain is going to end in tragedy, especially a so-called expert like Steffan. I don't need any of those fancy gadgets to navigate, but they do. And that's what's important right now. They may have a map, but I'd like to see Steffan navigate with one in deep snow and not knowing where about he is located.

I predict they won't make it two hundred yards before giving up and heading back. Have they ever walked through waist-deep snow before? It depends on how badly they want to leave. I let them go without a fuss, knowing that it won't be long until I see them again. They have enough food for perhaps a day or two, and I don't offer them any extra water to take. They won't need it. Either one of them will fall off a cliff, or the elements will get them.

I place the kettle on the metal stand over the fire and wait for it to boil. A nice cup of herbal tea is in order while I wait for either one or both to return. My money (if I had money) is on Bonnie returning alone.

Bonnie and Steffan whisper while they get their things together, but I have the hearing of an owl. They are afraid of me.

This is another thing about people nowadays. They believe only what's directly in front of their eyes. They don't bother to look beyond, to look deeper into what they're seeing. Their minds jump to conclusions without any proper thought, and they come up with answers that aren't there. It doesn't matter if it's the truth or not. People will believe what they want to believe, and nothing will change their minds.

That's why I'm allowing them to learn on their own. They won't get far and, when they return, they'll need my help. Like I said, I have something Bonnie needs, and she knows it.

While I rock back and forth in my chair, I stare into the flames. Bonnie says thank you and I reply with my warning, then they squeeze themselves and their packs through the gap Steffan has made in the snow near the top of the door.

The fire crackles and spits as the kettle whistles its high-pitched scream. I pour the water and allow the tea to stew as the aroma of the herbs fills the cabin. Now they've gone, it's rather nice to be alone again. It's amazing how quickly one becomes accustomed to having others around. I can hear the voice in my head again!

With every back-and-forth of the chair, a squeak emerges. Over the years, it's become my constant companion. It's funny how one's perspective can change on the little things in life that once brought you pleasure. Now, though, the squeak is a constant annoyance, like a drill into my brain.

'Now, where did I put the oil?' I say. 'I do miss your handiness around the cabin, dear Erik.' I think for a moment, as their voices grow fainter.

There's no light coming through the gap in the snow now.

Darkness has well and truly settled in.

They are both fools for leaving. If they don't end up returning, no doubt I'll discover their frozen corpses not far from the cabin once the snow thaws enough for me to get out.

It's only a matter of time.

I'm nothing if not a patient woman.

32

BONNIE
ONE YEAR AGO

During the drive to Hannah's, my mind is a mess of questions and disbelief. I just can't understand what Chris is thinking by hiding this mysterious box in his house, under Hannah's nose. We always grew up promising we'd never lie, especially when it came to big things like this. The address he's texted me is about five miles from my house in an industrial estate that I know quite well, but I have no idea why I need to take the box here.

Perhaps something has happened while they've been away. Is it money-related? I know Steffan has had gambling issues in the past, but what would that have to do with my brother? He's the most switched-on person when it comes to finances I've ever known. Even better than me. After what happened with our dad, we both decided we'd never gamble our money or make risky investments or anything like that. So, if it's not about money, then what is it about?

I pull up in the driveway next to Hannah's family car, and let myself in using my key.

'Hey,' I call out.

'Hey! We're upstairs in the bathroom!'

I take the stairs two at a time, following the excited shrieks and shouts. I reach the bathroom door and find water all over the floor and a half-drenched Hannah kneeling next to the tub. The twins both have bubbles in their hair, attempting to make it stick up as high as possible in a mohawk style.

'Wow, nice hair, guys,' I say with a chuckle.

Hannah shakes her head at me as if to say, 'Don't get me started.'

I sigh and lean against the doorframe, crossing my arms. 'I brought wine. It's in the fridge. How much longer are you going to be?' I ask as casually as I can.

'Oh, I don't know. About as long as it takes to wrangle two five-year-olds out of the bath and into their pyjamas, so I'm guessing between five minutes and five hundred hours. Why?'

'Just wondering whether to pour you a glass of wine now or later.'

'Better make it later, once they're out.'

'Okay. I'll be downstairs, loading the dishwasher.'

'You're a star. Thank you.'

'No problem.'

I always help with the chores when I visit. But this time I can use them as a smokescreen to buy me some time to find that damn box in the main bedroom.

Ensuring Hannah is once again preoccupied by her screaming children, I tiptoe along the hallway to the end where the master bedroom is. The door is already open, so all I need to do is walk through. I walk to the other side of the double bed and glance down at the floor. It's not carpeted, like all the other rooms, but beautifully finished with mahogany floorboards, but right in the corner where the board meets the wall is a small circular gap big enough to fit my finger. I hook my finger inside and give the plank a tug. It does move, but only barely. Clearly, I'm not putting enough effort into moving it, but I'm worried it'll make too much noise when it comes free.

The kids are still splashing and laughing and screaming, so I wait for a particularly noisy moment, then pull the board as hard as I can. It pops out of the floor, revealing a gap below.

I can't believe I'm doing this.

Shaking my head, I reach my hand into the hole and feel around for the box. It only takes me a moment to find it, so as quickly and as quietly as I can, I remove it and replace the board, then tiptoe out of the bedroom and down the stairs, not releasing my breath until I'm at the bottom.

I head out to the car and place the box in the passenger footwell. It's locked, so there's no chance of me opening it, but when I shake it gently, something moves around inside. It's heavier than just sheets of paper, but not as solid as, God forbid, a gun.

Once back inside the house, I head to the kitchen and make good on my promise to load the dishwasher and do a general tidy. I get out a wine glass ready to be filled. My heart rate only barely returns to normal by the time I hear a herd of elephants running down the stairs, followed by shrieks.

Hannah emerges a minute later, her t-shirt soaked. I hand her a glass of wine. She takes a slurp. 'Thanks. Did I hear you go outside earlier?'

'Oh, yeah. I just needed to get something from my car.'

'You not having one?' she asks, nodding at the fact that I'm not drinking anything.

'Oh, no. Changed my mind. I forgot I have this work thing I need to get done tonight before tomorrow, so I'm going to need to head off. Sorry. My head's all over the place lately.'

Hannah frowns at me, as if she's trying to read my mind. I've never been a good liar, and she knows that, but luckily, she doesn't push the matter further, which I'm eternally grateful for.

'Well, thanks for doing the dishwasher and stuff.'

'No problem.' I move to walk past her, and she grabs my arm to stop me.

'Everything okay?'

I blink several times and nod, probably too overenthusiastically. 'Absolutely. Yeah. Sorry, I just forgot about this work thing.' I hate this. I hate lying to her. Why is Chris making me do this? What's he hiding from her? He shouldn't be forcing me to choose between doing him a favour and lying to my best friend. Should I tell her? What harm would it do? Then, we could be angry at him together and work out whatever is going on, like we did at lunch earlier.

'Okay, well... Have a good day at work tomorrow.'

'Thanks. I'll call you later, okay?'

Hannah nods and lets go of my arm.

'Bye, kids!' I say, giving the freshly bathed children a wave.

'Bye, Auntie Bonnie!' they chant in unison.

I leave the house, get into my car and drive to the industrial estate, feeling like the worst best friend in the whole world. When I reach the destination, I pick up the box and hold it on my lap while I stare at the large building in front of me. It's not marked with any business sign or logo, like most of the other buildings on the site.

Why does this suddenly feel like it is to do with drugs? Most things are nowadays, right? But even thinking that word makes me immediately think I'm crazy. Steffan and Chris wouldn't be mixed up in anything like that. I'm sure, whatever this is, it has a perfectly reasonable explanation that will reveal itself in time.

My weak attempt at making myself feel better does nothing to soothe the nervous gurgles in my stomach. I replay Chris's phone call in my head. He sounded like Chris, all cheerful and upbeat, but what he was asking me to do sounded nothing like anything he'd asked me to do before. When he was a teenager, he'd ask me to pick him up after parties and gigs, most of the time drunk out of his skull, and there was one time he asked me to hide Hannah's birthday present at my house, but this favour is full of secrecy and vague details.

I don't like it, and the longer I sit here, the more I want to turn the ignition and drive out of here as fast as possible. Minutes pass. I can't catch my breath. Just sitting in my car, it feels as if I'm running at a nine-minute mile pace.

I take a breath. In through my nose. Out through my mouth. Calm. Controlled.

A knock on the window startles me. My heart rate spikes and my muscles tense, as if preparing for fight or flight.

Ensuring the door is locked, I gulp back the lump sticking in my throat and wind down my window.

33

BONNIE
NOW

Steffan crawls up through the snow hole first, then reaches through and pulls each of our packs up. I go last. It's a tight squeeze, and once we are out on snow, we sink quite far at first until we manage to sort out our snowshoes and put them on, which works well, even though it feels like I have tennis rackets strapped to my boots.

The bracing cold steals my breath away. It may not be snowing, but the chill factor is easily minus ten. There might not be another storm on the way, but it's not safe to be out here either. The snow is so deep that even though our snowshoes are stopping us from sinking through to the ground, it's still like trying to wade through thick custard, and we sink to halfway up our thighs.

God, this is impossible.

And the darkness is creeping closer by the minute. We haven't got our head torches on yet, as we need to save the batteries, but we're going to need them soon. Everything looks the same, covered in a thick blanket of white.

We have no choice but to keep plodding forwards

because either we face the deep snow or we go back inside the cabin and face Annalise and, quite frankly, I'd rather take my chances with the snow. The idea of going back inside that cabin fills me with dread. Not only because of Annalise, but the claustrophobia, the way the walls kept feeling like they were caving in on me.

What she said to me just before I left echoes in my mind.

'I have something you need.'

What I *need* is to find my brother, so unless she can tell me his exact location, I decide she only said that to try and get me to stay. I have his watch. I don't need anything else from her.

Steffan is doing most of the work, using his body to carve out a trench through the snow so it's easier for me to follow. It must be taking a lot out of him. He keeps stopping to catch his breath.

I'm not sure if Steffan has a plan for where we're going, but the first thing we need to do is get out of the deepest snowdrifts and find a path. The cabin appears to be sandwiched between trees and rock, hidden in a bowl-shaped valley, so we need to get up and out somehow.

An unknown amount of time later, we reach a rocky outcrop where we're forced to climb up the snowbanks to get on top of the rocks and drifts. With our heavy packs, we continue to sink down with every step. My body screams with exhaustion, but I know better than to complain. I don't say a word as we press on. Everywhere I look, there's white, fluffy snow. It's beautiful, but it could kill us if we are trapped out in it. The minutes tick by slowly and the darkness closes in further.

When I look back to see how far we've come, I can no

longer see the cabin. I squint into the gloomy darkness, unable to make out any discernible shapes.

I turn and plod on, but just as I take my next step, the ground beneath me shifts and I topple sideways. An almighty scream rips through the air, sending a jolt of adrenaline straight through me as I fall and tumble down... down...

'Bonnie!' Steffan calls my name from somewhere above, but I can't see him. I can barely hear him because when I land, I face-plant the snow and it's in my ears, nose and mouth. I spit it out, flailing my arms around, and that's when the shock of pain makes me cry out again.

My shoulder is on fire and it's difficult to breathe. Fighting back the panic, I take a breath, now I'm no longer falling. I don't think I fell far, but it was a steep drop.

'Bonnie!'

'Steffan!' I cry out, scared and cold.

'Don't move, okay? Try and stay calm. Are you hurt?'

I blink back tears. 'Y-Yes! My shoulder and... and... I think my ribs are broken.'

I look around me, but it's so dark, there's nothing to see. I'm on my back, lying awkwardly against my pack, which is anchoring me into the snow. I need to try and get it off, but when I try and manoeuvre my right shoulder, the pain makes me almost black out. I take a couple of deep breaths to bring myself round.

'I think you've fallen down a cliff,' says Steffan from somewhere above me. 'Can you put your headtorch on, so I know where you are?' Then, a flicker of light comes through the darkness above, and I can just make out his silhouette. I switch my own headtorch on and direct the beam so he can see where I am.

'What do we do now?' I ask.

I'm injured, and he's weak from whatever fever he had. We're now in an impossible situation that we shouldn't even be in. I rest the back of my head against the pack and stare up at the sky. Time stands still. We're caught in a never-ending loop. How many days ago did we start our trek? How many days were we trapped in the cabin with Annalise? How many more days will it be until we reach safety and get home?

I can't think about that now, though. The idea of being safe and warm seems like a distant dream that will never come true, not at this rate. Not unless Steffan can rescue me from the bottom of this cliff. I know we have ropes in our packs, so I assume he'll fashion some sort of rescue device with it. He has the experience and the knowledge.

He had the experience and knowledge to save Chris too...

The thought enters my mind before I can do anything to dispel it. He wouldn't... He couldn't...

'Steffan? Are you still there?'

A few moments go by and all I hear is the wind through the nearby trees.

'Yep, I'm here! Just sorting some stuff out,' comes the reply.

Relief washes over me as I sink against my pack. It's fine. He hasn't abandoned me.

I really need to get the pack off me. Steffan's not going to be able to lift me up with it still attached to my back. It's literally pinning me to the ground because I don't have the strength to stand up and move with it on. My first attempt at rolling over on my side doesn't go well when my rib feels like it snaps all over again.

I bite back my scream as I take a deep breath and do it again, this time somehow managing to roll onto my left side.

My right arm just dangles helplessly at my side, which means it may be dislocated at the shoulder joint. I don't know what hurts worse, my ribs or my shoulder. Both injuries make it almost impossible to move around. I just need to get the pack off.

With extreme difficulty, I eventually wriggle my arms out of the straps and collapse in a heap from exhaustion and pain.

'Bonnie,' calls Steffan. 'I... I don't think this is going to work.'

It takes me several seconds to understand what he's said.

'Wait... What do you mean? Just throw a rope down and I'll grab on, and you can pull me up.' It will be difficult and probably hurt like hell, but I don't see why it wouldn't work, especially now I'm free from the extra weight of the pack.

'It's too steep. I'm going to go and get help, okay?'

'Steffan, you're making no sense! Are you... are you seriously going to leave me here like this?'

His silence tells me everything I need to know.

He's really going to do it. He's leaving me in the exact same way he left Chris.

'Steffan! Don't you dare. You hear me? If you leave me here, it's over. Do you understand? It's over. How can you do this to me?' My voice is hysterical.

'Bonnie, I'll get help, I promise.'

'I'll freeze to death by the time you make it back. Please. Can you at least try and get me up?'

'Even if I did, I'm in no state to carry you to the nearest path. I'll be able to move quicker on my own.'

'You don't need to carry me. I can walk. I can... Steffan, please!' Snot and tears stream down my face, mixing with the cold snow. Panic is clawing its way up my throat at the idea of Steffan leaving me to die. Because that's what he's doing. I'll never make it till morning, not in these temperatures.

We should never have left the cabin.

Annalise was right.

Annalise...

'Steffan, we can go back to the cabin!'

'There's no way I'm going back there. Bonnie, just erect your tent and stay warm, okay? I'll be back with help in the morning.'

'Steffan! Don't leave me. Please! Steffan!' He doesn't answer. 'Steffan,' I whisper in floods of tears. This is how Chris felt being left behind by a trusted friend, but this is worse. He's my husband. He's supposed to do anything for me, lay down his life for me, in sickness and in health, till death do us...

'Fuck you, Steffan!' I scream into the snowy night. My voice echoes back to me. I hardly ever swear, but I feel this situation warrants it. I don't want the last words Steffan hears from me to be begging him to help me. I want him to know I'm angry and I hate him.

I thought we might be able to work through our issues, through his gambling, his lies and the fact he left Chris to die out here, but this... this is a deal breaker.

I'm going to die the same way my brother did. Because of Steffan. He'd much rather save himself than risk his life to save us. To save me. His wife.

He says he's coming back for me, but I'm inclined not to believe a word that comes out of his mouth anymore. No one is coming to save me. If I'm going to live, then it's up to me to rescue myself. I close my eyes, gaining a moment of composure.

I can do this.

I have to go back to the cabin. Back to Annalise.

It's the last thing I *want* to do. I place a hand over my heart, steadying my breathing, trying to feel for a sign from Chris. Just knowing the watch is there soothes me, bringing my heart rate down enough for me to see clearly.

Even if I can get myself up this cliff face, there's no point in trying to follow Steffan. It's a suicide mission. I'd never make it, not in my condition. I don't even have a map. He has it. The quickest and easiest route to somewhere warm is the cabin. I'm already feeling the effects of the cold seeping through my layers of clothing, having laid in the snow for several minutes already. One of my snowshoes has fallen off during the fall, but the other is still on. I remove it, then crawl and fetch the other. I'm going to need them.

Shuffling awkwardly, I manage to get to my unsteady feet, my right arm hanging limp by my side. The thought of the shoulder joint popping out of its socket makes my stomach heave. I've never been good with injuries or blood. Once, Chris fell off a swing when he was eight and bit through his lip. I'd never seen so much blood, and I don't think I have since. It poured out of his mouth like a tap had been turned on. After I'd stopped freaking out, I ran to the house and told Mum and Dad, who then, thankfully, took over. Chris always made fun of me for having such a weak stomach, and it was often a story he would tell around the dinner table at large family gatherings, such as Christmas or birthdays. What I wouldn't give to hear him tell that story again, to embarrass and make fun of me.

But he never will because Steffan left him out here to die.

Maybe Chris managed to make it a little way before he

succumbed to his injuries. I don't know his fate, and right now, I may not ever know, not if I stand around here and feel sorry for myself. It's time to get my head in gear.

'I have something you need.'

Annalise knows something. And I'm going back to find out.

I scan the beam from my headtorch around the area, looking for the least steep section of cliff that I tumbled down. If I can get out on the side I fell from, then it should be relatively simple to trace my steps back to the cabin, since there's no snow falling to cover them up.

There is a tree growing out of the side of the cliff, wedged between rocks about halfway up, that I might be able to use to my advantage. I return to the pack and retrieve my own rope. It's difficult to do everything with only one hand, but I can barely do anything with my right arm. I quickly search in my pack for anything else I can use, but there's nothing. Our ice picks are still missing. I assume Annalise has hidden them somewhere at the cabin.

When I do get back to her, I'm no longer going to be Little Miss Nice Guy. Steffan has just proved to me that even the people I thought I could trust don't care about me. I'm not going to tiptoe around Annalise anymore. I want the truth from her, especially when it comes to Chris's watch. I need to know what happened to him. I need to know where he is. Steffan is clearly refusing to help me anymore.

Leaving the pack half-buried in snow, I take the rope and stand underneath the slanted tree. If I can hook the rope over one of the sturdier branches, then I can pull myself up from there, but with only one working arm, I'm not sure if it's even possible.

I don't have a choice.

It takes ten attempts until the rope catches on a branch. I test it with my weight, and it holds. Just as I take a step, I remember the snow and ice boot grippers in my pack. They'll help! Several more minutes pass before I can attach them. My body is already showing signs of seizing up.

I will not die like this.

The grippers aid my climb by biting into the ice with each step. I wrap the rope around me and pull with all the strength I have left in my working arm. Even though it hurts like hell, I use my injured arm to hold onto the snowshoes. I'm in reaching distance of the tree now. Just a few more inches. I stretch further as my ribs burn, but I don't give up. I grab the tree branch and haul myself onto it, grabbing the cliff face for support.

I was right. I didn't fall down a long way. It's just very steep.

I'm not sure how I managed to fall off, considering I was following Steffan's footsteps.

The top of the cliff edge is roughly shoulder height now, but with nothing but snow and ice to cling onto and nothing to use to dig in for leverage, I'm at a loss for how I'm going to pull myself up. If I had the use of both my arms, it wouldn't be as difficult a task, but since my muscles are close to freezing and my injured arm is incapable of doing anything, I'm pretty much screwed.

Then, an idea comes to mind.

The grippers on my boots. If I remove one and use it in my good hand, leaving the other on my foot, it might be enough to help me up. Balancing on the tree is precarious as I remove the gripper from the left boot. I slide my hand into it and dig it into the ice at the top of the ridge. I dig in with my other foot and push with my leg and pull with my arm.

It takes time and saps all the strength left in my body, but eventually I make it up the cliff and collapse onto my back, puffing and panting. My pack is below. It'll have to stay there. I suppose I could have tied the rope to it somehow so I could pull it up after me, but I only had one rope, and I'm not sure it would have been long enough anyway.

Knowing I only have minutes before hypothermia well and truly sets in, if it hasn't already, I sit up and attach my snowshoes, then stand on wobbly legs and head back the way I came, using my and Steffan's footprints.

I see his footprints leading off in the other direction, and for a moment, I wonder if I'll ever see Steffan again. Will he make it to the main path and find help?

Deciding not to waste another minute thinking about my liar and traitor of a husband, I make my way slowly back towards the cabin. It's now so dark that the torch beam does little to pierce it. One foot in front of the other. That's all I need to keep doing.

But my whole body is betraying me.

It's failing, one muscle fibre at a time.

I'm so cold that I don't even feel the pain in my ribs and shoulder anymore. I'm just numb as I fumble and trip up to the roof of the cabin, which is sticking out of the snow up ahead. The top of the door is still visible, but barely.

I collapse next to it and hammer my fist against it.

For a moment, I wonder if Annalise will even let me back in again.

But then the door opens and a familiar face peers up at me through the snow hole Steffan and I dug earlier. I slide down into the cabin, back inside my prison of warmth and safety.

34

ANNALISE

NOW

As soon as I open the door, an icy wind whips through the cabin, almost extinguishing the fire. Bonnie collapses in a snowy heap on the floor, groaning like an injured animal. I'm annoyed she's letting all the warm air out. The fire is crackling away, but the hole she and Steffan climbed out of has got bigger thanks to the warmth from inside the cabin. From the looks of it, the snow is still at least waist height outside.

Bonnie garbles something indistinguishable.

Dear, dear, what a mess.

I wait a few moments, but it seems there's no sign of Steffan. I don't know what's happened, but I can take a wild guess. They can't have been gone more than two hours. I wonder how far they got.

Snow is everywhere again inside the cabin, and it's already melting and causing large puddles across the floor. It's going to take weeks to dry this place out.

I bend down next to Bonnie and try to roll her onto her back. She cries out and grabs her shoulder, curling up into a ball on her left side.

'Are you hurt?' I ask, even though I can see just by her body language that she is.

Bonnie takes a moment, then turns her face to look up at me. Good God, the woman is half-frozen. I should let her lie on the floor in her misery and do nothing. She should have known better and listened to me. I told her that leaving the cabin would be a mistake and would be dangerous.

'Where is Steffan?' I ask.

'G-Gone.' Bonnie shuffles herself into a seated position, still clutching her right arm. 'I was following him and... I slipped and fell off a small cliff. He didn't even attempt to rescue me. He said he'd go and get help and come back for me in the morning.'

'I see...' He sounds about as delightful as Erik used to be. 'You made the right choice, Bonnie. You'd be dead by morning if you'd stayed out there.'

'M-My pack is still out there. It has all my first aid stuff in it.'

'Never mind. I've treated broken bones before without all the fancy medicines.'

Bonnie blinks up at me, snowflakes sticking to her eyelashes. 'I... I think my shoulder is dislocated and I have a broken rib.'

'Hmm, I'm afraid not much can be done for the rib, but the shoulder will need to be popped back into the socket and then strapped up. It will be quite painful, but don't worry, I've done it before once, when my dear husband dislocated his shoulder after falling from the roof.' Bonnie wipes her face with the arm of her jacket. She's a complete mess, soaking wet and shivering. 'But first, you need to get out of your wet clothes or you're going to get sick.'

'T-Thank you,' she says. Bonnie begins the arduous task

of removing her jacket, wincing with every movement. 'I appreciate you letting me back in.'

'Yes, but never mind that now. I'm afraid to say, but I don't think Steffan will survive out there. He's much further from the main path than he thinks. You never would have made it.'

Bonnie hands me her wet jacket, which I take with a smile as I feel around in the pockets. I turn my back on her, sliding the watch into the folds of my own clothing. She starts unlacing her boots with her blue-tipped fingers. 'Right now, after leaving me like that, I couldn't care less what happens to him,' she mumbles as tears stream down her cheeks.

Once her boots are off, I help her into a comfortable position by the fire. She doesn't look good. Not only is her face as white as a sheet, but she's sweating and hot to touch.

'This isn't going to be pleasant,' I say. 'Can I offer you some herbal tea to dull the pain?'

Bonnie gulps and shifts her weight uncomfortably. 'No tea.'

'As you wish.'

I feel around her dislocated shoulder with my fingers, manipulating the muscles and assessing the damage. I then lay her on her back and adjust my hands either side of her shoulder joint, ready to use all my weight to pop it back into place.

'Okay, I'm going to go on three. One. Two... Three.'
Crack.

Bonnie's screams fill the small cabin, almost rattling the boards against the windows.

But that may just be the wind.

35

BONNIE

NOW

The pain, combined with the cold and shock, makes my body shake uncontrollably. Annalise's swift but strong movement pops my shoulder back into place. It sounds like a branch snapping. The noise that erupts from my mouth is animalistic in nature. Goddamn it, I should have taken her offer of the drugged tea. I'm on the edge of passing out as it is. The tea may have dampened the pain.

Annalise works fast. She grabs a long stretch of fabric from her bedroom and then creates a makeshift sling for my arm to rest in. I sit by the fire with my knees pulled up to my chest, but that hurts my ribs. Black spots dance in front of my eyes as I try not to faint.

'Are you sure you don't want something for the pain, to help you sleep?' asks Annalise again, taking a seat in her rocking chair across from me.

I lick my dry lips. 'Water,' I mumble. I'm severely dehydrated, something I didn't think was possible being surrounded by so much snow.

Annalise fetches me a cup of water and hands it to me. I take it, sniffing it before taking a sip. It smells normal. The cool water hits the back of my parched throat and makes me splutter. It's a welcome relief, but the pain still ploughs on, pushing me closer and closer to the edge.

Do I trust her? She's got what she wanted: me back in the cabin, but what's her plan now? What's *my* plan?

I need to keep my wits about me, but it's difficult to do when all I can focus on is the pain in my shoulder and ribs. It's up to me now. I can't depend on Steffan to get me out of here anymore. He's long gone and may be half-dead already. It's time for me to step up and take control of this dire situation.

My pack is several hundred yards away, buried in snow at the bottom of a cliff. My expert mountaineer husband has left me to fend for myself. And I have only one working arm and a broken rib, which feels like I've got a knife wedged in my side every time I breathe in.

The only thing of use to me in this cabin is the GPS that Annalise has taken and hidden. There's no way in hell I'm going to be able to navigate without it. It would be a suicide mission. I'd be blindly wandering around the Swiss Alps in the hopes I'll stumble across a random hiker who could help me. Not worth the risk. I can't believe it's come to this.

Annalise and I don't speak for a while. There's not a lot I can say. I'm thankful to her for helping me, but she also scares the life out of me because I don't know what she's thinking or what she has planned. I need her to tell me about Chris. Without Steffan's guidance, there's no way of me finding his body. It would be like searching for a needle in a haystack. Only Annalise can help me now.

The wind howls down the chimney, which almost causes the fire to go out. Annalise sighs and fetches a blanket, handing it to me.

'It's going to be a cold night,' she says. 'The temperature is going to drop rapidly.'

My thoughts jump to Steffan.

'Maybe next time you'll listen to my warning,' she says quietly before settling into her chair and closing her eyes. 'I'll see you in the morning, Bonnie.'

Cold shivers rush down my spine.

I'm literally at her mercy now. She's not leaving me alone in the cabin, preferring to sleep in her chair, watching over me all night. It's like she's waited for this moment all along. I don't know whether she's my saviour or my captor.

She barely stirs all night. The wind howls all night long, never letting up even for a minute. For all I know, it could be snowing a gale out there again, covering the cabin in even more snow. I think of Steffan, out there alone. Has he made it to safety? Is he a frozen corpse now?

Tears spring to my eyes at the thought. How did it all change so fast between us? When we entered this cabin, I thought he was saving me. I trusted him with my life, but since being here, all his secrets and lies have come to the surface. He not only lied to me about the gambling and whatever he'd got himself involved in, but he admitted he left Chris alive on this mountain to save himself. It's as good as killing him himself.

It's exactly what he's just done to me.

I don't even know who Steffan is anymore.

When he came back from the hiking trip a year ago, after telling me and Hannah about the accident, he was a broken man. He blamed himself over and over. He went to therapy for it. Therefore, at the time, I didn't feel it was appropriate to bring up the whole thing with that Irish man again, and the box which Chris asked me to get just before he died. It never even crossed my mind. My brother had just died and my husband blamed himself.

I never did get to the bottom of what was going on at the time, but Steffan's blatantly lied to me about so many things. And since Chris died, nothing ever came of whatever was in that locked box, but what Steffan said earlier has cemented the fact that he and Chris were mixed up with something dodgy to do with Steffan's gambling debts.

A day after I handed over the box, Hannah and I got the news that Steffan and Chris had been involved in a mountaineering accident and only Steffan had survived. At the time, we'd been overcome with grief and had put the entire thing with the weird phone calls and the box out of our minds. In fact, I never told Hannah about the box because it didn't seem to be of any importance after Chris died.

I've got this all wrong.

I should have questioned him about it. I should have fought harder for answers rather than brushing them under the rug. Now, Steffan has left me here and taken the chance of finding out the truth with him. Did he leave me here intentionally? What if he knew exactly what he was doing when he led me out of this cabin?

The thought makes my head spin.

One thing's for sure: I do not know who my husband is anymore.

I spend the rest of the night blaming myself for believing Steffan's story. I remember him crying to me about how he tried his best to reach Chris, how he refused to leave without his body, but the rangers and the emergency services convinced him it was too dangerous to return for him because of the impending weather.

It was all lies.

36

ANNALISE

THEN

She works quickly to pack a bag for each for them, but she has no idea what she's supposed to bring with her. Clothes. Food. Money. Where are they supposed to go? The police are on their way to arrest her for something that she can't remember doing. If she'd stabbed him in the house, then what had happened? Had he left in search of help and then died elsewhere? Where's his body?

It would explain all the blood. Yes, some of it has come from her own body, but not all of it. Is that why she found the knife under the table earlier? It wasn't her fault, though. It was self-defence. Surely, the police would be able to understand that. Why do they have to run? Surely, that makes her look more guilty, like she has a reason to run away?

Erik grabs her arm and pulls her towards the door, taking the bags from her. She has no choice but to follow him. She knows she'll follow him to the ends of the earth, but never did she think they'd be on the run together.

But Erik is serious. He keeps saying she's killed him, that

the police are on their way, that she'll be arrested and locked away. Perhaps they both will.

She's killed a man.

That's the bottom line.

But rather than staying and fighting, to try and explain what happened, Erik is forcing her to flee the scene of the crime before she's had a chance to take a breath. Annalise takes one last look at her home and heads out the door, knowing already that she'll never return.

Erik drags her along the streets. They have no vehicle or any way of travelling long-distance. Her legs are already close to giving up, but she can't. Not yet. They need a place to hide, somewhere they can rest for a while until this blows over. But will it blow over, or will they be running for the rest of their lives? This wasn't how her life was supposed to be. How has everything changed so fast in a matter of hours?

This morning, she'd been blissfully happy, with a long and happy marriage to look forward to, children to raise and nurture, but now there is nothing but a black, empty hole where her future should be. She just has to trust her husband. He will make everything better in the end. She's sure of it.

As they make their way through the streets, she keeps her head down, staring at the pavement under her feet. She expects to hear shouts from police any minute as someone spots them, but there's nothing. Didn't Erik say the police were on their way to arrest her? Where are they then? How were they able to escape from their house so easily without being spotted? The way he'd rushed back inside the house earlier and told her to pack made it sound like the police were merely minutes behind him. Yet, here they are, on the outskirts of the village already, walking along the road with no sign of being followed.

'I think we're safe now,' says Erik, finally letting go of her hand and allowing her to walk without being dragged. He has the bags in his other hand, storming ahead with no sign of slowing down.

'Can we rest a while?' she asks. She's exhausted and the pain inside is still there, causing her to walk with a cumbersome gait, almost bent over double.

'Soon. We must get as far away as possible first.'

'When you left the house earlier, where did you go? Why did you leave me?'

'I told you. I tried to get some help, but I found him. I found the body. I ran. They think it was me.'

'You found him?'

'Yes. He'd collapsed just down the road, unable to get help in time.'

'But you said the police were on their way to arrest me. How did they know what happened?' Erik doesn't slow his pace, and now she has to jog to keep up with him. 'Erik! Talk to me.' She stops in her tracks. 'I'm not moving another muscle until you tell me what happened.'

Erik stops and turns. He drops the bags to the ground. 'No one was coming. I just said that to get you to hurry.'

'But...'

'Annalise, why don't you trust me? If we'd stayed there, then you would have been found out eventually.'

Tears bubble up behind her eyes. 'Who was that man? Why did he attack me like that? He works – worked – with you, didn't he?'

'I can't tell you that. Not now, but I will soon. We need to get as far away from here as possible, and then I will tell you everything, I promise.' He holds out his hand for her to take.

She hesitates, unsure what to do, but then she steps forwards and takes her husband's hand. She has no reason not to believe him. He will keep her safe. He's always kept her safe. She might not agree with him keeping secrets from her, but she believes him when he says he will tell her everything once they are far away from here.

Now, they can run off into the sunset together and start a new life somewhere else.

Just like they always planned.

But that's not what happens next.

Far from it.

37

BONNIE

NOW

Somehow, I survive the night. I don't have a thermometer, but I don't need one to know that my temperature is dangerously high. Too high. I'm still in a lot of pain and, on several occasions, I've almost buckled and woken up Annalise, begging for whatever concoction of herbal remedies she has. I curse myself for leaving the pack behind. I should have at least grabbed the first aid kit with the paracetamol and other various medications inside.

Annalise sleeps in her rocking chair with me nestled just off to the side. She's a very sinister presence, sitting there, her elbows resting on the armrests, her hands clenched on her lap, her bony fingers interlinked. Her head is laid back against the chair and she's rocking gently all night.

Squeak. Squeak. Squeak.

How she keeps rocking while she's asleep, I don't know, but with every squeak of the chair, my nerves fray and jangle even more, until I'm so on edge and exhausted from keeping my eyes open that I feel like a pressure cooker ready to erupt. Why does it feel like she's watching me with her eyes closed?

Is she even asleep? If I were to try and move, would she wake up?

The next morning, my eyes flutter open. Somehow, I must have fallen asleep. Or maybe *passed out* is a better explanation. My head pounds and my mouth is dry again, but not only that, the pain is so bad that I'm sweating through my light jacket.

I'm not sure I've ever felt this bad in my life, not even when I had the flu combined with tonsillitis and ended up in hospital on a drip. With no access to any sort of medical expertise or drugs, I'm not sure how I'm even going to survive the day, let alone leave at some point, trek several miles across the mountains and find help.

Because that is what I need to do. As soon as the snow clears a bit more, whether it be in two days or two weeks, I will be getting out of here somehow.

Annalise is still in her chair, rocking. Merely seconds after I open my eyes, she lifts her head from the back of the chair, opening her own at the same time and looking directly at me. She's like a possessed doll.

'How did you sleep, dear?'

'I-I didn't,' I say, my teeth chattering. I'm not cold but boiling hot.

Annalise gets up, then kneels beside me, reaching out her frail hand to my forehead. I try not to recoil. Her caring gesture feels like she's baiting me.

Annalise stands up then sighs heavily. 'Bonnie, you're burning up. I know you don't want to use medicinal herbs, but I highly recommend it right now. I am very good at mixing herbs and know the exact amounts it will take to help you, but you have to trust me.'

I clench my teeth as vicious tremors and sweats take over

my body. I'm so cold yet feel as if I'm on fire. 'N-Not until y-you tell me the t-truth.'

'The truth about what, dear?'

'Like I s-said before, I found a watch belonging to my brother, C-Chris, in your wooden box. About a year a-ago, he died somewhere out here and I'm here s-searching for his body. H-How did you find the watch?' I would hold it up and show her, but it's still in my jacket, which is hanging by the fire. It's the first time since being back in the cabin that I'm parted from the watch, but I'm too weak, too feverish to stand up and fetch it.

Annalise narrows her eyes at me, dark shadows creeping over her wrinkled face as she does. 'Steffan left him here, didn't he?'

'I... Yes.' There's no point trying to deny it now. I have no reason to protect Steffan anymore.

'And now he's left you to the same fate, but at least he'll never make it back home.'

I'm not sure how she knows that so definitively, but I don't question her judgment.

'I-I need you to answer my question, Annalise. How did you get his watch?'

Annalise sighs. 'I'm afraid I found it on a body.'

I look away from her. I knew he was dead. Obviously, I knew, but hearing it so bluntly feels like a dagger piercing directly into my heart. I suck in a breath, even though it hurts to do so.

'Where abouts did you find him?'

'I found him roughly two miles from here at the bottom of a steep crevice, but I don't believe that's where he fell. The lack of blood splatter and the drag marks on the ground nearby told me he'd pulled himself along from wherever he fell, seeking help. He was dead when I found him, though.'

My stomach clenches. The thought of Chris dragging himself along the ground, trying to find help, is more than I can bear. He must have had broken legs, and God only knows what other injuries. Did he die from his injuries, or did he die from exposure to the elements and dehydration? There's no way I'll ever know.

'I buried him near where I found him, but to be honest, there wasn't a lot left after the wildlife...'

'Stop. Please. I can't...' The tears come thick and fast.

'I did search through his pockets for anything of use.' Annalise stands up and moves away from me. 'His backpack was nowhere nearby, so I assume he must have left it behind where he fell, but I was never able to find it.'

'W-What else did you find on his body besides his watch?'

Annalise looks down at me and blinks once. 'Nothing of importance,' she says.

'Do you remember where you buried him?'

'Yes, of course. My memory is very good.'

'Please. You have to take me there once the snow clears. It's why I'm out here. I can't go home without him.'

'As I told you, there was barely anything left.'

'But...'

No. This can't be happening. This can't be it. I can't have come all this way, risked my life, been stranded and left behind by Steffan, broken my ribs and dislocated my shoulder, all to come away with nothing.

'Besides,' continues Annalise. 'You're not going anywhere for the foreseeable future.'

'Are you keeping me here against my will?'

'Let's just say that it's in your best interest to stay here for as long as possible.'

'But why?'

'I do not trust you, Bonnie, but I don't plan on killing you. I'm not the evil witch everyone seems to think I am. All I've ever wanted was to be left alone, but people constantly trespass on my property, let themselves in and start asking questions and accusing me of things that aren't true.'

'I... But we didn't have any other choice. We would have frozen to death. I'm sorry about accusing you of killing and eating your husband or whatever else...'

Annalise bursts out laughing. 'That's what you thought?'

'Honestly, yes, it did cross my mind, along with many other things. I'm sorry. I misjudged you, okay? But I can't stay here.'

Annalise grins, resembling an evil witch as she shows her full set of rotten teeth. 'You will stay here, Bonnie. You don't have any choice in the matter.'

And that's the moment when I realise I've made a terrible mistake coming back here.

'Why are you so intent on keeping me here?' I ask. 'Surely, I'm a hindrance to you.'

'Yes, you are, indeed, but after being alone for so many years, it is rather nice to have company.'

'I can't stay here forever, Annalise. You know that, don't you?'

Annalise leans closer, grasping my arm, my injured arm, and squeezes it. 'I told you, I can't let you leave, Bonnie.'

'W-Why not? Steffan's gone.'

'Your husband is dead.'

'How do you know that for sure?'

'I have lived up here over forty years. I know the weather

on this mountain better than anyone. It reached minus twenty last night with a wind chill of minus twenty-two. The snow is over ten feet deep in places and we are over three miles from the nearest path. If he didn't freeze to death from the exposure, then he probably fell off a hidden cliff. You, my dear, were the lucky one. I shall look after you now.'

She stands up and moves away from me.

'You can't keep me here against my will,' I shout again.

'You are about to lose your fingers to frostbite. You have an injured shoulder and broken ribs and a fever that, if it doesn't come down soon, will render you immobilised and delirious. But please... feel free to leave. I guess I'll be finding your frozen corpse in a day or two when the snow clears.' She points to the door, testing me.

Does she want me to go or doesn't she? What would she do if I called her bluff and just got up and left? To be honest, I'm in no position to go anywhere, let alone trek through deep snow with no clue where I'm going. I wouldn't last five minutes.

'Once the snow clears, I'm leaving,' I say, sounding a lot more confident than I feel.

'We'll see.'

I grind my teeth together as she turns and begins sorting stuff out in the kitchen area. My stomach growls at me, signalling my hunger, but I'm not eager to eat what she has on the menu. Has she forgotten I'm a vegetarian, or will she make something with only vegetables?

My pack, along with all my rations, is freezing at the bottom of a nearby cliff.

I am literally depending on her to survive the next few days. Even though she's menacing and is refusing to let me leave, I don't think she wants to kill me. The whole cannibal thing was made up in my head, so why else would she want to kill me if not to eat me? I don't take her for a deranged serial killer. She's just deranged because of being alone for too long.

'What happened to Barry Bolder?' I ask as she starts chopping up vegetables.

'I don't know who you're talking about,' she replies.

'He came looking for the White Witch.'

'Did he now?'

'Did he come here? Did you speak to him?' As soon as the second question leaves my lips, my vision blurs and my head swims. I gulp back the saliva that fills my mouth and my head bobs forwards, my chin almost touching my chest. I jerk upwards again, waking myself up.

The fever rages through my body like a charging army. I'm not sure how much more my immune system can take before it relents completely, and the walls collapse.

'You don't look well, dear.'

I close my eyes for a moment, just to rest them, but when I open them again, everything looks different.

There's no fire.

It's pitch black and much colder.

Also, the smell of raw meat fills my nostrils, instantly making me retch. Where the hell am I? What's going on? I closed my eyes for a second...

Didn't I?

Or did I pass out?

I glance at my Garmin. It's now six in the evening. I've been unconscious for over nine hours. I tap my watch again, which illuminates the darkness for a matter of seconds with the light-up dial before switching off.

I'm in a cramped hole of some sort. There's hardly

enough room to stretch my legs in front of me, and when I attempt to sit up, my head hits the hard ceiling.

She's moved me.

Why?

Where am I?

What am I lying on? I feel around in the dark with my free hand and find cold earth between my fingers. The stench is making my eyes water. What is going on here?

'Annalise?' I call out.

There's no immediate answer, but I can hear footsteps above me.

That's when my location clicks into place.

The cold hole.

She's buried me down in the cold hole underneath the floor of the cabin.

Is she seriously keeping me prisoner now? How long can I survive down here?

'Annalise!' My throat burns. I don't remember the last time I ate or drank anything apart from a sip of water.

She really has locked me down here with her meat and food. That's what the smell is. I can't feel any lumps of meat, so perhaps the smell has seeped into the earth.

'Are you ready to accept some food and water now?' Her voice sounds above my head. I look up, hoping to see a glimmer of light, but there's nothing. The darkness is so disorientating.

'Annalise! You can't treat people like this!'

'Why not? It's no worse than how I've been treated for most of my life by someone who was supposed to love me.'

I close my eyes, but it's no different than having my eyes open. 'Look, I'm sorry for whatever your husband did to you, but it doesn't mean you can treat people like animals, locking them away.'

'All I'm offering you is food and drink so you don't die. If you won't keep yourself alive, then I have no need to help you.'

'But you could have poisoned it.'

'Then I guess you'll just have to trust me. If you search around down there, you'll find a cup of water and some stew. Don't worry, I made it without meat this time. It's your choice, Bonnie.'

I sit in silence for a long time after that, going over my choices.

Trust her.

Or die.

PART 3

38

ANNALISE

NOW

Over the past few days, I've come to realise that Steffan is more like my dear husband than I first thought, almost exactly like him in fact. Bonnie is better off without him. I saw the tension between them, long before it rose to the surface.

My husband, God rest his soul, was a difficult man to live with, especially towards the end, but I still loved him. He's much easier to live with now he's dead, though. Plus, I no longer live in fear of him. Now, I have something else to fear. Everyone else.

There's not a chance Steffan made it through the night, and even on the off chance that he did, would he really tell people that he left behind his wife to save himself? No. He wouldn't. I think I'm safe, but the whole idea of Steffan telling people about Bonnie is moot because he won't have survived, no matter how hardy and resilient he thinks he is. When it comes to the raw elements and exposure of the mountain, Steffan wouldn't have stood a chance.

But Bonnie...

She's a different story.

She seems to have this romantic idea that everyone must tell the truth. I overheard a lot of their conversation through the walls of the cabin about Steffan lying to her. He lied to her about gambling, and he lied about the accident with her brother. It therefore didn't surprise me when Bonnie came back to the cabin without him, injured and close to death. Men like Steffan (and my husband) only ever think about themselves when it comes to life or death.

Bonnie cares about others, even me, although I'm sure she's reluctant to admit it. I had to lock her up for her own good. She needs to eat and drink, or she's going to die. I'm merely making it an easier choice for her.

I keep an ear out for any sounds coming from the cold hole. I'm sure it smells bad in there, and it must be freezing, but that's the least of her worries if she doesn't eat or drink anything in the next few hours. Otherwise, the next time she passes out, she may never wake up.

I don't want her to die.

I'm an old, lonely woman. It would be nice to have company for the remainder of my days here. But she has to *want* to stay. Time locked in the cold hole will help change her mind. I'm sure of it.

Rustling sounds tell me she's moving around in the dark below, then I hear large gulps as she swallows the water in the mug.

I grin. She's trusted me. She probably thinks that I have drugged her food and drink.

Maybe she's right. Maybe she's wrong.

We'll just have to wait and see.

39

BONNIE

ONE YEAR AGO

The man staring at me through the car window has dark hair that's matted and greasy. A few wispy strands curl around his forehead and ears. The wind has picked up and cloud is covering the once warm sunshine. It's almost like the weather is copying my mood. It wouldn't surprise me if the heavens opened and drenched the area.

The man grins at me with crooked, rotten teeth. I don't like to judge books by their covers or people on how they look and dress, but this man is either homeless or a drug addict. Is this who I'm supposed to hand the box over to?

I cautiously lower my window, only a couple of inches, enough to be able to speak through. 'Can I help you?' I ask.

'You got the money?' he asks in a gravelly, smoky voice.

So, it is money in the box.

It's not the same guy I saw earlier, not the Irish guy, so who is he? Is he even connected to the Irishman and whatever Chris and Steffan have got themselves involved in?

'Um, yes, I think so.'

'Hand it over then.' He attempts to open the car door,

but thankfully, the automatic lock is enabled. My heart rate spikes as I clutch the box tighter. He gives up when he can't open the door and steps back, his arms folded, staring at me with cold eyes.

'Come on then. I haven't got all day.'

This cannot be a legitimate transaction. This guy is not trustworthy in the slightest. How are my brother and Steffan mixed up with someone like him? Despite the muggy weather, my armpits and forehead are sweating. My stomach twists and clenches.

I lower the window the rest of the way. 'What's your name?'

'Doesn't matter what my name is. All that matters is that your hubby owes me money. Now, hand it over.' Wait... *Steffan* owes him money? Not Chris? Why was Chris keeping this money at his house?

Every part of me is screaming to turn the key and drive away, leaving this guy in the dust, but I can't. What if he doesn't leave us alone? If the Irish guy knows where we live, then maybe he does too. I've seen movies and TV shows where money deals go bad, and things get ugly. I don't want that in my life.

One thing's for sure: Steffan and Chris have some explaining to do when they get home.

I lift the box through the open window and pass it to the man, who takes it. He doesn't seem concerned that it's locked. Does he have a key to open it, or will he just bash it open by force?

'Tell your hubby it better all be here.'

I nod, my throat dry. The man turns and walks away into a nearby warehouse. Only then do I release my breath. Only then do tears fill my eyes.

MORNING ARRIVES, and with it, a building sense of dread of going to work. My job is not very exciting – a customer service position – but it pays the bills, and since Steffan seems to be having money issues that I don't know about, I expect we'll need every penny we can make soon. How much money was in that tin? Why was Steffan storing it at Chris's house?

I do my best to push these questions and negative thoughts aside as I drink my coffee and prepare for work, but they keep tickling the back of my mind like an annoying itch that won't go away. I really need to speak to Steffan and Chris face-to-face, but they aren't due home for several weeks yet. The phone signal is patchy at best out there too, and it would cost a fortune to call them.

This is one of those times where I must learn to be patient, but patience was never my forte. Just as I pick up my handbag and keys to leave, my phone rings. I lock the door while simultaneously searching for the phone in my bag, which is in dire need of a clean-out.

When I finally find it, the screen shows me it's Hannah.

'Hannah. Hey, I'm so sorry I didn't call you last night, but I was super tired and...' I stop when I hear my best friend sobbing on the other end of the line. 'Hannah? What's wrong? What's happened?'

Everything stops.

I don't even care that I'm going to be late for work. I stop in my tracks, clutching the phone tight to my ear. Something tells me that nothing is ever going to be the same again.

Hannah's cries are like nothing I've ever heard before. She can't catch her breath.

My first thought is that one of the kids is hurt. Or both of them.

'Hannah. Where are you? I'm coming over right now. Are you at home?' I start moving again towards the car, my destination now different from what it was several seconds ago.

'T-There's been an a-accident,' she stutters.

I get in the car, slam the door, slot the key into the ignition. 'An accident? Are the twins okay? Are you at the hospital?'

'N-No. The twins are fine. I-It's C-Chris... He's dead, Bonnie.'

My whole world turns upside down.

After that moment, the money, the secrets, the box, the Irish man, everything gets shoved out of my head and replaced with Chris's death.

Nothing else matters.

40

BONNIE

NOW

I eat and drink what Annalise has provided, scoffing it down like it's my last meal. It could well be. I don't know when she's likely to feed me again. The darkness means I can't see what I'm eating, so when my teeth bite into a stringy texture, I immediately spit it out.

She's fed me meat, which means she's done it on purpose, as a test. Eat it or starve. It's a power play if I've ever seen one.

I choose to uphold my beliefs and cautiously bite into each chunk of food after that. If it's meat, I spit it out. If it's a vegetable, I swallow it. My stomach clenches with every mouthful and, when I'm done, it gurgles, signalling my continuing hunger.

The warm tea soothes my sore throat, and the mug feels good clenched in my trembling, freezing fingers. The cold is unlike anything I've ever imagined or experienced. Without the warmth from the fire in the room above or the extra layers from my outer jacket and fleeces, my body is unable to generate and keep any sort of heat.

My toes are numb, and my fingertips burn as if they've been dipped in acid again. I'm not holding out much hope that my fingertips will survive this experience. Once I've finished the tea, I tuck my hands underneath my armpits, but it's no use. If frostbite hasn't set in already, it will soon.

There's no use in calling out for Annalise. We're at a stalemate. Her versus me. As soon as that trapdoor opens, I'll be launching myself up at her and fighting my way out with the little strength and energy I have left. She's gone too far now. She's keeping me here against my will, and I'm not ready to be kept here, trapped like her pet.

TWO HOURS HAVE PASSED since I woke up down here and there's not been even a peep from upstairs. She's trapped in this cabin too, so she must be up there, unless she's managed to climb out the door like Steffan and I did earlier, but where would she go? She's an old lady. I can't imagine her traipsing through deep snow, especially since she doesn't have snowshoes or proper equipment.

My teeth chatter together so hard that my jaw aches and I keep biting my tongue. My whole body is rigid with cold as I cower in this hole with my knees hunched up to my chest. I'm trying to make myself as small as possible, to try and keep my body heat in, but I can feel it seeping out of my skin, evaporating into the air. My ribs and shoulder constantly pulse with pain, which keeps me from slipping into unconsciousness.

I'm done for. I'm going to freeze to death in here. Annalise will drag my frozen corpse out of this cabin and bury me somewhere on this mountain, along with whoever else in the past has been stupid enough to fall into her trap. I'll never see Steffan again. He's either dead or close to it. My niece and nephew will never see their auntie again, never get the chance to say goodbye to their father properly. And Hannah will lose her best friend. All because I was stupid enough to believe Annalise was helping us and...

All negative thoughts stop.

Wait...

I may have walked straight into my own grave by returning to the cabin after escaping with Steffan, but I've kept something on my person for the past however many days we've been here, something I kept inside my jacket in a hidden pocket in case of emergencies. It turns out, I didn't need to defend myself from a physical attack or need it to cut myself free from anything, but I do have something that can help me get out of this place.

Hands still shaking, I feel around for the Swiss army knife I have hidden, then let out a frustrated and hysterical laugh when it dawns on me that I'm not wearing my jacket. My brain is shutting down, forgetting simple things.

My brain ticks over and over. The knife isn't there... The knife isn't there... What does that mean? I'm trapped, yes. No way out. Nothing to defend myself.

The knife was in my pocket.

Why won't my brain work?

Then, it's like Chris himself has whispered in my ear.

Chris's watch.

I don't have it.

It was in my jacket pocket next to my knife; the same jacket I gave to Annalise when I arrived back inside the cabin, freezing cold and soaked through.

I clamp down on my bottom lip to stop myself from wailing like a child. I place a hand over my heart, but the watch isn't there to give me a warm, safe feeling. I need it back. It's out there right now. My jacket is hanging up by the fire, drying, and it's cocooned inside.

If I can get out of here somehow...

Don't give up, Bonnie.

Rather than allowing the minutes and hours to slip by, along with my life, I need to start switching on and figuring a way out of this mess. Annalise may never open the trapdoor again. She may wait for me to pass out and then open it, which means I'll miss my chance to overpower her and escape.

No more sitting around.

There must be something in this stinking hole that can help me.

Forcing my frozen limbs to move, I go in search of something – anything – that I can use. I don't know what I'm looking for, but I'm certain that I'll know it when I find it. The lingering smell of meat and rotten food lodges itself at the back of my throat and keeps threatening to make me gag. I can see why foul smells are used as torture methods in some countries. I think I'd do just about anything to get away from it.

Feeling my way along the soft walls of the hole, I let the fingers on my good side search blindly for a miracle. I catch myself on something sharp on the back of my hand as I pass by the trapdoor on the roof, which rips at my skin. Yanking my hand away, I return to the area, concentrating, feeling again for the culprit that stung me.

There.

A nail sticking out of a plank of wood on the underside

of the trapdoor. I grasp the nail between my fingers and give it a tug. It's loose, but my fingers are so numb and don't respond properly to my brain signals. Even if I do get this nail out of the wood, then what? What am I seriously expecting to achieve with a single nail?

I'm losing the plot.

Can I stab her with it if she opens the trapdoor? I'd have to aim properly because she's wearing lots of layers, so a nail wouldn't cause much damage if I went for her body. I'd have to stab it into her eye or something to cause enough pain for her to back off, then I could make a run for it, grab my jacket and escape. But launching myself up and out of the hole isn't going to be easy. She has the upper edge when it comes to who's in control here.

It's all I have.

Only a nail stands between me and defeat.

I have to focus on something. Anything. Despite the plan being ridiculous.

I chip away at the nail embedded in the plank for hours. My fingernails chip and snap until blood trickles down my fingers and collects in my palms. I even try and pull it out using my teeth, but fear of yanking a tooth out makes me stop.

Eventually, three hours after finding the nail, it springs free from the wooden board, and I grasp it like it's my only lifeline before collapsing in a heap on the cold earth. My watch tells me it's 11 a.m., a Thursday, not that the day matters, but what does matter is that it's daylight outside, which means if I can find a way to escape, I'll have the advantage of at least being able to see where I'm going.

The snow must have thawed more over the past few hours too.

Now, it's only a matter of waiting for Annalise to open the trapdoor.

She has no way of knowing if I'm awake or asleep.

I have to stay alert, ready for her. I have my trusty nail.

I'm ready...

41

BONNIE

NOW

Five agonising hours later, there's movement above. The trap door creaks open, and a faint glimmer of firelight flickers into the hole. The nail is still gripped tight in my hand on my good side. I'm delirious with pain, exhaustion and hunger, but the trapdoor opening is enough to kick me into action.

I don't give Annalise a chance to speak.

I push myself to my feet, now there's room to stand, and launch myself up and out of the hole. Seconds later I throw myself at her, my body exploding with pain as I do so. I've barely moved in five hours, bar moving my fingers and toes to keep the blood flowing. I'm heavy and cumbersome, but my bodyweight slamming into Annalise is enough to send her off balance. She totters sideways.

Her eyes widen as the cup and bowl she's holding go flying and I land on top of her with a thud. Raising my arm as high as I'm able, I bring the tip of the nail down, over and over, stabbing any piece of pale flesh I can make out in the faint glow of the fire embers and the single candle she has lit.

Annalise howls as I feel the nail embed itself in something soft. Her eye, perhaps? I'm like a woman possessed, stabbing over and over. Then, when Annalise brings her hands up to her face to shield herself, I make a run for it, tripping over my own frozen feet as I do so.

I launch myself towards the fire, grab my jacket and then throw myself at the front door, tears streaming down my cheeks.

'Bonnie!' Annalise screams behind me.

She's hurt.

That's when I realise I'm no longer holding the nail. Perhaps it's lodged itself into her eye socket. Good. I hope it hurts.

There's no time to feel sorry for her. She's got what she deserves.

I don't even have time to stop to put on my jacket, so it remains clenched in my hand as I scramble through the doorway and out into the frozen world beyond. It's still light outside and the snow has thawed considerably, which enables me to climb on top of it much easier than before. I sink several feet, but I don't have time to grab my snowshoes. I just needed my jacket.

I'm shocked to find that when I get outside, it's snowing. Not a snowstorm, but a tranquil, beautiful snowfall.

Great. Just what I need. More snow.

Leaving the howls of Annalise behind, I surge forwards but instantly collapse in a heap.

I try again. And again.

Left foot. Right foot. Left foot...

I stop for a moment and put on my jacket, but my bad shoulder makes the movements near impossible without considerable pain. I place a hand over my heart and feel the hard lump of the watch through the layer of fabric.

A calm washes over me.

It's okay now. I'm free.

The snow falls around me like sparkly, delicate crystals dancing in the wind that whips around my face, causing my skin and eyes to sting with pain. In any other setting, on any other day, at any other time, I'd be admiring the beautiful scenery around me, revelling in the silence of the mountains and the crisp, icy air, but not today. Not now.

Today is not the day to admire the snow that's still so deep, I can hardly take a step without collapsing. My legs just aren't strong enough to keep ploughing through the deep drifts. My legs buckle like matches snapping in half with every step. My energy is fading fast. But it's not just that.

My body is on the verge of giving up. It doesn't feel like it belongs to me. I'm generally fit and healthy, and I've been in tough situations before during long runs, freezing cold and soaked to the skin, but that was different to now. During a run, I always had a clear marker to follow. I knew the right direction to travel and that, with every step I took, I was moving closer and closer to the finish line. There were also people out there waiting for me at checkpoints with a hot cup of tea, especially during proper official races. My phone was always fully charged too; help merely a call away.

Out here, in the vast wilderness, I don't even know if there is a finish line. But there must be, or I'm going to freeze to death. I don't know how it's going to be possible for me to find it because my brain is so numb, I can't focus on anything but what's directly in front of me.

This is how it ends.

Buried deep in the snow, frozen to death, most likely never to be discovered until the snow thaws. Whenever that will be. Up here, in the Swiss Alps, the snow doesn't even thaw in places. What if my body is never found? What if I'm discovered, not by a rescue team, but by a bear or a pack of hungry wolves? There won't be anything left of me to find.

It's getting dark yet again. Why is it always dark up here?

With every passing minute, the freezing temperature is affecting my coordination and muscle control.

Is this how he felt? Christopher.

I can barely move my legs one in front of the other. Progress is non-existent. I'm inching forwards, away from the cabin, back the way Steffan and I went, but it's not enough. It'll never be enough. My strength is gone.

I slip beneath the snow, unable to keep my head above the drift. The freezing flakes are like fire against my skin. It burns. I've never felt pain like it. I'm torn between wanting to feel the pain to know that I'm still alive and not wanting to because it hurts too much to keep breathing. If the pain is there, it means my extremities and nerve endings are still working properly and functioning as they should. It's when I can't feel anything that the danger sinks in.

I open my mouth to call for help, which I know is pointless and will give away my position, but I do it anyway. Nothing comes out. Not even a squeak. All I hear are my teeth chattering together.

I don't want to die like this. I want to live. I need to find him.

Forcing my frozen muscles to move, I drag myself out of the snow hole I've collapsed into and shuffle up a small incline, dragging my body through the snow that feels as if it's trying to pull me down into its icy depths.

My plan is to go back to fetch my pack at the bottom of the cliff, then climb back up and attempt to follow the trail left by Steffan. I can see it quite clearly, but now it's snowing again, it will only be a matter of time before it's covered.

Have I passed the cliff edge somehow? How is that possible?

I was barely paying attention as I stumbled out of the cabin. I think I've gone too far.

This is the way Steffan went, though. Thanks to the footsteps we made, I can just about manage to keep on top of the snow.

Minutes later, I realise that I've overshot the cliff where I fell, and I'm following Steffan's footprints only, not mine and his combined. The idea of turning around fills me with dread, so I keep ploughing forwards. Maybe I'll find Steffan huddled under a tree or overhang somewhere.

Then again, he did leave me to die out here...

What will I do if I find him?

There's a slight decline ahead, so I scoot down on my bottom because I don't trust my legs to hold me up as I descend. I need to find shelter. Exposure to the elements will kill me fast, but all I can think about is getting as far away from the cabin as possible.

As I shuffle to my feet after sliding down, a dark shape emerges ahead. It sticks out of the white snow like a beacon. Solid. Not moving.

As I approach, my brain fills in the blanks of what I'm seeing.

It's a body.

It's Steffan.

I've found him.

Annalise was right. He didn't survive his escape after all.

Whether he died from exposure or fell down the slope and broke his neck, I don't know, but it doesn't matter.

I kneel next to his body, but dehydration has removed my ability to cry. I don't know how to feel, but in a cruel twist of fate, I realise that Steffan's death has saved my life. I can use his pack to continue onwards towards my own freedom.

I don't know how long he's been dead, but thanks to the frozen temperatures, his body is already stiff and difficult to manipulate into positions that enable me to remove his pack. I slowly and awkwardly peel off his pack, then his outer jacket. I put it on; an extra layer couldn't hurt. His jacket swamps me, and the relief from the biting cold is minimal at best, but it's a start, and it means my body has a chance at keeping whatever warmth it generates from the exertion of walking.

His pack is heavier than mine. My injured shoulder means there's no way of lifting it, not without causing extreme pain. I don't have a choice. I can't drag it, so I place it on the snow, and I get on my back, then shuffle into position, sliding my arms through the straps, almost biting through my tongue when my bad shoulder is stretched beyond its limit.

Panting from the effort, I crawl onto all fours with the pack on my back and stare down at Steffan. He doesn't look like Steffan. I barely recognise the man I married. So much has changed in the past few days. I found out he lied to me about so many things, then he left me to die.

I should be glad he's dead, that he's paid with his life for what he's done, but I'm not. I'm ambivalent. In fact, I'm more upset that he can no longer lead me to my brother's body.

I sit for a moment in the snow. With tears in my eyes, I slide my hand into the inside jacket pocket. My knife is missing...

I clasp the watch in my fist. I bring it out to look at it, to remind myself why I'm here.

No.

No. No. NO!

This isn't Chris's watch.

My stomach flips.

Annalise switched his watch for some random one in her wooden box.

The warm, fuzzy feeling vanishes and is replaced by cold, sharp anger.

I hurl the stupid watch into a nearby snowdrift, lift my face to the sky and scream.

I scream for Chris. For Steffan. For Annalise.

Fucking Annalise.

What more does she want from me? Why is she torturing me like this?

I have to go back for it. There's no other option. Leaving the watch behind feels like I'd be leaving Chris out here, just like Steffan did. I can't do that to him. It's the only thing I have left of his to take back from here. Without it, without something to show for it, this whole endeavour has been for nothing.

I don't care if it's reckless, or stupid, or crazy.

There's no hope of ever finding his body, not now I know she's buried it. But I need his watch. I need *something*.

I'm going back to the cabin.

The idea brings a hysterical chuckle as well as a sob. But this time I'm ready because inside Steffan's jacket pocket is another knife just like mine. I have something substantial to defend myself this time, and I'm not leaving without that watch.

If Annalise has to die, then so be it.

Better her than me.

This just got personal.

42

ANNALISE

THEN

Two months they've been on the road, constantly on the move, only stopping to eat and sleep. She feels like wounded prey, forever hiding and keeping quiet in case a hungry predator finds her, devours her whole. She thought she was safe with Erik, that he was her protector, her place of refuge, but now she knows she's wrong. So very wrong about that. Erik has never been her protector, but the hunter himself; a crafty predator, a patient one, who lulls his prey into a false sense of security so she lets her guard down around him. That's the worst kind of predator.

She's not sure how much longer Erik's going to force her to keep running, keep hiding, but surely, they can't go on forever? He keeps saying it's his job to protect her, keep her safe, but she feels anything except safe as she follows him blindly from town to town. She always keeps her head down, never allowed to speak to a single person, forbidden to interact or even look at someone else other than him. He ensures they are fed by working cash-in-hand wherever he can do physical labour jobs on farms and anywhere else that will hire him. He's clever, skilled and strong. He can do anything he sets his mind to. It used to be one of the things she loved most about him, but over the past couple of months, she's seen him in a different light, and it's not doing him any favours. Has he always been like this? She questions herself over and over. Why hadn't she seen it before? His power, his control over her. She'd been happy, so happy before the attack happened. Now, she wasn't sure if she even knew what happy felt like anymore, or whether her past happiness was indeed happiness. Perhaps it was something else entirely, hidden under a shiny exterior.

She bled for almost two weeks before the pain and discomfort finally dulled inside her. She couldn't say a word to Erik because she knew he wouldn't take her to a hospital to be treated. Annalise kept her pain silent, crying tears at night by muffling them against her palm or pillow. She has no idea what internal damage has been done, and she won't until many years later when no children ever come.

They sleep wherever they can, like street urchins, under canopies or inside barns, then wake up early and keep moving. Annalise doesn't understand who they're running from. The police? No. He told her that he lied about that. Erik's fellow work friends? Are they even his friends? He still hasn't explained why that man came after her, and she doesn't think he intends to tell her. Perhaps it's best she doesn't know.

Eventually, after another week of the same thing, the relentless day in and day out of running from an invisible enemy, she confronts her husband.

'Erik, I can't do this anymore.' She's filthy from head to toe, wearing old rags they found in a barn several weeks back. She's never in her whole life smelled this bad. Erik's beard is long and unkempt, his hands dirty, dry and cracked. She's lost weight and barely has enough energy to put one foot in front of the other most days.

'I have a plan, Annalise.'

He keeps saying that, but it's not enough of a reason anymore.

'I've been thinking… We should head up into the mountains. It makes perfect sense because there aren't many people living up there. We can hide out. I'll build a cabin for us to live in. We'll grow our own food. I'll teach you to hunt. We'll never have to see another living soul unless we want to ever again.'

Annalise's eyes flood with tears. 'But I don't want to hide away for the rest of my life, Erik. I love talking to people. My whole life, I've met people, made friends and laughed with strangers. I can't hide away. I can't. It's not who I am. I'll wither away and…'

'Well, you should have thought of that before you murdered my friend in cold blood!' His hate-filled words explode out of his mouth. Spit flies with them, splashing her in the face. He's never raised his voice to her, not like that. Not ever.

'It was self-defence! I don't even remember doing it,' she cries. 'He attacked me! He raped me, Erik!'

'Don't!' He points a finger at her. 'Don't use that word, Annalise. He did not rape you.'

'He did!'

'Call it whatever you want, Annalise. The point is you're damaged goods now. No one will ever want you. You're lucky I'm even still hanging around. No one in their right mind would want to be friends with someone like you now. Do you realise you've made yourself an outcast?'

'B-But...' She stops, thinks. Is Erik right? Will people shun her because of what's happened? But how will they know? She'll never tell another soul, not in a million lifetimes, so surely, that will be okay? That would mean she'll be safe from their judgment and ridicule, right?

'But nothing, Annalise. It's over for you, do you hear me? I have to protect you now. You're ruined. You've disgraced me.'

She's disgraced him? What is he talking about?

'How could you say that! I'm your wife, Erik. I thought you loved me no matter what.'

'I did love you, Annalise, but if you'd just... if you'd just shut up and taken it, then this wouldn't have happened. By killing Alarik, you've put us both in danger. They will never stop looking for us now.'

'Alarik. That's his name? Who's *they?*' she asks as she jogs to catch up with Erik, who has now turned and walked away from her as if he thinks the conversation is over. It's far from over. He's hiding something from her, and she won't rest until he tells her.

'The men I worked for,' he replies. 'I needed to get a certain job finished and I failed, so they sent me a message to get me to work faster.'

Annalise stops in her tracks. 'I was the message.'

'Yes, and now you've fucked us both because you killed Alarik, and now they'll think I did it. We can never show our faces anywhere. I worked for very powerful men, men who will stop at nothing to get their revenge. Do you understand now? Do you understand how utterly fucked we are?'

She runs to catch up with him again, grabs his arm and pulls him back so he stops. 'We can get this straightened out,' she says. 'Please. I'll take the blame for everything, I promise.'

Erik won't look at her. He turns his head to stare into the distance. 'No, Annalise. It's my fault. I shouldn't have been so easy on you all these years. Maybe a firmer hand is what you've needed from the start. I was stupid for thinking you could be my perfect little wife who follows my every command. You need to be punished.'

Annalise doesn't know how to respond. Everything she's ever known about her husband is a lie. He's always been the sweetest man since they've been together. Why has he changed so drastically now? Her life, her marriage had been perfect, and in the blink of an eye, it's all gone. She doesn't recognise Erik anymore. She doesn't recognise herself.

'Come on,' he says, taking her chin and squeezing it. 'I'll build you the perfect cabin in the mountains. We'll spend the rest of our lives living off-grid. We'll raise our children right. I promise.'

'B-But my family...'

'Forget them. You'll never see them again. You owe me, Annalise. You're my wife. It's your duty to do as I say.'

HE KEEPS HIS PROMISE, not about raising children but finding them the perfect location to live, a beautiful spot off the main path, miles away from anywhere, deep in the Swiss Alps. It takes them almost a week to hike there from the nearest town. Despite it being the height of summer, the higher they climb, the colder it becomes.

How are they supposed to survive out here? It's so barren and secluded. Before they start their hike, Erik steals an axe, a shovel and various other building materials that he knows he'll need, as well as a hunting knife and some warmer items of clothing. He says that if they ever need anything, he can trek back to the nearest town, but Annalise is never allowed to accompany him. She must stay at the cabin, complete the chores, make the food and tend to the land. He'll ensure she has everything she could ever want. But what she wants most, she can never have again.

Erik works tirelessly, creating and building a small cabin made of wooden planks, which he chops down and planes himself using the tools he took from the villages down in the valley. It's the height of summer, so while Erik builds the cabin, they sleep under a makeshift tent made of blankets and other items. He works fast in preparation for the colder autumn and winter months ahead. Up here, he says, when the snow comes, they could be trapped for months at a time. The cabin takes him almost two months to finish. Annalise worries about all sorts of things, such as how they will keep the cabin warm and how they will find food, but Erik insists he can handle everything.

She must admit it is the most beautiful location she has ever seen. The cabin is built within a bowl-type valley, but after a short hike to a nearby hill, she can see for miles across the Swiss Alps. She's not sure how far they've travelled over the past two and a half months. A hundred miles? Two hundred?

She'll never see her family again and it's all her fault. Erik is right. If she'd only not fought back and killed Alarik, she wouldn't be here now, but it's the words Erik said that cut her the deepest. She's damaged goods. Should she be grateful to him for staying with her, or afraid of him because he's changed so much since it happened?

Despite what he says, living out here in the wilderness

has certainly improved his mood. Perhaps he knows they are safe. There's no way anyone could find them. What would happen if those men he worked for did ever find them? Would they kill them both? Annalise still isn't sure what happened, but it doesn't sound like Erik merely worked in a sawmill. What has he been doing behind her back?

Then, a thought hits her that takes her breath away. Did he know what Alarik was going to do to her? Did Erik allow it to happen to try and pay off whatever debts or mess he'd got himself into? She doesn't want to believe her husband is a monster, but the signs are all there.

Perhaps this new way of living will be a fresh start for them, and they'll find a way to co-exist and live the life she's always dreamed of. One day, they can have children, but what sort of life will they have being brought up away from other people? She mustn't dwell on the negatives. She is, after all, a positive person, and she must make the best of this bad situation. Perhaps it will all work out in the end and they'll spend the rest of their lives growing old together and living in harmony.

As she gathers wood for a fire, she wonders what her life will look like in five years' time, ten years, twenty...

Does she seriously see them still living here? Will it ever be safe to return to civilisation? What if one of them gets sick and needs medical treatment?

Only time will tell.

Erik is a good man, deep down, and she's sure he'll provide for her.

But, once again, she's wrong, and even after forty years, long after Erik is dead, she'll find herself still trapped within the walls he built for her.

If only things had worked out differently.

If only.

43

ANNALISE

NOW

Bonnie is more resilient than I give her credit for. I didn't drug her food or water, and yet she repays my generosity by sabotaging me as I open the trapdoor, then attacks me with a rusty nail. The last I see of her out of my intact eye is her scrambling out of the door into the deep snow, without a jacket or any sort of protection or provisions. Foolish girl.

When she landed on top of me, the air whooshed from my lungs. It felt as if I'd been hit by a car. She's strong, or maybe she's just determined to survive. If only she'd been willing to stay quiet, to stay here, then I wouldn't have had to resort to such drastic actions. Locking her up had never been part of my plan. None of this was part of the plan. I had no plan.

She and Steffan brought this upon themselves. They were the ones who came here and forced their way into my home, the home I've been trapped in myself for so many years. I told Erik at the start that I'd lose myself along the way if I didn't talk and interact with people. Now, look what's happened.

I've transformed into a monster of my own creation. People fear me. They run from me. They stab me in the eye with a nail to get away from me. I never wanted this. All I ever wanted was to be safe from the men who my husband told me would kill me if they ever found out where I was. That's why I've remained hidden for so long.

I refuse to kill Bonnie in cold blood. I am not a killer, but she's refusing to play by my rules. It's my home, yet she's treating me like some sort of wild animal with no feelings or emotions. Erik was right in one way. People do look at me differently now because of what I did, because I killed that man, Alarik, all those years ago. He used to tell me that they'd never understand, they'd never believe me.

I see that now more than ever.

AFTER BONNIE HIGHTAILS it out the door, I scream and writhe around on the floor, covering my injured eye with my hands. I need to remove the nail, but I fear if I do, my eyeball could come with it. Once I stop screaming and groaning, I keep one hand over my injured eye and use the other to pull myself across the floor towards my rocking chair. The fire is still burning, but it's fading, giving off only a faint glow.

Seated, I take a deep breath, composing myself. First, I must tend to my wound, but before I can do that, I must remove the nail. Bonnie won't make it far before she perishes. She has no protection from the elements, nor food or water. Once the snow has thawed enough for me to leave the cabin, I shall go in search of her body. I expect I'll find it along with her husband's too.

I smile, wondering if she'll notice I switched her brother's watch with another before she dies.

I grab a cloth, down a mug of strong herbal tea to dull the pain and senses, then grab the end of the nail and yank it out. Better to get it over with quickly. Thankfully, my eyeball stays put, but the pain swallows me whole. I scream into the empty cabin, a guttural, throaty noise that echoes for several seconds before petering out. I hold the cloth against my eye, stemming the blood flow. Then, after it's slowed, I fashion a make-shift eye pad and tie it around my head like a patch.

I slurp more tea while staring into the dying flames.

The tea starts to take effect, and my remaining eye slowly closes. I don't sleep, but drift into a sedated daze as I remember all the horrible things Erik did to me over the years while living here.

44

ANNALISE

THEN

During the first year, things are mostly calm. We focus on getting the cabin habitable and preparing the land for planting. But after a year, the reality begins to sink in like damp through a wall. The isolation is affecting Erik. He gets angry. A lot.

The first time he hits me, it's just a slap, but it comes out of nowhere. I never see it coming. He's said horrible things to me in the past year but never raised his hand. He is very sorry and apologises over and over, saying it will never happen again, that he loves me and he only lost control for a second. I'm wary, but, like I always do, I believe him. I shouldn't have. More fool me.

It happens more and more after that and gets worse and worse. It isn't only a slap anymore. He pushes the boundaries of what he can do and get away with. I become afraid of my own husband, so I daydream of my life before everything changed. I pretend he and I have the perfect marriage, the perfect relationship. I suppose it can be said that I'm deluding myself, shielding myself from the harsh truth, the harsh reality that is my marriage, but it's better than accepting I am living with a vile man who now takes to abusing me every single day just because he can and there's no one around to stop him, not even me.

The beginning of the end starts one day when I'm out picking herbs in the valley. Erik is nearby, watching me, but even under his watchful eyes, I love spending time outdoors. I enjoy gathering food for dinner and preparing meals. It keeps me busy, and I'm learning all the different edible herbs, flowers and vegetation that grow in abundance around our cabin.

I pick a herb I haven't seen before. I don't show it to Erik, who seems to know all the names of everything. Even years later, I don't know why I don't show it to him, but I stew the herb in hot water that evening and take a sip. Its flavour is subtle and delicious, so I drink the whole cup. I wake up to Erik shouting at me with fire in his eyes. He's shaking my shoulders and slapping my face.

It turns out I picked valerian root, which can be a highly effective sedative. He says I am lucky I didn't make it too strong and mixed it with the other herbs I'd gathered because it can become toxic. He tells me there are many poisonous plants around, so I begin to make a list of them. From that day on, I drink valerian tea every day in very small amounts to numb the pain and dull my mind from his assaults. I even sneak it into his drinks sometimes so I can have a few hours of peace from time to time. I use this time wisely.

Another three years pass in the same way. Nothing ever changes. During this time, Erik continues to brainwash me into believing that every person is out to get me.

The first time I see another human being since I arrive is a year later. I stare at them while crouched on top of a nearby hill, carefully hidden but able to watch them as they chat and laugh while strolling along the path.

I almost shout out to them, wave my arms in the air to signal for them to come and save me, but I don't. I stay rooted to the spot as they become specks in the distance.

But then, not long after that, the worst happens.

Erik and I are sitting by the fire after eating, and a knock sounds at the door. It startles us so much that, at first, neither of us moves a muscle. I think that maybe it hasn't even happened, that it's merely a figment of my imagination after drinking too much valerian tea, but then it comes again.

And again.

'Stay there,' Erik says to me.

Even if I wanted to move, I can't. Fear holds me in place while Erik grabs the axe by the fire and approaches the door with it raised by his side, ready to strike.

He opens the door to find a lone hiker.

All I can think about is that they've found us – the men who want to kill me for killing Alarik. Our cabin isn't invisible. I knew it was only a matter of time before it was discovered, but what I hadn't been prepared for is the mind-numbing fear that grips my insides like a vice.

This man is here to kill me.

It doesn't matter who he is.

'Hi,' he says. 'I didn't know there was a cabin this far up the mountain. My name's Barry.' He locks his eyes on me. 'It's you... the White Witch.'

Those are the only words he speaks before Erik buries the axe head into his skull and Barry's brain splatters across the walls of the cabin.

I scream and close my eyes at the gruesome sight.

Erik tells me it's my fault for travelling too far away from the cabin in search of food and herbs. This man must have spotted me and followed me back here.

I help Erik bury the body deep in the mountains. After that day, I'm not allowed to go anywhere without Erik. He says he's been stupid and put too much trust in me again. That I have failed him. Failed us.

More people might come now.

But they don't.

Another year passes after Barry is killed. I spend my days pretending to be happy. Sometimes, I even believe it. It's hard to distinguish between reality and what my mind makes up to protect me from my husband.

One evening, I offer him some herbal tea. I make it slightly stronger this time because I'm still sore from his last beating and I can't take another night of it, so I stew it until I'm sure he'll be out for several hours. I misjudge the strength of the tea.

He never wakes up.

I curse myself for never thinking of doing it before.

Even in death, Erik has a hold over me. I thought after his death, I would be sad for a while, then pack up the few things I had and find the nearest town, but I never do. It's easier, safer, to stay here. On my own, I can make my own rules, create my own life.

So I do.

I speak to Erik as if he's next to me, as if we're in a loving marriage, because the thought of facing the truth is too difficult. It may seem crazy to some, but these people haven't been through what I've been through.

All these years spent in solitude have changed me into someone who's less than human.

Perhaps I am the White Witch of the Alps after all.

45

BONNIE

NOW

If I didn't know any better, I'd say that my fingers are on fire, the skin burning and peeling. In my mind, I'm screaming, over and over, as I make my way back to the cabin. I've never felt pain like it. It overwhelms my senses, even rising above the pain in my ribs and shoulder.

But when I arrive at the cabin and face Annalise, I can't show an ounce of weakness. She knows I'm injured and weak, but I bet she won't expect me to return for the watch. Will she? I'm pretty sure I stabbed her in the eye with the nail. She'll be weak herself, off her usual game. She's an old woman. I can overpower her, I'm sure.

The closer I get, the more I realise that I'm out of my depth here in the wilderness. I always have been, but I needed to come here for Chris. I was supposed to bring his body home and lay him to rest, but now I have nothing to show for my time out here other than a dead husband and the tips of my fingers freezing off.

I need that watch.

It's like a fire inside me, and I'm unwilling to extinguish the flame. Not now.

After what happened a year ago, I should have fought harder to understand what happened, but I believed Steffan over my own doubts. Steffan and Chris had been involved in something, and I never did figure out what it was. After Hannah called me with the news of his sudden, accidental death, everything else stopped. Nothing else mattered.

Now, they are both gone. Steffan and Chris. Will I ever know the truth about what happened, or am I forced to be in the dark for the rest of my life? I thought finding his body would bring me closure, but instead, it's brought me nothing but pain, suffering and more questions.

No answers.

The sky is completely dark by the time the cabin comes back into view. The snow is still roughly waist-deep in places, and it's a monumental effort to keep going and not sink down into the depths. I'm not sure where my strength and resilience are coming from, but they're there, pushing me onwards, towards either my freedom or my inevitable death.

Will Annalise kill me if she has the chance? She's had several chances over the past few days to end my life, but she hasn't, which tells me she wants me alive. Why that is, I don't know. Nor do I really care. All I care about is finding my brother's watch and getting the hell out of this giant freezer. I'll be happy to never see another snowflake ever again.

There's no way of getting into the cabin without Annalise seeing me. Only one door in. Crouching just outside the door, I awkwardly take the pack off and dump it on the ground. I arm myself with the knife, then reach for the door handle, taking a breath before pushing it down and opening the door.

'Annalise,' I call out softly.

The fire is barely ablaze now, but a couple of candles flicker nearby.

There she is.

She's sitting in her rocking chair. Squeak. Squeak. Squeak.

Back and forth. Back and forth.

The sight sends a shiver of fear through my body. She's made some sort of rustic eye patch and is staring blankly ahead with her one remaining eye. What is she looking at?

I step over the threshold, barely daring to breathe.

'Annalise,' I say again. 'I'm just here for my brother's watch. Just give it to me and I'll leave. You'll never hear from me again. I'll never say a word about you to anyone or about what happened here. I promise. Just give me back the watch.'

An eerie silence follows my speech. Then, she makes a small movement, her head turning slightly in my direction, but her gaze never leaves whatever it is in the far corner she's staring at.

'Your promise means nothing to me,' she says, her voice gravelly and low.

I take another step, the knife held tight in my fist. Scanning the area, I search for the watch, but it's nowhere to be seen.

'I am tired,' she says. 'I am tired of running, of hiding, of people lying to me, of people hurting me.'

Her tone of voice and words take me by surprise. I'd expected her to fight more, to shout, to scream, to attack me, but she's just sitting in her chair, completely at my mercy. I could easily surge forwards and plunge this knife into the side of her exposed neck, making my job of finding the watch that much easier. But I don't.

I don't know her full story, and I'm sure as hell sure she won't tell me.

I want to tell her that she's free now from whatever prison she thinks she's in, she can return to civilization without fear, but I can't because if she returns, she won't recognise the world we live in. She won't know how to use a mobile phone or the internet or anything like that. It will be like freeing her from one prison only to lock her up again in another. Perhaps she's better off here. She may collect technology from hikers, but she has no idea what it is or how to use it properly.

Is that why she won't let me leave? She's afraid of people coming here, taking her away from the only safe space she's ever known?

'I'm sorry,' I say after another long stretch of silence. I have no idea what I'm supposed to say to this woman. Am I supposed to make her feel better somehow? Make her trust me so she'll give me the watch and let me go? Become friends with her? There's nothing I can say. Nothing she'll want to hear anyway. I arrived here angry, but looking at her now, I can feel my emotions cooling. 'I'm sorry for whatever happened to you, but all I'm interested in is taking my brother's watch and leaving this place.' I pause for a moment, then add, 'Steffan is dead. You were right.'

At this, Annalise turns her head fully to face me. She stares at me with her eye. She notices the knife but doesn't appear to be concerned.

'Then you are lucky your husband died before he had the chance to twist you into someone you don't recognise.'

'Just give me the watch, Annalise.'

'No, but I shall tell you something.'

'What's that?'

Annalise reaches slowly into the folds of her clothes and pulls out a scrap of paper. She holds it up into the light. 'Along with the watch on your brother's body, I found this, tucked into his jacket pocket.'

My stomach plummets and my heart batters itself against my chest cavity. What the hell?

'I'm guessing he wrote it before he died, in case his body was ever found. I expect he wanted you to know what his final thoughts and words were.'

A hard lump forms in my throat. All I can focus on is the piece of paper in her hand. From this distance, there's no way of seeing what's written on it, but I can just about make out some swirly writing.

Chris's last message to me.

I hold out my hand towards her. 'Annalise … Please.'

She keeps the note held aloft and grins. 'An eye for an eye,' she says before tossing it on the smouldering embers, where it catches alight almost instantly and burns before my eyes.

I let out a gut-curdling scream, throwing myself towards Annalise and the fire.

46

BONNIE

NOW

Annalise doesn't move a muscle as I push past her sitting on the chair, sending it rocking again, and collapse to my knees in front of the fire. I cautiously use the blade of the knife and attempt to flick the burning paper out of the fire, but it only partly works. The paper disintegrates as the blade touches it and only a small section survives.

My eyes burn from the heat and tears as I pick up the charred slip of paper. Even in the dim light, I recognise Chris's handwriting. I always made fun of him because it looked like a child's, all wobbly and uneven. It's there, as clear as day, but only a few letters are left. The rest of the paper is gone.

I turn from where I'm kneeling and glare at Annalise. 'How could you do that!' My voice trembles. I thought I could understand her somehow. Maybe I even felt sorry for her, but now all I see is the woman who has robbed me of my brother's last words. He'd no doubt written them as he lay dying, in considerable pain, all alone and lost in this wilderness thanks to Steffan.

The mere thought makes me want to explode into hysterical sobs. Did he want to tell me he loved me? Or maybe he was trying to tell me Steffan left him to die. Was it a message back to Hannah and his children?

Now, I'll never know. I should have stormed into the cabin and stabbed Annalise where she sat. This is my fault. I'm too trusting of people, too easily swayed by their emotions and struggles. But what about my own? I have to live the rest of my life now knowing that Chris wanted to tell me something in his final moments.

And Annalise, this old woman in front of me who has both saved me and kept me captive, is the only person who knows what he wanted to say.

'Tell me,' I say. I awkwardly get to my feet, holding the knife in front of me in defence. I keep the scrap of paper clenched in my other hand. The knife bobs up and down as I struggle to contain my emotions.

Annalise doesn't blink. She doesn't stare at the knife, but right at me. She barely looks human anymore. I thought I could reason with her, convince her to trust me, but we're beyond all that now. She's taken something from me that can never be replaced. She knows where my brother's body is buried. She knows what he wanted to tell me, what was on that piece of paper, and she still has his watch.

'Tell me what it said,' I say, this time my voice sterner.

'I'm afraid I can't,' she replies flatly.

I shove the knife right up close to her face. 'Tell me!'

'I can't read, Bonnie. Not English, anyway. I think I recognised your name, but other than that, I'm afraid I have no idea what it said.'

A half-sob and half-laugh escape my mouth before I can stop it. Is that even true? She can speak English, so a part of me doesn't believe that she can't read it too. I wouldn't put it past her to be playing me for a fool again.

The knife lowers a fraction of an inch. It's like all the fight has left my body. Whatever was on that note, no matter how insignificant it was, Chris had wanted me to know it.

I turn my back on Annalise and face the flames, pulling out the slip of paper I pulled from the fire. I can only make out one word.

Me.

Before it are three final letters of a word.

Led.

Led me.

It's not enough. Not by a long way. He was talking about himself, perhaps about what happened up on the mountain, about how he fell and Steffan left him. But there's more. I know there's more.

I have no idea what to do now. I need to leave this cabin, but I have no compass, no GPS, no working phone, only the map in Steffan's pack to lead me to safety. The darkness has settled like thick smoke, and with only a small headtorch, finding my way through deep snow and treacherous terrain is almost suicide.

I turn back to Annalise, who now has her eye closed. She doesn't appear concerned that I'm standing nearby, having only moments ago threatened her with a knife to the face. If I have to, I'll take out her other eye, I swear it.

'Just give me the watch,' I say as calmly as I can muster. Everything inside me wants to explode at this woman. 'It's all I want. You've taken everything else. Just give me his watch.'

Annalise opens her eye, continuing to rock back and forth. 'You cannot leave, Bonnie.'

'I cannot stay here with you.'

'I'm an old woman. I don't have many years left, but it would be nice to have company in my final time. Real company.'

I ignore her plea. 'Give me the watch.' I point the knife at her once more.

'You will have to kill me.'

'I don't understand you, Annalise. You want company, yet you locked me up. How do you expect me to trust you, to like you, to want to stay, if you treat me like an animal?'

'I have been treated like an animal for my entire life. My husband told me I was a murderer when all I did was defend myself.'

I want to ask her questions, find out what she means by that, but I can't focus on her issues, her past. I have my own future to focus on, to live for. Whatever happened to her, whatever she's been through, she's beyond help now. I'm past the point of caring.

Annalise uses the arms of the rocking chair to push herself up to her feet. She steps towards me, slowly, like she's stalking me. Her single eye doesn't blink, doesn't even flinch.

My automatic reaction is to step back.

Her movements are odd, like she's a combination of drunk and high. How much herbal tea has she drunk? It's almost like she's possessed. This isn't the Annalise I've come to know over the past few days. She's walking towards me like a hungry animal...

'Annalise... Stop. I'm warning you.'

She doesn't.

'Stop!'

She grins a second before she rushes at me. My body is too frozen, too numb with fear to react quickly enough to dodge her attack. As she collides with me, the knife is knocked from my grasp. It skids across the floor out of reach. She lands on top of me and begins slapping and clawing at me like a savage beast, letting out the most feral scream I've ever heard.

It's now a matter of fight or die.

Her or me.

47

BONNIE
NOW

Annalise may not weigh very much, but my weak muscles and injured ribs and shoulder means she feels like a tonne of bricks on top of me. A long nail of hers slices through the pale skin on my cheek, bringing with it a sting of pain. There's blood still oozing from underneath her makeshift eye patch, and dried rivers of it are staining her cheek on that side.

I must kill her. There's no other way around it. She's left me no other choice. Live or die. I want to live. *Need* to live.

Annalise somehow manages to grab my left hand while it's flailing about and instantly sinks her rotten teeth into my numb fingers. She bites down hard as I let out a long scream, desperately attempting to yank my hand away from her mouth, but when I do, it comes away minus two fingertips.

She's bitten through my almost black and frozen fingertips on my middle and ring finger.

'Fuck you!' The vile word sounds alien in my mouth as I continue to scream and hit her.

Using the last of my strength, I shove Annalise off me. She rolls, grunting as she lands awkwardly on her side, but she's quick to right herself. Her mouth is dripping with my blood as she spits my two fingertips at me.

Swallowing back another vicious word, I scramble to my hands and knees, trying to crawl across the floor to the knife, which has landed about five feet away, barely visible in the dim firelight.

But Annalise isn't ready to back down. I don't think she ever will now. The animal in her has been unleashed. She grabs my left boot with both hands and holds on tight, her claw-like hands clenched together in a tight grip.

I shake my legs to get her off, but she only loses concentration for a moment. It's enough to enable me to scramble away from reach, but within seconds, she's after me again, but not before I grab the knife with my uninjured hand, turn on my back, and hold it upright against my chest, just as Annalise launches herself on top of me once more.

She knows she's made a mistake the instant the blade penetrates her body, sliding in below the rib cage through her stomach. Due to her thick clothing, I don't think it goes in all the way, but it's enough for her to stop in her tracks.

She spits my own blood into my face.

Now she's weakened, I shove her off once more, then attack her with the knife, this time aiming for her exposed neck. I miss and she slaps the knife straight out of my hand. My injured fingers are bleeding and there's nothing I can do to protect them.

The knife lands too far away for me to attempt another retrieval, so I turn my attention to whatever else is lying around. Annalise groans, blood dripping down her mouth, clutching her stomach with one hand. The fire is ablaze in her single eye and her teeth are bared. She's like a rabid dog. She's losing strength and blood fast, but whatever concoction of herbs she's on is keeping her lucid enough to stay conscious.

My eyes focus on something that's propped next to the fireplace.

The stick she's been using to stoke the fire.

Without waiting another moment, I skirt around Annalise on the floor and grab the stick with my good hand. Try as I might, without my fingertips, I can barely do anything with my other hand, which happens to be on the side of my non-injured shoulder.

Holding the stick high, I feel the muscles in my bad shoulder scream as I force them to stretch more than they're physically able. Annalise continues to clutch her stomach with her hand while attempting to drag herself along with the other.

With one quick movement, I swing the stick as hard as I can across her head, hearing a loud smack as it connects with her temple. She collapses instantly to the floor, leaving me panting and groaning in pain. I stop and watch for any sign of life, but Annalise is down. She makes no movement to get up and continue her relentless attack.

The witch is dead.

Or, at least, just knocked out.

She's still breathing.

Only when I'm satisfied she can't attack me anymore do I lower the stick to the floor and collapse to my knees, clutching my fingers against my chest. I need to stem the bleeding and wrap them up. Thanks to the blackened nerve endings from frostbite, the pain isn't as bad as it probably should be. It's highly likely I would have lost the tips anyway.

Staggering to the front door, I grab Steffan's pack, which I left outside, and drag it down into the cabin, slamming the door shut behind me. I need to get Annalise tied up, but if I don't stop my own bleeding, I'm in danger of passing out.

I get out the first aid kit in Steffan's pack and tend to my wounds as best as I can, swallowing three painkillers dry. One of them gets caught in my throat, which makes me gag, but once they're down, I turn my attention to Annalise.

What do I do with her?

If I'd killed her during my attack, it would have made my decision easier. As it happens, she's still breathing, so I have two choices: finish her off in cold blood or leave her here. The way I see it, I can't make the mistake of leaving the cabin again in the dark. It's already been proven twice that it's a risky and stupid decision. Therefore, I must wait out the night and leave in the morning, but there's no guarantee Annalise will stay unconscious the whole night, and I'd rather not have her wake up while I'm here.

My eyes drift down to the rug on the floor, the rug I know is covering up the cold hole in the floor. The same hole she shoved me into. It's rather a poetic end for her.

I pull back the rug and flip over the trapdoor.

Turning on my headtorch, I stand over her unconscious body. She's bleeding from the wound in her stomach, but without checking underneath her layers of stinking clothing, there's no way of knowing just how bad it is. If I leave her, is she going to die? Have I ended up inadvertently killing her, but in the most slow and painful way?

I can't allow my compassion to cloud my judgment. She attacked me. She tried to kill me. I don't owe her anything.

Should I search her? Would she hide the watch on her person or elsewhere?

Since she hid the note from Chris in her pockets, I'm betting she'd want to keep the watch close by too. Holding my breath, I angle the headtorch down and begin to search through the various items of clothing she's wearing for the watch.

It doesn't take me long to find it.

The relief of feeling the cool metal between my fingers makes me almost break down in tears. I hold it against my heart and breathe deep.

I then crouch and grab her shawl with both hands, then drag her inch by inch across the floor. I stop several times to compose myself as my shoulder threatens to pop back out of its socket. I shuffle backwards and drag her into the hole. She hits the damp earth with a thud. She stirs slightly, groaning something I can't make out.

I slam the trapdoor closed, bolt it, then drag the rug over.

Damn it, I should have tied her up before locking her inside. What if she wakes up and somehow finds a way out? Would she be strong enough, especially with her injury? No. I was in there long enough to know there's no way she's getting out of there.

I'm safe from another of her assaults, but I have a lot to do to make sure I have the best chance of surviving this ordeal. Despite exhaustion threatening to drag me into a never-ending sleep, I rummage in Steffan's pack and pull out a sealed pack of vegetarian casserole.

I don't remember the last time I ate something substantial. The stew she fed me has been a couple of mouthfuls at best. My mouth is bone dry, so I open his water bottle and take a drink. It's half-empty already, so I need to preserve it and the other rations. It takes all my restraint not to down the rest of the bottle in one go.

I tear open the pack of food and eat it cold, using a spork from his bag. The fire still emits a faint glow, so I turn off my head torch to save the battery. I eat and drink what I can afford to use, then sit near the fire, in sight of the rug hiding the trapdoor.

I dare not sleep.

My watch beeps, signalling a low battery. Great. If it dies, I won't even be able to tell the time. All I know is that the minute it starts getting light, I'm leaving this cabin behind, this time for good. Nothing will make me come back here for a third time.

I make it through the next five hours. During that time, there's not a peep from below the trapdoor. My watch dies around six in the morning, but it's as good a time as any to start my trek. After swallowing another dose of painkillers, I perform the most painful and awkward manoeuvre of lifting the pack onto my back. I have everything I need, including Chris's watch tucked safely into my jacket pocket. I find my phone and GPS in the wooden chest, but both are dead, so are of little use to me. I take them anyway, along with Steffan's electronic equipment.

I don't know when Annalise is going to die or even if she's already dead, but as I turn to leave the cabin, a sadness washes over me that makes my eyes brim with tears.

Despite what she's done, she's still a person. A human being. I don't know exactly what her story is, but over the years, it's clear she's become a very sheltered and misunderstood person.

I do feel sorry for her, but she made her decision, and I've made mine.

Sighing heavily and bracing myself for the arduous trek through the deep snow back towards civilisation, I close the door to the cabin, leaving the White Witch to die in peace.

48

BONNIE
NOW

Twenty-Six Hours Later

My body is tired to the point where I don't know how it's still functioning. 'Tired' is a term I am guilty of throwing around a lot without any real reason. I used to be tired after a long day of work or even after a ten-mile run, all normal experiences in which the body has a right to be weary, but what I'm feeling now, what I've experienced over the past few days, is not tiredness. It's beyond that.

Exhaustion is real; where the body begins to shut down one muscle fibre at a time, the brain stops sending signals properly, reflexes falter, and it's almost impossible to concentrate on any one thing. I thought I'd been exhausted before when Steffan had been leading the way across the mountain, before we'd come across Annalise and her cabin, but it's nothing compared to how I feel now. When I'd been hiking with Steffan, I hadn't needed to worry about where we were going (even though I should have). I'd allowed him to take the lead, which enabled me to take my eye off the ball completely with regard to navigation. Now, I wish I'd spent more time learning how to properly navigate, but he'd always insisted on him doing it.

Even if I did have the ability to read a map efficiently, I'm not sure my brain would allow it. Every time I look down at the squiggly lines, the contours and various shapes, they all move and blend together into one giant blob or vibrate in front of my eyes so I can't even see them.

How am I supposed to find my way back like this?

At this point, I'm not even following the map, merely walking in one direction with blind hope that I'll stumble across another hiker. I haven't found a proper path yet because the snow is still too deep, hiding most of the landmarks that would usually help determine where I am.

Without a GPS telling me where to go and when to turn, I get confused easily, and by the time I realise I've made a mistake, it's already too late to turn back, so I try and make ground elsewhere. There's very little food and water left, and I haven't stopped to sleep for more than a couple of hours at a time. I can't. If I stop, there's a chance I'll never get going again. Sleep is one of those things that I can't afford.

I'm not out of the woods yet. Or, more appropriately, the mountains.

For all I know, these mountains are never-ending. The snow makes everything look the same, but on the plus side, the sun has been out during the day and is thawing the ice and snow with every passing minute. My worst fear is an avalanche coming down on top of me, burying me under hundreds of thousands of tonnes of snow.

I hear one in the distance as I cautiously traverse a snow

ridge – a crack and a thunderous roar. I've been heading downhill now for several hours, still in search of an elusive path to freedom. I must be getting close. I've run out of painkillers now, and I'm barely able to put one foot in front of the other, hobbling along at what may as well be a snail's pace.

My mind drifts to Steffan on several occasions, and now I know exactly what I'm going to say to the authorities and rangers when I see them with regard to why I'm alone and no longer hiking with him. I'm going to tell them the truth. There's absolutely no point in trying to cover up what Steffan did to Chris a year ago. Chris deserves to have his story told.

It's the lying that has pushed me over the edge with regard to Steffan. He refused to tell the truth, over and over. He had so many chances. He watched me for months as I grieved and came to terms with my brother's death on that mountain. He pretended that he'd done everything he could to save him, even put on a show of blaming himself, making me believe his grief and guilt were real. It was all lies.

There's one story that I have no idea how to tell, and I can't quite make up my mind. Do I explain to the local rangers about the old woman living off grid high up in the mountains? Do I go back and tell Johan that the White Witch is real, or do I lie and tell people that Steffan and I stumbled across an old, abandoned cabin and hid inside while the storm buried us, and that's why we've been uncontactable for days? She never told me if she knew what happened to Barry, so I can't even divulge those details.

I want her to rot down there the way she lived: alone. But there's a high chance that when the rangers come to collect Steffan's body, they'll find her cabin. And I'm not about to start lying through my teeth now about what happened up here.

I'm telling everyone the truth about the White Witch, and they can discover her cabin and her body, and maybe they'll find out what happened to Barry. All those items in the wooden box will be found. Maybe the families of those people will finally get the answers they've been searching for.

It's the least I can do.

AN HOUR LATER, I find myself climbing a huge hill covered in rocks. The only saving grace is that the snow has finally thawed enough to see parts of the earth beneath. The air feels crisp, warm and clean. I'm not sure what's on the other side of this hill, but if I can get to the top, it will hopefully provide a good vantage point from which to scope out the surrounding area.

It's my only mission now – to reach the top. Steffan's pack forces me down with every step, as if I'm constantly battling a static enemy, hell-bent on ensuring I faceplant the ground. Not today. Just a few more hours. I have to find something soon. My water is almost gone, and the food is minimal, but I'm more worried about running out of energy.

It's so steep towards the top that I'm no longer walking upright, but scrambling on my hands and toes, using every rock I can find as leverage to pull me up. When I finally haul myself to the summit, I collapse to the ground, too exhausted to take in the breathtaking scenery.

It's the middle of the day, and even though there's still plenty of snow around in places, the sun is out at full strength, which is melting the surrounding ice quickly, perhaps too quickly.

Scanning the nearby rocky ridges and mountains, I check for any signs of life. It truly is barren out here. I need to reach a cabin or village soon, before the darkness approaches again. I don't want to be out here another night. I've already heard the howl of a nearby pack of wolves several hours back. It made my blood run cold as I imagined being stalked by the pack animals, who are designed to hunt and kill, to tear their prey apart with dozens of razor-sharp teeth, leaving them in pieces. I'd become one of those mountain statistics or headlines in the news: *Woman discovered half-eaten by wolves.*

As an eagle circles overhead, my ears pick up some sounds that make my heart rate spike.

Voices. Definitely voices.

I spin around, scanning every direction in search of their origin. Despite not being able to see anyone, I can *hear* them.

'Hello!' I call out several times, bringing my hands to cup around my mouth to help transmit the sound further. Whether that helps or not, I don't know, but I keep shouting, ignoring my sore throat, then waiting for a few seconds to listen for a response. My stubby fingers sting with pain through the makeshift attempt at a bandage, which is filthy and stained red.

'Hello?'

There! A faint voice below me.

'Hello! Yes! I'm here!'

I stumble in my hasty attempt to climb down from the ridge I'm standing on. The backpack weighs me down and sends me off balance as I jump off a rock to the ground below. My ribs explode with pain, but I don't care. I know there's a path somewhere. Even if these people are going in the opposite direction, I just need to see another human being to know I'm not alone. To know I'm rescued and not going to die.

'Hello!' I keep repeating the word as I jog and trip down the slope, cursing silently as my body responds in pain and pure exhaustion. What I wouldn't give for a long, hot soak in a bath right now, overloaded with Epsom salts.

'Well, hello!' calls a voice ahead of me.

I stop and take a breath, which I fully need after holding it the whole way down the slope. A group of hikers are on the path ahead, and I almost sink to my knees and weep with relief. Tears sting my eyes, but I burst into hysterical laughter as I catch sight of the group, all of whom look fresh, clean and upbeat. Clearly, they haven't been trapped in a cabin with a mad woman for the past however many days it's been. Three? Four? I've no idea. Time has stood still, and now I'm just happy and relieved to be alive and out of that cabin, which had felt more and more like a prison with every passing minute.

'Boy, am I glad to see you!' I say, stopping and leaning over, resting my hands on my knees to catch my breath.

'Are you alone out here?' asks one of the group, a tall man with a rugged beard.

'I... Yes, I am,' I reply, stopping myself just in time. As far as anyone knows, I *am* a lone hiker. I don't need to explain anything further right now. I'll save it all for the rangers and the authorities. If I tell them about Steffan and Annalise, they'll ask questions, and I don't have the energy to answer them right this second. I'm not lying. I'm just omitting the truth. Isn't that what Steffan said?

Steffan and I had been planning to trek across the Swiss

Alps to Lake Geneva, but according to my map, I think I'm still miles away from there. Once my phone is charged, I'm going to call the rangers' lodge and inform them that there's been an accident and that Steffan's body needs to be recovered.

'You're an awful long way from the nearest marked path,' the man replies. He nods at the map clenched in my hand. 'Good God, what's happened to you?' He notices the crude bandage. I probably don't look well either.

'Yeah. I got lost and... I think I may have lost some fingers to frostbite.'

'Ouch. Were you trapped out here in the storm?'

'Yes, but I found an isolated cabin to hide out in for a day or two. I'm running low on supplies, though.'

'No worries. You can share ours.'

The group stops and we take off our packs. I wince in pain as I do so, and the nearest man helps me with my pack, setting it on the ground.

'Thank you so much,' I say as they hand me two water bottles, some dried food and energy bars and biscuits. I want to cry with joy.

'No worries. Do you want me to take a look at your hand? I'm a first aider.'

My first and immediate instinct is to say yes, but I stop myself just in time. If he looks at my fingers, will he notice that they've been bitten off? I don't want to answer questions I'm not ready for yet, so I shake my head with a smile.

'Thank you, but I've got them wrapped up tight. I could do with some painkillers though, if that's not too much trouble.'

'Not at all. Here.' He hands me a blister pack.

I swallow them with several gulps of water.

'Where are you heading?' asks the only woman in the group. She's very smartly dressed in the latest designer hiking gear – top of the range and very expensive. Her long blonde hair is tied back in a tight ponytail, not a wisp out of place. It doesn't even look as though she's breaking a sweat. In fact, she looks vaguely familiar.

'Um, to be honest, I just want to get off these mountains. I was doing the Alpine Passes Trail, but my best friend has left a message on my phone saying there's an emergency at home, so I need to cut it short. What's the easiest way down to the nearest village?'

'You were doing the Alpine Passes Trail? You're miles off course.'

'Yeah, I know.'

'And you were doing it by yourself?' the woman asks.

'Um, well... yes. It's been on my bucket list for years. It was my thirtieth birthday gift to myself,' I reply without missing a beat.

'Impressive! Well, we're passing a village in about eight hours' time, according to our expert navigator.' She nods at the man who handed me the painkillers. 'You're welcome to join us until then. I can't promise there will be adequate transport out of there if you need to get home fast, but it's a start and you can contact whoever you need to.'

'That's great. Thank you.'

The woman nods. 'I'm Gabby,' she says, extending her hand.

I take it with my good hand. 'Bonnie.'

We spend a few more minutes conversing and swapping supplies. I must look an absolute state, but I devour an energy bar and a banana within a minute. I dare not tell them about my injured shoulder and broken ribs. I don't want them to know I've been attacked by a crazed lunatic. As far as they know, I'm just a silly woman who decided to hike one of the longest Alpine trails in Switzerland by herself, has got lost and is now needing some help to reach the next village. I'll leave it all for the rangers and authorities.

Once everyone is ready to leave, properly hydrated, I turn and stare back the way I came. Somewhere out there are the bodies of my husband and brother, not to mention a recluse mountain woman whose sad story has meant she's been hiding away out here for over forty years.

It seems like an eternity since I arrived here. So much has happened in that time. I feel like a different person altogether. My husband is like a stranger to me. Did I really know him at all?

'You ready?' asks Gabby, jolting me out of my gnawing thoughts.

'You have no idea,' I reply.

I hobble next to Gabby as we make our way across the terrain. They keep the pace slow, which I'm grateful for.

'It's beautiful out here, isn't it?' she says to me when she sees me staring into the distance.

'Oh, yes... makes you wonder... I'm sorry if this sounds rude, but... I'm sure I recognise you,' I say. 'Your face is so familiar.'

Gabby laughs. 'You might! I'm a TikTok influencer.'

'Ah, that explains all the amazing hiking gear.'

'I'm sponsored by lots of big brands.'

'Ah. I think my husband follows you.' A lump forms in my throat as I say the word and use the present tense.

'Ah, cool. He didn't join you on your trek?'

'Um, yes, he did, but he got injured early and had to call it quits,' I say with a half-hearted laugh. It dawns on me that lie after lie is spilling off my tongue as easily as the truth, which makes me almost as bad as Steffan, the notorious liar. I'm losing sight of myself.

'I'm out here looking for something,' continues Gabby. 'Well, actually... *someone*.'

My heart rate doubles. 'Someone?'

'My older brother, Barry.'

I gulp back yet another lump in my throat, attempting not to show that I'm about to hyperventilate. I feel as if I've just walked into a massive trap and now, I want nothing more than to turn and run from it.

'Um, is he... missing?' I ask as casually as I can muster.

Gabby nods. 'Have you ever heard of the White Witch of the Alps?'

'Actually, yes, I have.'

'Sixteen years ago, Barry came looking for her himself. He never came back. He was a good hiker. Our parents told him not to go alone, but he was adamant, but that's Barry... I guess I've just always wanted to have closure; you know what I mean?'

I squeeze my lips together and bite my tongue in a feeble attempt to stop the tears. 'I know what you mean.' She has no idea how much I know.

'Hey, are you okay? Have I upset you?'

I half laugh and half cry as I wipe at my eyes. 'Oh no, sorry, I... it's just I know how you feel. To be honest...' I stop, take a breath. 'I haven't told you the whole truth about why I'm out here. My brother is lost out here too. I know he's dead, but his body is still here.'

Gabby gasps. 'Oh wow! It's like we're on the same journey, you and me. Do you believe in fate?'

'I'm not sure...'

'I feel like it's fate that you and I have met.'

I give her a weak smile, touched by her compassion. 'Yeah, I guess it is. Do you have any idea where Barry went?'

'That's why we're heading for the village over on the other side of the mountains. These guys are like my tour guides.' She giggles, pointing to the men in the group. 'Barry called me from the village, so I'm hoping someone will remember him. I know I'll probably never find him, but... I'll never forgive myself if I don't try. Plus, it's great exposure for me on TikTok. I've gained a tonne of followers and have several large sponsors. Hey, maybe you and I should make a video or something! Let people out there know about your brother too. We can search for your brother together at the same time.'

I wave my hand, feeling my cheeks warm. 'Oh no. That's okay.'

'Well, can I talk about your brother in my videos? What's his name?'

'Chris.'

'I'll use the hashtag Find Chris alongside Find Barry.'

I smile again at her enthusiasm and kindness, even though I know it's almost hopeless that we'll ever find Chris, knowing that Annalise has buried him. 'Thank you. So... the White Witch who Barry was searching for? Do you reckon she's real?'

Gabby shrugs. 'I hope not. She sounds downright terrifying, don't you think? Imagine... She could be watching us right now.' Gabby cranes her neck and glances around her, then shudders overenthusiastically. 'Creepy.'

I stop and stare out into the vast snowy wilderness. 'Yeah... creepy.'

'If she is real, though, I'd love to know her story,' continues Gabby. 'Wouldn't you?'

'Actually... I already do.'

Gabby's perfectly plucked eyebrows shoot up, and she listens as I tell her everything that happened. Once the truth starts coming out, it sets me free, and the weight comes tumbling off my shoulders.

49

ANNALISE

NOW

When I wake up, the area around me is dark, cold and silent, like it has been for the past forty-odd years. For the first time, I don't know what the time is. My routine and rhythm are off. My head pounds with the hangover of too much herbal tea. As my good eye blinks open, the ache under my eye patch intensifies, as does a sharp pain in my stomach and the throbbing at the side of my head.

What's happened? I can barely remember anything.

I reach my hand up and touch the side of my head, my fingers coming away sticky and warm. A groan escapes my lips as my head lolls to the side. It's so heavy. I'm so tired. I just want to go back to sleep where there was no pain and no loneliness.

That's when I remember something...

Bonnie.

Where's Bonnie?

By the stench and dampness around me, I can guess I'm now in the same situation and place as I placed her in. I suppose I can't blame her for that, but what happened? I'm assuming I drank too much herbal tea again to dull the pain in my eye when she stabbed me with that nail. When was that?

The disorientation is too much for my brain to handle. Every memory and flashback rolls around like marbles pinging off walls and I can't make heads or tails of any of them. Did I do something bad again? Did something happen?

All those years ago, I killed a man in self-defence, but Bonnie wouldn't have attacked me, would she? Unless I attacked her first. If I did, I didn't mean to. I just wanted her to stay with me. That's all. What's the harm in an old woman wanting a bit of company?

I adjust my position so that I'm sitting up rather than lying on my side, but it brings about a coughing fit so bad I feel blood spurt from my mouth. I'm not sure which of my injuries hurts more, but all of them combined are causing me to almost slip back into unconsciousness.

If I had access to my herbal remedies in the main area of the cabin, I'd be able to dull the aches and pains flooding my senses. The high dose I took however many hours ago is all but gone, leaving me with a pounding head and a fuzzy memory.

I have a conundrum to face now.

Do I try and find a way out of this hole and save myself or do I accept my fate and finally die? I have no idea if my stomach wound is bad enough to kill me faster than dehydration, but whatever the case, I have roughly three days before I succumb to it.

Perhaps I deserve this.

I've done my best to keep away from people, for my own safety as much as theirs, but when they knock on my door and force their way in, what am I to do? I tried to be a good host, but everyone takes one look at me and immediately thinks I'm a bad person. Is it because of the way I look, or because of how I live my life?

Am I a bad person? Or am I just a person who has had bad things happen to me?

As I lie alone in the dark, I listen as the cabin above me creaks and groans. I'm not sure if Bonnie is up there or whether she's left already. If she has any sense about her, she'll have waited until the morning before taking off again.

I know I could have handled things better with her, but I did try and warn her and Steffan about leaving in the dark. I did try and take care of her, but she seemed adamant that she wanted to leave, that I wanted to hurt her in some way. It's not true. I only wanted her to stay.

The pain is too much. I can barely move or take a deep breath. I don't think I have much longer in this world, and I'm strangely okay with that. I've made my peace and I'm ready to face whatever awaits me in the afterlife. I just hope my husband isn't there waiting for me.

My eye closes and I listen to my shallow breathing. It's cold, but my body has become accustomed to the low temperatures over the years.

A memory flashes across my mind.

Bonnie crawling away from me on her hands and knees. Then…

I lick my lips, remembering the coppery taste of blood.

Oh God…

I've turned into a monster.

It wasn't me. It was the herbal drugs in my system. I took too much, and it changed me, made me think and see things that weren't real. It happened once before, many years ago.

Perhaps I've been depending on the numbing effect of the herbs too much over the years. I always thought I was safe here, away from the human population who wished me harm, but I was wrong.

People aren't the enemy.

I am.

At least now, I get to rest.

The pain sends me into a deep sleep where I dream of a happy life, the perfect family, including three children who laugh and play around me as I sit and watch them. It's the only thing I've ever wanted. Erik smiles at me from afar. He's tending to the vegetable garden, which is in full bloom. It'll be a fine harvest this year.

'Mummy!' shouts my youngest daughter as she runs to me and wraps her arms around my waist.

I kiss the top of her head, breathing in her wonderful scent.

In the darkness, in the cold, dreary hole of my own making, my mouth curves into a happy smile as I take my final breath of this life and enter the next.

EPILOGUE
BONNIE

One Year Later

The past year since the trip to the Swiss Alps to find my brother's body has been one of many challenges, but it has also made me realise whom I can really trust in my life.

After reaching the next village, I contacted the ranger hut where we started from and spoke to Johan, who arranged for Steffan's body to be recovered. I then spoke to the local authorities and, with Johan translating, told them everything that had happened. Gabby filmed parts of it for her TikTok too. The hashtag #TheWhiteWitch started trending on X and TikTok overnight. Her story became headline news, and I was ushered from one news station to the next to tell my story.

The items found in her wooden box were photographed and put online. The families of seven different people came forwards, claiming they belonged to them. Their bodies were never found. Neither was Barry's, but it did bring them some form of closure, no matter how small.

Annalise's body was found in the cold hole, and the body of her husband in a nearby grave. It appeared she didn't eat him after all, although her body underwent numerous tests and scans, and it was never ruled out that she hadn't consumed human flesh at some point in her life. As she once told me, if there's a choice between life and death, she'd do just about anything to survive.

Netflix contacted me to do a documentary and a miniseries regarding my time in the Swiss Alps. I turned them down, despite the astronomical fee they were willing to pay. All I wanted was to tell the truth, and that's what I did. I don't need to make money from her pain and suffering.

As for Steffan, a postmortem was conducted, showing that he died from a broken neck after tumbling down the slope and crashing into the rocks at the bottom. A terrible accident, they said.

His funeral consisted of only me, Hannah and the twins and Hannah's brother, George, who told me afterwards that Steffan had messaged him several times asking to borrow money over the years. George did give him a small loan, which was never repaid. He told me that Steffan and Chris had got themselves involved with a loan shark. The police have my description of the Irishman and are still searching for him.

Steffan and I didn't have a mortgage or own a property, so there wasn't a lot of paperwork or admin to do with regard to him dying. He didn't believe in health insurance, so I received no compensation for his death.

I found out after searching through the drawers in his locked bedside cabinet that he was in several thousand pounds' worth of debt and had six other bank accounts other than our joint one. All of which were overdrawn. Since I had no idea of their existence and wasn't a guarantor, I wasn't liable for his debt. His guarantor for all his debts was Chris, but since he's also dead, the money has been erased.

I told Hannah about the box of money I found under the floorboards in their master bedroom. She was rather angry at me for keeping it from her, but understood why I never brought it up, especially as it all happened on the same day we found out Chris had died.

Hannah also discovered that Chris had got himself into debt, but it was all because of Steffan, who'd been blackmailing him to hand over more and more money. After a bit of digging, Hannah and I found out that Chris had been embezzling money from his place of work in order to pay Steffan. It had ended up being a vicious circle for Chris, who couldn't find his way out of the mess he'd got himself in, all because Steffan had needed money to pay off his own debts.

My mind keeps drifting back to the note Annalise burned. I hope she rots in hell for what she did. Hannah came to terms with the loss of the note quicker than I expected. There's no way of ever knowing what was on it, but it's something I have to live with now.

Sometimes, I lie awake at night and wonder if it was all some massively messed-up dream brought on by vivid hallucinations and cold exposure, but then I look at the two missing fingertips on my left hand. She bit them clean off. That was no dream.

The doctors were able to sew up my fingertips neatly and save the rest of them – a lifetime reminder of my time in the cabin when I met the White Witch.

I just want to put everything behind me. I gave Chris's

watch to Hannah. It felt right that she have it and not me. She asked me to move in with her to help look after the twins, which I wholeheartedly accepted.

I love them all to bits and now, without Chris, loved ones are even more important. I feel as if I sometimes took family and friends for granted when he was alive, but now I'm determined to always put them first.

IT'S my day off today, and I'm going for a long-distance run. A few months ago, I decided to start training again for the Dragon's Back race across the mountains of Wales. I may never go for a hike again, but at least during a planned race, there's limited risk of going off course and getting trapped in deep snow and held prisoner by a deranged mountain witch.

Garmin on and trainers laced, I set off at a leisurely pace. There's some rain forecast in about two hours' time, so I'm hoping to be finished by then. I settle into the miles easily, enjoying the well-trodden paths and the slight breeze that ensures I don't overheat too quickly.

My phone buzzes in my bum bag. I check my Garmin, and a notification pops up. It's a number I don't recognise, so I ignore it. A few minutes later, another call comes through. Then another. On the fourth call, I answer.

'Yes, hello?' My breathing is laboured. I don't stop running as I wait for the response.

'Is that Mrs Phillips?' comes a female voice.

'Yes, this is she,' I say, deciding not to correct her. I went back to using my maiden surname of Wilkins a few months ago.

'Hello, Mrs Phillips. I'm Detective Sergeant Warrington.

I am the detective in charge of your husband's death and involvement with your brother.'

'Yes, hello.' I remember her voice now. She'd been very patient and understanding with me while I poured my heart out about what I'd found out about Steffan while we'd been trapped in the cabin, awaiting the storm to pass.

'There's been a development in the case.'

I stop running. 'What sort of development? I thought it was closed.' My heart leaps in my chest.

'Well, it was, but Christopher's body has been found and, along with it, there's evidence to suggest that your husband was directly responsible for his death.'

'You've found him!'

'Yes.'

I cover my mouth with my hand not holding the phone, stifling my gasp. Is this real? I'm not dreaming? 'I... I don't believe it... H-How?'

'I'd prefer to explain everything in person...'

'No, please. Tell me now.'

'Very well, but I'd still like you to come into the station. A group of hikers came across a scavenging animal digging in the ground. Upon inspection, they found the remains of a body. The ID found confirms that it's Chris.'

My stomach lurches. 'Oh God... Wait... You said there was evidence of Steffan being directly responsible for his death. What do you mean by *directly responsible*? We already know he left him out there to die.'

'Yes, but along with Christopher's body, we also found the rope he was using when the accident happened. It was purposefully cut with a knife.'

Time seems to stand still as I absorb her words. 'What are you saying?'

'I'm saying that Steffan didn't just leave Christopher out there to die after he fell. I'm saying... it's likely your husband killed Chris on purpose.'

A sob catches in my throat. 'M-Murder. Are you saying Steffan *murdered* Chris?'

'I believe so. As I said, I'd like you to come into the station as soon as possible and I can explain everything in further detail.'

'Yes, of course. Where are his... I mean... Where is his...' I can't say it. I can't.

'The remains have been bagged and are on their way back to the UK as we speak. We'll carry out further tests once they've arrived, and then, once we've completed our tests, we can hand the body over to you for a proper burial.'

Tears flood my eyes and stream down my cheeks. 'T-Thank you, Detective. You have no idea how grateful I am.'

'It wasn't me who found him. He was found by pure luck.'

'Well, thank you anyway. I'll be at the station within the next two hours.'

'See you then.'

I hang up and stare blankly ahead as a rabbit crosses the path in front of me. It stops and watches me, its nose twitching.

Steffan murdered Chris. He murdered him. He killed him.

Then, like a puzzle piece slotting into place, I realise exactly what was on the note that Annalise burned. Chris had been trying to tell me that Steffan had killed him.

Led me.

Kil*led me.*

Steffan killed me.

THANK YOU FOR READING

Did you enjoy reading *I Will Find You*? Please consider leaving a review on Amazon. Your review will help other readers to discover the novel.

ABOUT THE AUTHOR

Jessica Huntley is an author of dark and twisty psychological thrillers, which often focus on mental health topics and delve deep into the minds of her characters. She has a varied career background, having joined the Army as an Intelligence Analyst, then left to become a Personal Trainer. She is now living her life-long dream of writing from the comfort of her home, while looking after her young son and her disabled black Labrador. She enjoys keeping fit and drinking wine (not at the same time).

www.jessicahuntleyauthor.com
Sign up for her newsletter on her website and receive a free short story.

ALSO BY JESSICA HUNTLEY

Inkubator Books Titles

Don't Tell a Soul

Under Her Skin

The Good Parents

I Will Find You

Self-Published Titles

THE DARKNESS SERIES

The Darkness Within Ourselves

The Darkness That Binds Us

The Darkness That Came Before

THE MY…SELF SERIES

My Bad Self: A Prequel Novella

My Dark Self

My True Self

My Real Self

STANDALONES

Jinx

How to Commit the Perfect Murder in Ten Easy Steps

COLLABORATIONS

The Summoning

HorrorScope: A Zodiac Anthology – Vol 1

Bloody Hell: An Anthology of UK Indie Horror

Printed in Dunstable, United Kingdom